Jeff Arnold has lived in the UK and Italy and is now retired in France. He is the author of the blog JEFF ARNOLD'S WEST (jeffarnoldswest.com) which has been going since 2010 and which reviews Western movies and books. A history major and a passionate reader and writer about the West, he is also widely traveled there, especially in Arizona and New Mexico.

This book is dedicated to all my heroes of the Western movie – and their fans.

Jeff Arnold

STAY AND DIE

A NOVEL

AUSTIN MACAULEY PUBLISHERS™

LONDON • CAMBRIDGE • NEW YORK • SHARJAH

A CIP catalogue record for this title is available from the British Library.

ISBN 9781528982689 (Paperback)
ISBN 9781528989121 (ePub e-book)

www.austinmacauley.com

First Published 2023
Austin Macauley Publishers Ltd®
1 Canada Square
Canary Wharf
London
E14 5AA

I am grateful to the people of that fine town Las Vegas, NM, especially those who talked to me there about the old times and provided me with invaluable information and insights.

I found the book *Wildest of the Wild West: True Tales of a Frontier Town on the Santa Fe Trail* by Howard Bryan (Clear Light Publishers, Santa Fe, 1988) to be especially useful and interesting.

Many of the people who appear in this story really existed, including the hero, Josh Webb, and some of the events that occur in the narrative actually did happen, but the work is essentially fiction, and what the characters did, said and in particular what they thought have been imagined.

Prologue

He knew it would come to violence. With such men, it always did. Mind, Josh was hardly a saint. He was not a man to back down from a fight, never had been, whether in the right or in the wrong. He knew that. And when the mood came over him, as it sometimes did, a blackness descended over his spirit and there seemed no point in goodness or truth. But the man that Josh faced now was beyond redemption, with no saving grace. An arrogant son of a bitch, dishonest and appallingly aggressive when drunk, which was often. Despite his great wealth, he stole from everyone he could. The Indians, he cheated; the tradesmen, he did not pay; the farmers, he swindled. And he had swindled Josh too. But he was going to pay what he owed to Josh. He was going to pay.

There wasn't much official law in Wyoming Territory in 1870. You made your own law. Very well, let us see what Mr. High-and-mighty will do. Josh went tooled up—downright foolish to do otherwise. His Colt, a Winchester, the bowie knife. He wasn't going to start an armed fight. But he'd finish it.

The interview was short, in the hotel in Cheyenne. It was a matter of seconds, it seemed, before they were shouting at each other and that turned to cursing, which wasn't Josh's way, normally. There seemed simply no room for reason or rational discussion and no possibility of it. The man was not going to pay, that was clear. But he was not going to turn away either. Josh's effrontery was to be punished. The rancher was a man who could not brook even the slightest opposition. Would not stand it. That was why he beat his children and his wife, and his servants and animals whenever he could. And he was in drink. Josh ducked the first blow. It wasn't difficult; it was a wild swing. But the fellow was a fighter, and strong, very strong. Not big (no more was Josh) but wiry, lean, muscled and with great arms. The man was armed but drew no gun, yet at least. He aimed to beat Josh to a pulp. Well, we'll see about that.

They were quite evenly matched and the fight was bitter. A crowd gathered and some men began to lay bets. No one appeared to support Josh but several cried out encouragement for his opponent: "Come on, Michael! Whack the fellow!" They were maybe Irish. The hotel manager was distressed and urged them all outside. But the crowd ignored him and the combatants had only eyes for each other. When Josh finally beat the man down, he nearly fell himself. Blood ran down from his eye and his whole face was already starting to swell. He felt giddy. But his opponent fared worse. He was a mess. His jaw looked to have been broken and he could barely see. Josh turned away, leaned against the bar, and took some deep breaths. Then he asked for water.

The bullet slammed into the back of Josh's shoulder. It felt like a train hitting him. He turned and saw the cattleman drawing back the hammer on his long-barreled .44 for another go. Josh took out his own pistol and shot the man, right where he lay in his bloody mess. In the head. There. That was an end of it.

Later, when he was limping out into the street, he thought he should have looked at the man's pocketbook and taken what was owed him. But that felt wrong, somehow, like robbing a corpse. Well, it was over.

Two days later, in great pain but his shoulder bandaged and his cuts washed, he headed down to Kansas.

Part I

Chapter One

The arrival of the first train started it all. The noise of the celebrations almost drowned out the snorting and grinding of the 4-4-0 as it panted to a halt. Wild whoops and yeehars, accompanied by the flat loud cracks of six-shooters fired into the torrid air, sought to overcome the metallic shrieks of the huge steel wheels against the rails and the giant bronchial wheezing of the boiler. But it was the triumphal roar of the train whistle which finally ensured that the railroad won this little competition and the engineer, his begrimed rosy-cheeked face under its striped cap beaming down at the welcoming crowd, held onto the whistle rope for all he was worth and turned the jubilations of the welcoming crowd into mime.

The Fourth of July. But what a Fourth of July! The entire population of Las Vegas, New Mexico Territory, had turned out to greet the first ever train of the Atchison, Topeka and Santa Fe Railway, and mark the most important day so far in the history of the township.

The No. 14 Pittsburgh, the gleaming pride and joy of the engineers, delivered in January of '73 by the Baldwin Locomotive Works of Philadelphia, had come a long way. The AT&SF had run their line over the Raton Pass from Trinidad, time the enemy, coolies and surveyors and gang bosses toiling in the heat and the cold, through mountains and desert, to lay track and reach that terminus of Santa Fe. They had set themselves the goal, meaningless really but important to them nevertheless, of reaching Las Vegas by July 4th. Many residents of this well-established Santa Fe Trail town were mortified that the track was to pass through a wheat field a good mile and a half east of their central plaza, on the other side of the Gallinas River, but it meant little in the long run for a new town of East Las Vegas was already springing into life, with creamy timber buildings appearing like pale mushrooms almost overnight, parallel to the tracks along the new Railroad Avenue, along Center Street and up towards the Gallinas to join up with the old town.

Veteran track followers poured in, anticipating as always golden rewards at each end-of-track town. And they were right. The railroad would bring prosperity, with trade goods and livestock moving in and out, new farm equipment arriving, new settlers too, and of course increased mobility for the townsfolk. Look what it had already done to Trinidad. Las Vegas was next and the inhabitants knew it. The Exchange Hotel had a pianoforte which must have weighed half a ton. It had come out from New York to St. Louis by rail and then, in pieces, by wagon down along the Santa Fe Trail, through Kansas and Colorado and New Mexico, braving gradients and thirst and Indians. Incredible, really, and the cost was prohibitive. Now, pianos by the score would come trundling in if they were wanted. And anything else. The future had arrived.

Of course, among the track followers were also saloon keepers and gamblers and whores and pimps and bunko men. The usual frontier riffraff. Thieves and gunmen and vagrants. You couldn't avoid it.

The tracks beside the half-built skeleton of a depot were invisible for the throng. The town dignitaries to the fore were surrounded by gentlemen in their best hats, many of which were thrown into the air and then retrieved to be thrown again, ladies in all their finery, waving handkerchiefs and parasols, farmers, tradesmen, small boys wildly out of control, and cowboys, dashing in chaps and checkered shirts and large soft hats, nearly all emptying their sidearms into the summer air. Mexicans, Anglos, Indians; a smiling clergyman; the ladies of the town's Temperance Committee with their embroidered banner; several younger and rather less respectable females from some of the saloons; a salesman of patent medicines up on a soap box, trying to profit from the crowd but without success. They all seemed to have forgotten the almost unbearable heat and ignored the flies. A band struck up the Battle Hymn of the Republic, which may not have been appreciated by a totality of those present. The appropriately portly bass drummer, his already considerable belly hugely extended by the large drum, whacked the skins rhythmically with all his might. Cornet and trombone and tuba clashed out their tune, the orchestra's trumpeting essaying to be heard over the din. The engineer gave another blast of the whistle which was greeted by yet more gunfire and cheers. It was a joyful pandemonium.

"Dutchy, make a way for me here." A huge gorilla of a man, almost shaven-headed and with a chest like a pork barrel, duly thrust crowd members to each side with little ceremony, using his tree-trunk-like arms to create an alley down which Hyman Neill and another man could comfortably walk. Neill

14

had spotted a distinguished gentleman in a dark gray suit begin to descend from the first car, followed by various flunkies. He had divined that this was the esteemed representative of the railroad company and he wished to be first to shake his hand. There was no difficulty: 'Dutchy' Schunderberger was not to be obstructed or gainsaid and his master and the other fellow passed easily towards the railroad man. Behind, well back, the mayor and marshal looked affronted but were powerless to approach.

"Welcome, sir, welcome. Welcome to East Las Vegas, the new township. As distinct from old West Las Vegas yonder," he added, loudly, almost as it were underlining the point, for the benefit of the dignitaries behind him. "You are most welcome. And allow me, in the name of the new town of East Las Vegas, to extend the most heartfelt greetings of its presently few but soon-to-be oh-so numerous denizens to your most estimable self and the fine railroad company which you represent. Yes, sir, you are indeed welcome and I, Hyman G. Neill, dare I say premier citizen of this fine new community, do most heartily greet you." He smiled so broadly that the newcomer was afraid that his face might split.

"Thank you, sir. It is, I am sure, a great day for this town, and the Atchison—"

"It is indeed a great day, my dear sir, it is indeed. And may I add that while this Territory may not, yet, officially at least, be part of the United States of America, nevertheless the most fortunate happenstance of your arrival here upon the fourth of July, our sacred and honored national day, adds, sir, significance and weight to this most happy occasion. Furthermore…"

Although the noise had somewhat abated in respect for this exchange of pleasantries, it had not subsided to the extent that any but the closest could hear what was said. Certainly, the town worthies who had assumed that they would have been the ones to deliver the official welcome, some of whom had even indeed memorized small speeches, heard nothing. But they needed no actual words to understand that this upstart Brown (why did he call himself Neill?) had clearly and brazenly usurped their functions. "It is not that I mind personally," said the mayor earnestly to the marshal, "perish the thought, but it is an affront to our office!"

"Yes, Mayor, yes. My sentiments exactly."

"Well, let us move forward, at once."

"Yes, well, we can try. But it won't be easy getting past Schunderberger."
As the Mayor looked, it was clear that the marshal was right. Dutchy
Schunderberger's back presented a huge wall-like bulwark to them, like the
ramparts of Fort Stanton to a bunch of Apache boys.

It was in any case too late. The grandees of the Atchison, Topeka & Santa
Fe were being ushered towards the newly erected establishment, first on
'Railroad Avenue', of Hyman G. Neill, known, however, to all by his preferred
name of Brown and to most Las Vegans by his soubriquet of Hoodoo Brown.

Hoodoo Brown was a tall Kansan, and the first and most noticeable feature
of him was his piercingly blue eyes. They were of a washed-out blue, almost
gray, yet their lack of pigment betrayed no weakness, no lack of grit. On the
contrary. Steel, rather. His dark hair did not somehow match. One expected
fairness. But these auburn, almost raven locks flowed long behind his neck in
an elegant wave. His black eyebrows met in the middle. His mother had always
said that this meant that he was born to hang. It certainly gave his face a
curiously primordial mien. His teeth were good and he often displayed them
with a smile. This smile did not always, however, include his eyes. It appeared
to be restricted to the lower part of his face. He had a slight stoop, as very tall
men sometimes do. So Josh reckoned.

John Joshua Webb had descended from the train later and further back than
the Santa Fe big shots. But he was close enough to observe the exchange
between Hoodoo and the railroad Vice-President. The Vice-President was a
gray man in every sense (most especially his clothes) but this leader of the
welcome committee, now there was an interesting fellow. Josh observed
discreetly, as he always did, and registered everything. The man accompanying
Neill seemed curiously faceless, a nonentity. Some kind of valet or servant
perhaps. Or a secretary. Hoodoo referred to him as Carson.

Josh placed his carpet bag in a rare space and pulled out of his pockets the
makings of a smoke. He leant down and struck a match on his boot then stood
quietly inhaling and looking around. Not much here. Railroad tracks, which
stopped abruptly only yards ahead. Piles of railway sleepers, shovels and picks.
Groups of Chinamen clustered silently round tents. To the west, a few
exceedingly new-looking wooden put-me-ups lining a dusty 'street', saloons
and dancehalls by the look of them. Over in the distance what looked like a
better town. Well, it would do for now. A base. He needed a base for his
investigations.

He looked back, towards the end of the train. A man of about thirty was descending, holding a leather valise. He held on to the rail with his right hand and it kept his muscular body taut. He seemed watchful, even wary. He wore a discreet black frock coat and flat shovel hat. No gun, at least visible. A gentleman? Not quite. Josh's attention was jerked back to his own condition.

A small, rather oily man stood in front of him.

"Can I help you, sir? A hotel, for example? We are delighted to accommodate all new visitors."

Josh looked down scornfully at first, then considered. "What have you got?"

He followed the little man, scarcely listening, just picking out an occasional 'Mr. Brown will be pleased to...' They arrived at a wooden shanty just west of the railroad 'station' whose frame of timbers was still green, raw lumber as far as Josh could see. The clerk, clutching Josh's bag to his bosom as if it were a treasured family heirloom, mounted the three steps onto the boardwalk and waved his new guest in.

Josh waited. "How much?"

"Oh, very reasonable rates, I do assure you."

"How much?"

"Well, with the railroad and all we are now asking five dollars a—"

"May I have my bag, please? I will continue into town."

"Oh, but please, sir, please, I do assure you—"

"My bag. Now."

"But Mr. Brown said—"

Josh took a step forward and the clerk took fright. This worm wasn't worth even loosening his Colt for. He simply took back the luggage and turned away.

He found a goodish hotel, the Exchange, up by the plaza in the old town and installed himself. He needed somewhere he could send a wire from. After shoving a few shirts and other items in some drawers, he sat down and wrote on a yellow pad ADAMS EXPRESS COMPANY BOSTON AM IN LV NMT WILL REPORT SOONEST ON ROBBERIES WEBB. He would have to bribe the telegraph clerk to keep quiet but that was normal.

***

"My name is Howard."

"Si, Señor Howard. And the first name?"

He ignored the question and looked around. A miserable squat adobe doss house. He picked his leather valise back up. "Is there a better hotel in town?"

"Well Señor, this is a good hotel, clean and—"

"I said, is there a better hotel in town?"

"Well, I suppose you might get slightly better lodging in the old town."

"Which is the very best hotel?"

"The best hotel, Señor, is The Adobe House out at Montezuma Hot Springs. However, it is—"

"How do I get there?"

The man sighed. "Well, it is about five miles out to the north. You would need a carriage, Señor."

"Call me one."

***

No one expects New Mexico to be cool in summer. It isn't going to happen so you might as well get used to it. But it did truly seem as if this summer of 1879 was more than just hot. The word hot just didn't suffice. You would need some word like Sahara-like. Or something to do with Abednego and those Shadrak boys. It was as if New Mexico were in the last stages of a terminal fever. The air was bleached of oxygen and it pressed on the breast, like when you pass the open door of a furnace and get a taste of it, dry on the tongue. Coming down on the train, the horizon had been indistinct. And the land seemed like the skin of a jaundiced man, pallid, unnatural and yellow. The earth was drained and barren. You would need ten acres to keep a cow. You would need the Maxwell land grant to support a small herd.

He lay flat on his back on the bed. It was building up for a July evening thunderstorm. Or for thunder anyway. Most nights it deceived. The parched land waited for a downpour but it was all just piss and wind. Like taunts. And the thunder would roll away and leave another dewless night and a baked morning. Josh followed the path of a small spider across the ceiling, moving steadily across the huge expanse, going for some reason known to itself from nowhere to nowhere else. Josh reflected that he knew the feeling. Well, he was here now. He would stay for a bit. Las Vegas was as good as anywhere else. Better, if he was any judge. A brand-new town, the railroad just arrived and a town boss shaping up to run things. He was in on the ground floor. He might give up this Adams detective work.

How many times had he given up on an occupation? Too many. He could hear Masie berating him. "You've no sticking power, Josh!" Aye, and she was probably right at that. Count them off: freighter, buffalo hunter, lawman, business owner, surveyor, soldier, scout, saloon keeper, gambler: the list was fairly long—even mercenary, if you counted the Colorado railroad war as that. But he had always had itchy feet, was never satisfied. He was born a month premature, as if he could not wait to begin life, and he was born at just before midnight in late December, as if too impatient to await the right day or year. He wanted to get on with it. It was always a basic principle with him. He had, all his life, been ready to move on to the next stage, been early for appointments, anxious to try something new. People said he was energetic, dynamic. Maybe he was. Except of course when the moods descended on him.

But his family was the same in a way. They had moved from Illinois to Iowa, from Nebraska to Kansas, his father always looking for better opportunities, or just different ones. His eleven brothers and sisters were just the same, scattered now all over Kansas, Missouri and Oklahoma. He'd lost touch with them all over the years. And now the only other person he had really known, properly known, and who understood him through and through, was gone. It was too painful to think about Masie now. At any rate, looking at it from another point of view, he had had an interesting and varied life. Thirty-two years old and he had been around alright. Yessir. The best time? Maybe as part owner of the Lady Gay up at Dodge. He had most friends then anyway. Will especially, but also Bat and Wyatt. Luke, Ben, the others. Doc, as far as anyone could ever be his friend. Doc was said to be here in town now. Josh would look him up shortly. No hurry there. And he had had money in his pocket in those Dodge days too. Yes, it had been a good time. But that had grown stale, like everything else. He needed to be moving. What was he looking for? He found difficulty in answering. He found difficulty in answering even such basic questions as 'Where are you from?' or 'What do you do?' He usually grunted 'Kansas' but he didn't feel himself a Kansan. And he said he was 'a businessman'. Businessman, hell. He was little more than a gun for hire. Well, enough. What about now?

He got up. July 4th. He smiled. He often smiled. Let's see what the saloons have to offer.

He started downstairs in the bar of the Exchange. It was mighty jolly. The place was packed and full of noise. A man in shirt sleeves and a derby bashed out Oh, Susanna on a battered piano, surrounded by a little gaggle of saloon gals singing along. There were gaming tables and waitresses weaving between them with large trays of glasses, neatly avoiding the occasional hand stretched out towards their rear quarters. In a large back room, a ball was in progress. But most men were crowded up at the bar, two or three deep. It took some time for Josh to arrive at the counter.

Everyone was crying, "Henry! Henry!" to get the barman's attention, so he joined in. "Henry, here!" Finally the young bartender came over and, with a brimming beer mug in one hand and a shot glass in the other, Josh turned back and regarded the scene. There was no one he knew. Maybe he would get in at a table and play a bit.

The light blow on his shoulder was totally unexpected. Had he not a glass in each hand he might have been tempted to put one on a gun, in case. That was unusually careless of him. But as he spun round, he saw a familiar beaming face with a large mustachioed grin and knew no weapon would be necessary.

"Wyatt! You son of a gun. I didn't know you were in town."

"Nor I you. What are you doing here?"

"Oh, the work in the Royal Gorge war ran out. Thought I'd see what was happening down here. You?"

"Doing a bit of business with Doc. Thinking of heading on down into Arizona later. James is here too."

"Well, good. I was just beginning to think I was on my ownsome. Let's have a drink. Maybe you can fill me in on how things stand here too. Hoodoo Brown seems to be running things as far as I can see."

"Yes, in East Las Vegas anyway. Here, this side of the river, it's all rather more regulated, and law 'n' order is what they like. The new eastern part near the railroad is a separate precinct unincorporated by the old Las Vegas. Hoodoo Brown, our own Mr. Hyman G. Neill, has somehow gotten himself appointed as mayor, coroner and justice of the peace. All in one."

"Yes, I've heard of Hoodoo, back in Kansas. The reputation was not one to shine out like a beacon over a sea of iniquity. In fact, he was one of the biggest sharks to swim in such a sea if half the stories I heard tell were true."

"You got that right. Still, it's good to have Kansas men running things, eh? Hoodoo seems to have cornered the market all himself, with only two sidekicks, that bear Dutchy and Joe Carson, have you seen him? Less impressive. Hoodoo has set Carson up as marshal. Probably wants someone obedient."

Josh reckoned that this was the man he'd taken for a secretary. Carson couldn't be any kin to Kit Carson, despite the New Mexico background. This Carson looked tall, even strong, but the eyes showed a lack of sand. The man was fundamentally flawed. He wouldn't stand up. At least, that was Josh's first impression. And he was used to judging men in frontier conditions and new towns. He could be wrong. The man anyway apparently had all the backing of the dominant clique. But it was Hoodoo Brown who ran this town. Hoodoo and his enormous minder. From what Wyatt was saying, no one would ever claim for Dutchy a high level of intellect or cunning. He wasn't there for that. But it was apparent that Dutchy was intensely and unquestioningly loyal, and strong as an ox. Dumb as one too.

But all three were perfectly capable of arranging or even carrying out robberies of stage or train. No doubt about it.

Josh thought he would stay for a bit. And he wouldn't give up the Adams job just yet.

Wyatt slapped him on the shoulder again. "Listen, Josh, let's go down to the other end, have a drink in Close & Paterson's—that's a Hoodoo joint. We could stop in at Doc's place on Center Street and pick up James if you like."

***

Doc Holliday's saloon was a narrow gin mill next to Huberty and Angell's bakery. It had little claim to distinction, being small, dark and rank smelling. Only its front window let in any light and the rest of the illumination came from badly smoking oil lamps that needed trimming. A boy was using a watering can in a vain effort to settle the dust on the floorboards. His efforts were admirable in their plucky resistance to the overwhelming, fetid heat but doomed to failure, nevertheless. Even on July 4th the place was not that crowded, most of the business being a little further down in the big saloons and dancehalls on Railroad. But Josh saw that all the tables were taken. He cast a professional gaze about. Faro and monte, mostly. The usual mix of inexpert cowboys and storekeepers losing money to the house or to men Josh could tell at once were professional gamblers. He saw one rather drunken fellow being ushered out back by two whores. He had an arm round the neck of each and in each hand was a bottle. These bottles thus hung down, one before the ample breast of each maid. There was a man who did not do things by halves.

John Holliday stood bent over the bar assiduously working his way through a bottle of some transparent spirit. He looked miserable and mean. Josh considered that was about right.

But when Wyatt approached, Holliday stood up and a smile broke out, transforming his face utterly. "Why Wyatt, I do declare!" He was clearly delighted to see his friend.

Josh never understood this relationship. Holliday was notoriously unreliable, cantankerous and vicious. He had alienated all the friends he had ever made and had a very long list of enemies. Yet he doted on Wyatt and Wyatt seemed to reciprocate this regard. It is true that Doc had saved Wyatt's life in a gunfight in the Comique in Dodge in '77 but that wasn't enough alone to explain it. They were just bosom pals. And they were intensely loyal to each other. Josh stood quietly while the greetings took place. Then Doc turned to him.

"Why, Josh. I didn't know you were in town. What a pleasure to see you again. Wasn't that fun up there in the Royal Gorge? Damn shame the Santa Fe lost out. If I'd've had my way, we'd still be up there shooting it out. Never mind, more money and just as much fun to be had here. Have a drink, won't you?"

"Thank you, Doc, don't mind if I do."

James Earp came up and they approached a table that miraculously liberated itself. There had been three sorry-looking specimens seated there, playing cards and drinking whiskey. Doc barely looked at one of them, a young man with appallingly ravaged skin which looked as though he had had a dose of the smallpox, kicked him on the side of the boot and the man rose, scooping up his winnings and his two friends got the hint and moved away also. Doc, Wyatt, Josh and James took their places at the table.

James was so evidently Wyatt's older brother. They were alike both in appearance and mannerisms. James had been in the war and Wyatt as a boy had idolized him but now it seemed almost the other way about. James took his lead from Wyatt. He had a darker disposition and was quieter. More bitter, perhaps. Or no, more hurt. But he was intelligent and acute. You couldn't help liking him.

The two Earps, Doc and Josh talked a little of old times, Kansas days mostly, especially of Dodge. It seemed to be an important time in all their lives. But it wasn't long before Doc was alluding more or less obliquely to pickings to be had from this new town. James smiled in a complicit way and once winked at Josh while Wyatt was more circumspect. Josh had told no one he was doing detective work but Wyatt was sensible enough not to say too much.

Doc showed no such restraint. "Hell, this place is wide open, fellows. Kansas boys in charge. Hoodoo is even justice of the peace and coroner so that should clear up any little legal difficulty, eh? Tame marshal as well. All this money coming into town. A good part of that is going to stick to our pockets, eh, lads? No damn noseless scout is going to stop me either." Josh did not understand this reference but did not question it. Doc continued, "Why, I can think of all sorts of activities that would make us rich. For example—"

"Well boys," interrupted Wyatt, "what say we walk down to Close & Paterson's. See what's going on."

Holliday looked up quickly and understood. "You boys go on. I got to stay and mind the shop. But have a good time." He rose and walked over to the bar where the three ruffians whose table he had taken stood at the counter. He started talking to them. They were gunmen, pure and simple.

Wyatt and James were on their way out but Josh went back for a moment to shake hands with Doc, and said, "So long, Doc," then followed them to the door. One of the gunmen gave him a gap-toothed grin. Josh reckoned that it was more of a sneer.

In the bustling street, skirting round wagons and mules and avoiding two barking dogs and cowboys on skittish ponies, holding handkerchiefs to their faces against the dust, suffering from the sweltering heat, Josh asked Wyatt, "Noseless scout?"

Wyatt laughed. "Yes, Gordon, Mike Gordon. 5th Cavalry scout. He got his nose bit off by a gambler he'd cheated. Took hold of both ears in a grip of iron and bit the fellow's nose right off. He's plumb ugly now! Mind, he weren't no oil painting before. I knew him up in Nebraska before he started in on the bottle. Decent enough fellow then. Brave man, I would say. Now he's just a drunk. And a mean one too. Threatened to shoot Doc's dick off. Said Doc had been interfering with his girl. Now you know Doc as well as I do. Doc's not the kinda fellow you threaten to shoot the dick off. Not if you want to live long."

Josh and James both nodded sagely at that.

***

There was a completely different atmosphere at Close & Paterson's. The place was huge, with two stories. A fancy bar went all down one side downstairs and there was space for tables and dancing too. Bright chandeliers lit the room and there was gaiety and laughter. A woman, Grace Rollia according to the placard behind her, was singing an operatic aria up on a stage and musical accompaniment was provided by the occasional pistol shot of appreciation and a fiddler.

The place was run by George Close and Billy Paterson. They were track followers. In more than one way, in fact, for they moved from racetrack to racetrack as well as trying always to be first when the railroad came to a new town. George had had a saloon in El Moro while Billy had sold his dance hall in La Junta. But everyone knew it was Hoodoo's joint. Hoodoo had put up the money and he used it as his office and home. He let George and Billy run the place and take a share of the profits.

There was a young girl with a limp sweeping in the doorway. She was maybe thirteen, very plain, and her frock was grubby. But she had a smile on her face. She looked, well, serene. The lass was singing a song, and Josh reckoned that it was a song suitable only for adults to sing, and only adults of a certain class at that, and ones who may have had intoxication as an excuse. But she was singing it without concern, not lustily or loudly but quietly between almost closed lips, doggedly, like a woman singing a hymn in church. The girl stepped back to let the men pass.

Once inside, they made their way to the bar. As they approached, they saw Hoodoo leaning against it down at one end, stooped in a huddle with Schunderberger and Carson. Josh figured that it was no doubt unintentional but it was a classic image of conspiracy. Exaggerated. Almost as if they had been up on stage in some melodrama with the audience booing and hissing them.

Wyatt bought Josh and James a drink and they exchanged news. Hoodoo caught sight of them and came over.

He nodded at James and Wyatt and put his hand out towards Josh. "I don't think we have met?"

"J.J. Webb."

"Ah, yes, Josh Webb. I know you. I know of you at any rate. Pleased to meet you. Here with Wyatt, are you? Ah, now isn't it nice to have all these Kansas boys together in this far western wilderness? Company, you might say. Tonight you boys drink on me."

The smile came out again. But the eyes remained implacable.

Josh's gaze strayed to a point above and to the left of Hoodoo's head and Hoodoo looked round to see what Josh was staring at. Coming down the stairs was as fine looking a woman as Josh had seen in a very long time. She was tall and erect in her long and tight green silk dress and she walked down the staircase like a lady. Dark-haired and white-skinned, she had a grace and poise. As she approached, Josh could see she had an almost perfect complexion, free of rouge or paint but with a little red rosebud of a mouth. There was a sparkle in her eyes, a sign of intelligence and humor.

"Ah, Mrs. Carson. What a pleasure. Allow me to introduce you. You know the Messieurs Earp, I think. This is Mr. Joshua Webb, of Kansas. Josh, Mrs. Carson is the wife of our esteemed constable here. Let me present him also." He turned and beckoned, rather peremptorily, at Carson to approach. "And this is my invaluable factotum Mr. Schunderberger. We usually call him Dutchy."

Josh took Mrs. Carson's gloved hand, covering the top of it with his thumb and lowered his head to it. It was a gesture he had been taught by his mother. Innocent Blue Webb had cared about such things and tried to teach all her children the social graces. Josh had forgotten most of them. Not much call for social graces as a teamster in Wyoming. But the gesture was appreciated by Mrs. Carson all right for she smiled, radiantly, at Josh and gave the slightest of curtsies. It was as if the sun had come out.

Joe Carson looked uncomfortable. Hoodoo smiled in a rather ugly way.

They sat at a table and Wyatt beat them all to holding out a chair for Mrs. Carson but this meant that Josh was able to seat himself next to her. James was self-consciously straightening his tie and smoothing down his hair with licked fingers. Mrs. Carson seemed to enjoy the effect she was having on the men. Joe Carson turned back to the bar and stood there with Dutchy.

The party ordered drinks and Mrs. Carson took a soda water. Wyatt rather led the conversation and was his usual winning self. But was it Josh's imagination or was the lady looking more often at him?

The shock of feeling her foot upon his own boot under the table almost gave him away. He coughed, as cover.

But then the limping girl appeared again, pushing through the throng and tugging on Joe Carson's sleeve, though addressing Hoodoo. "Mr. Brown, Mr. Brown, they need the marshal next door. There's a fight. Two girls. They going to do theirselves harm, Marshal. Best come right away."

Carson looked over at Hoodoo, who simply shrugged. The marshal put down his glass on the countertop and went out. Wyatt, James and Josh excused themselves and followed, for curiosity. As they left, Hoodoo was left sitting with Mrs. Carson.

The saloon next door was a low adobe Mexican place. They heard the shrieks from the street. Once through the door they saw two Mexican girls at each other's throats, rolling around on the floor, spitting, scratching and gouging. A barman was vainly trying to separate them with a broom.

"My, my," said Wyatt. "The daughters of Montezuma sure do know how to quarrel."

Carson hesitated, then stepped forward. "Now, now, stop that." Totally ignored, he raised his voice. "I said stop that. Right now." Finally, he sighed, leaned down and grabbed one of the girls by the upper arm. She tried to shake him off but he pulled harder and dragged her away from her adversary. This adversary, however, now decided to go to the aid of her erstwhile foe against the common enemy and she started to kick Carson. Carson looked at a loss, and didn't quite know how to handle it. The girl clawed her nails down his face. Exasperated, he knocked this girl down and turned again to the other, whom he still held by the arm. Two Mexican men rose from their seats. They weren't having this. One had an old pistol stuck in the sash round his waist. The other, an ornery looking younger fellow, had a knife in his hand. Others started to jeer at the marshal. It was starting to look ugly. Two other Mexicans came up from behind Carson and one kidney-punched him. Carson made an 'oof!' sound and went down on one knee. Josh thought that maybe the time had come to intervene.

It was like a whirlwind. Josh felt himself pushed aside. In a matter of seconds, Dutchy had all the Mexican men laid out on the floor. Every single one. One blow from his huge ham-like fists was enough for each. He disposed of two men by holding one in each hand and banging their heads together. It was over. Dutchy presented to Carson the two women, one under each arm. He had said nothing from the time he came in. When Carson had taken charge of the girls and was marching them up to the jail, Dutchy simply looked round, walked out, and went back to Close & Paterson's.

"Well!" said Wyatt.

***

Back in the bar at Close & Paterson's, they once again sat down at the table, interrupting a *tête à tête*. Hoodoo drew himself up and addressed them. "Dutchy sorted that out then? Good man, Dutchy, no doubt about it." He said nothing of Carson.

James chipped in. "You shoulda seen them hussies go!"

"Why do call them 'hussies', Mr. Earp?"

"Oh, well, ma'am, excuse the word, but I—"

"It's not your use of the word I object to, Mr. Earp, nor indeed the word itself. I just wondered why you employed it."

James looked at his brother for encouragement. Received nothing but a raised eyebrow. "Well, ma'am, I saw 'em and believe me, they was hussies."

"Because they were fighting?"

"Oh, they was fighting alright. Tooth and claw as it were."

"I often see men fighting in this establishment, Mr. Earp. And in other establishments. And in the street. Even in stores and by the railroad and in the plaza. In fact, gentlemen," (she now seemed to be addressing her discourse to the table at large) "it sometimes seems to me that American men do little else with their spare time *but* fight. When men fight, they are not 'hussies'. They are indeed esteemed even noble, certainly courageous. Fighting is the manly thing to do, it appears. There seems to be no male equivalent of the word 'hussy'. Correct me if I am wrong, I implore you, gentlemen. Yet it appears to me that women might fall to disagreements as often as men. But when they do so, they are 'hussies'. Does this seem equitable to you, sirs?" She addressed the question to no one in particular.

"Now, Mrs. Carson." Hoodoo was the first, indeed the only one to take up the gauntlet. "Please do not go troubling your very pretty head with these 'modern' ideas. It don't become you. It don't become you at all. Men is men and women, well, they are women, as far as my experience goes, and long may the difference remain, eh, gentlemen? You women sure do have your ways in any case, which ain't men's ways, that's for sure."

Mrs. Carson greeted this cogent statement of deep philosophy with a look which could not hide its contempt. She fairly bristled at the idea that her opinions expressed did not 'become' her, but she chose, for her own reasons, to say nothing. She retired behind a fan, which she briskly waved more towards Hoodoo than her own face, as if wishing to ward off his noisome opinions. She launched a brief smile of complicity towards Josh, as if to a kindred spirit. Why on earth, Josh could not tell.

Hoodoo turned to Josh. "Mr. Webb, I would be more than delighted were you to count yourself at home in this place. A Kansan with a reputation is always welcome here." Josh didn't much like the sound of this reputation but remained silent. Hoodoo went on, "You know there are very clear possibilities in this new young town, and both the mayor and the justice of the peace here, to say nothing indeed of the coroner, are eager, they are all eager to recruit as official or unofficial guardians of the peace men such as yourself, men of, how may we put it, initiative."

"I thought you were the mayor, J.P. and coroner all yourself, Mr. Brown."

"Why bless my soul, now that you mention it, I believe you are right!" He laughed loudly at his own joke.

"Well, I thank you kindly for your offer of a berth, sir. I appreciate it, and I will give your proposal due consideration. Right now I have just arrived and am looking around for a suitable occupation. If I may, I will take a few days and see what's what."

"Why of course, my dear Josh, of course. Take your time. By all means."

But it was clear that Hoodoo did not care for this stand-offish response.

***

Violent crazed lines of forked lightning sheeted down outside the window and almost immediately thunder rolled and roared.

"Don't worry. He'll be at least an hour yet getting those women up to the jail and charging them. It's right at the other end of town. And in this weather, he might stay up there. Here. What a good strong chest. I do like a good strong

28

chest." And she drew her no-longer-gloved hand downwards from his chin tracing an imaginary line down his sternum.

How had he got into this, in only half an hour? One moment he is kissing a lady's hand. The next he is upstairs and she is proving herself less of a lady after all. He didn't consider himself any Lothario. If anyone, that was Wyatt. Yet for the first time in he forgot how long he was in bed with a woman he had not paid for. And it was wonderful.

He had to admit, Lothario had nothing to do with it. Nor Don Juan or Casanova neither. She had done it. She had taken a fancy to him and decided to make love to him. Simple as that. It was done with discretion but without furtiveness or shame. She enjoyed it. And boy, so did he. He kissed her neck.

"Mrs. Carson," he murmured. He realized that sounded stupid. But he didn't know any other name. She seemed to take it as normal in any case.

"Yes, Joshua?"

"Nothing. I was just sayin'."

A little later, Josh woke. She lay serenely on the pillow, a smile upon her face, emitting the barest hint of a snore. He noticed now certain wrinkles he had not seen before. He stared down the big brass bed towards an ornate mahogany-framed mirror which showed the face of what he suddenly thought looked rather like an unhappy man. He felt curiously unsatisfied, even ashamed. He didn't understand it. But he wanted to get up and go.

So he did.

Chapter Two

Northern New Mexico gets most of its rainfall in July and August. And in those months, it sure knows how to rain. All through a hot day the clouds will build up until by late afternoon they are a massive, looming weight, like one of the black moods that sometimes descended on Josh. Then it will begin to rain a refreshing, light, dampening sprinkle. But don't be fooled and decide to start for home before it comes on strong because you won't have time. Before you know it, the water is coming down in torrents. Dusty streets turn instantly to mud. Horses struggle and wagons founder. Dry washes become running torrents. The water is warm, even pleasant if maybe you are a small shoeless boy playing in it. But it can wash out crops and roads, carry unsuspecting cows down into a river and drown them, undermine hastily erected buildings and of course it leaks through their often-green timbers. Drips and trickles are everywhere. You have to move to find a dry place and it isn't always easy.

All this was happening as Josh descended the stairs. Josh considered wryly that it was almost a sign of divine disapproval. That distinctive powerful smell of wet air leaked in through the batwing doors, which swung creakingly in the storm breeze. Inside the bar, the pungent odors of wet clothes and damp dog were added to the usual fragrance of a saloon in July.

Still no sign of Carson, thank God. Wyatt and James had gone off too, probably back to Doc's, and Hoodoo and Dutchy were not in evidence either. With no one to talk to, Josh went to the doors and gazed out at the gushing rain with pleasure then turned back and headed to the bar. With a beer in his left hand, he surveyed the tables, thinking he might join a game and wondering when Mrs. Carson might descend.

There was a skinny young cowboy, fair-haired and with a beaky nose, down at one end of the bar, all decked out in his slouch hat and fancy chaps. Spurs. One of those shirts with a rectangle of buttons which takes you all morning to get into, and a large drooping kerchief round his neck. He had some fancy Spanish gun belt on with a leather holster on each hip and bullet-filled cartridge loops.

Josh looked at him. Don't we just look the part! Straight out of one of them stupid nickel novels by Frederick Whittaker or whatever his name was. This fellow was close to drunk, it was clear. He kept laughing crassly at the men around him, though it was more like a girl's giggle. Probably thought he had said something really funny. The other men at the bar appeared to be cynically egging him on. The cowboy drew a pistol, a silver-plated Remington it looked like, and began twirling it. You could see the other men thought he was hopeless but they kept complimenting him and urging him on. The boy twirled and twirled that gun and Josh reckoned that if he didn't stop there was going to be an accident.

Sure enough, there was a loud bang and a fat man behind him slumped to the floor with a groan. The cowboy looked surprised. Josh felt that he was surprised rather than shocked. As if puzzled. They tried to get the fallen man to his feet but he was in a bad way and someone sent for the Doc. "I'm sorry! It was an accident!" the boy said, spreading his arms and opening his palms. Unfortunately, the pistol was still in one palm and men backed off fast, not trusting the gun to stay silent in the hands of this fool.

But he replaced the revolver in its scabbard, took another drink and then babbled, "Look, pards, it was an accident. I'll show you. I can do this." And he began twirling the damn pistol again in his hand.

One man put his hand on the boy's arm to restrain him and the gun went off again. This time no one was hurt. Or so they thought. But a man leaving stumbled across something. The limping girl was found stretched out in the doorway. She was stone dead. The bullet had entered her heart. Her broom lay beside her.

Josh reckoned that was enough. He went up to the cowboy and asked his name.

"Charley Beckworth, sir."

"Right, Charley Beckworth, give me them guns. We're going up the road to the marshal's office. I hear they got a good jail there."

"Oh, but honestly, it was an accident. I'm sorry. It was an accident!"

"Listen, 'pard', you just shot a young woman to death and this man here is also like to die and all you can say is it was an accident?"

"But it was! I didn't mean it! I'm sorry! It was an accident!" And incredibly he withdrew the gun again and was about to recommence his twirling. "Look, I—"

Josh had learnt the trick from Bat Masterson up in Dodge. Bat called it 'buffaloing' a man. You had to get it right. Bat's brother Ed had never mastered it and had been shot when he hadn't buffaloed a man named Shaw hard enough, there in the Lone Star. The fellow had gone down but remained conscious and had shot Ed in the chest, so close it set his clothes afire. Bat never made such a mistake. To buffalo someone properly you draw your pistol, preferably one with a bit of heft, like a cavalry .44 or something, you step in close and you whack the cowboy across the head with the barrel. Too hard and you crack the man's skull and he could die. Too soft and he will shoot you, as happened to Ed.

As he looked down at Beckworth groaning faintly on the floorboards, Josh held that he'd got it right.

He grabbed the boy by the scruff of his fancy blue shirt and dragged him outside to the boardwalk. A steel button popped and rolled. The kid's spurs left a trail along the floorboards. It was still pouring down. Josh sighed, asked to borrow a horse, slung the boy casually face down across its saddle and, leading the mare by the rein, set off, picking his way through the thick mud up the hill to the plaza and the town jail.

***

Over a well in the center of the large open plaza in the old town of West Las Vegas there stood a windmill. It was tall, perhaps forty feet high, and consisted of two parts. The pyramidical top section supported the turning vanes and pumping mechanism while the base was a simple square wooden frame, with a ladder leading up. It bore an uncanny resemblance to some gallows. And indeed, it served more than once as a gibbet when some of the townsfolk took it into their head to dispatch some less than satisfactory citizen.

The morning after Josh had handed Beckworth over to be locked up for trial—the boy still constantly repeating to all who would listen, "I'm sorry! It was an accident!"—his body was found hanging from the windmill. Attached to his fancy blue, buttoned shirt was a paper upon which was scrawled, WE ARE SORRY. IT WAS AN ACCIDENT.

***

Josh gazed at the swinging corpse in the early morning sunlight. The storm had freed the air and there was a watery wash of reds and yellows in the sky. A few weakling white clouds floated, high and impotent. One of those moods was coming upon him. But he was damned if it was going to get him this time. Grit, you needed grit. With grit, you could fight it off. A man is master of his own spirit. A man is not ruled by some external force, some vague power beyond his control. That is all bullshit. You are who you are and you are who you decide to be.

The corpse creaked in the wind. Look at that kid. He can't have been more than twenty. And they broke his neck as if he were a chicken for the pot. Shit.

He turned and walked down towards the bridge, up the rise and down over towards the other town. He began to sweat a little. He ought to get a horse. He passed Doc's place on the corner of Center Street and Grand but didn't feel like stopping and he just kind of found himself back at Close & Paterson's down by the railroad.

"My dear friend. Please, sit down. Let me get you a drink. You know, I heard all about last night. I want to thank you. For your grit and your common sense. Yes, and courage. You handled a potentially difficult situation with, how may I say, with aplomb."

Josh looked up at Hoodoo. The man was very shrewd. Very shrewd indeed. He somehow seemed to know how Josh was feeling. He knew and was playing on it.

"Now look, Josh. I understand you don't want to be rushed. You need space and time to think about things and sort yourself out. Sum up the situation. I understand that. I appreciate that. But on the other hand, you need an occupation, right? We all do. And well, you would be more than welcome here. You would be comfortable here. Don't worry about salary and wages and suchlike. I'll see you right. And if you are one of us, well, how can I say, you will not lose out. There are endless possibilities. All this money coming into town. A good part of that is going to stick to our pockets, eh? Think about it."

Josh was jolted. That was the exact phrase used by Doc Holliday. A good part of that is going to stick to our pockets. Had Doc copied it from Hoodoo, or vice versa? He looked Hoodoo right in the eyes. He expected the man to flinch but he didn't, not even for a second.

After a moment's thought, Josh replied. "Thank you, Mr. Brown. I think I will take you up on that. I shall, with your permission, install myself here and will be at your service. You may wish to swear me in as an officer."

"Oh, there will be time enough for that. Meanwhile, please do, as you say, install yourself. The gimp will…oh, I forget, she is no longer with us. Well, someone will show you to a room. Make yourself comfortable and at home, as it were. Yes, at home." He gave one of his glacial smiles. Josh returned one of his. It would be wise to be close to this Hoodoo feller for a bit.

***

 Standing in Hoodoo Brown's office, Josh knew of course that the smiling, rather prolix *bonhomie* of Hoodoo Brown which he had so far witnessed, or been treated to, was superficial. He just sensed the ruthlessness, the barbarity even, that lay beneath. But he was astonished at the speed at which it could all fall away and the true Hoodoo could be revealed. In a second, all the false smiles and counterfeit courtesy of Hoodoo Brown were dissipated. Like cigar smoke in a brisk wind. It was no longer there. It had never existed. Beneath was a face like flint or steel with not even an ounce of compassion or human feeling. The tied man gasped in his gag, clearly pleading. His brow was sweated and when Josh looked down, he realized with disgust that the man had wet himself. He didn't know whether the stench was that of fear or of urine.

"I wonder, Señor Barela, if you have ever seen a man walk, or rather try to walk, with no toes? No? Well, perhaps not. One would not necessarily expect toeless Mexicans to trip freely down the shitty little Santa Fe Trail. Well, anyway, let me enlighten you as to the unfortunate situation of the toeless man."

Josh hated this kind of display of *force majeure*. It was bullying cruelty. Like boys breaking the wings of a sparrow and laughing the while. It was a cruelty. Like that, what was he called, Marquis de Sade. If it went on, he would have to intervene.

"Well, you see, the toe may seem a minor and rather pointless appendage. After all, although the toes may be defined as the foot's fingers, we do not pick things up with our toes, do we? Nor do we use them to write or to hold our knife and fork. No, the toe appears, well, rather insignificant as corporal members go. But allow me to explain to you, dear Mr. greaser Barela, that the

34

humble toe does indeed have a rather important function in our physical functionality. You are following me? Good. Yes, you see the toes give us balance. Those who have lost their toes, perhaps through some unfortunate agricultural or industrial accident, for example, find themselves hardly able to walk. Barely able to stand, in fact. Curious, isn't it? One wouldn't have thought that the little twinkle toes made such a difference. But they do. If we were now to cut off your toes, Mr. Barela, which, to be perfectly honest, I think we will indeed do, with the machete that Dutchy here is holding, well, you would never walk again, except with the aid of sticks or crutches."

The man's eyes widened and if possible, he looked even more afraid.

"Let us come now to the matter of pain. I see that you, Mr. nasty-little-greaser Barela, are a man of substance, a merchant, a landowner. One who was born if not to riches, at least to comfort. I believe your father was also well off and doubtless you were brought up with all kinds of comforts. Pain, dear sir, will certainly not be a stranger to you, for we have all suffered pain. A toothache, perhaps, a broken limb as a child, oh, there are many kinds of pain. But you are not what one might define as a rough or tough fellow habituated to pain, are you? No. At least, not to the kind of pain I am talking about here. You see when Dutchy severs that first toe, you will scream as you have never screamed before. And of course you have ten of them!"

He signaled over to Schunderberger who raised the machete. Josh looked at Dutchy. There was no reaction. No recognition in the man's face of the horror of what was going on, no flicker at all. The giant approached and held out the machete ready, waiting for his master's order.

Josh thought it must all be a scene played out for his benefit. Brown could not be serious. And Dutchy would never…

"Well now, Mr. Barela. Of course you will wish to sign over to me all your properties in this precinct." At this important moment, Hoodoo's voice dropped and he spoke, or rather hissed, close to the man's ear. Barela furiously nodded, uttered stifled words. He was clearly doing his utmost to accept, agree, submit.

"Yes, yes, I know you will. But you see I think we will need to proceed in any case. To make a demonstration, as it were. Just one or two little pinkies. Oh, and to accord me a certain satisfaction also. Not to say, *ha ha*, pleasure. Yes, indeed. Afterwards you may make all the submission you wish and sign all the deeds prepared for you. You will doubtless survive. Well, possibly survive. There will be a considerable loss of blood, of course. But first let us proceed to the administration of, how may we call it, the correction, nay, even the punishment. For you were very naughty, you know, holding out on me for so long. Dutchy?"

"I think this has gone far enough, Mr. Brown."

Josh heard himself say these words. He hadn't planned them.

Hoodoo looked up. He thought for a moment. "Only just in my employ, Josh, and already contradicting me?"

"I ain't in your employ, Mr. Brown, not in any official sense. And I ain't going to allow this."

Hoodoo paused again. He was clearly weighing things up. His *bonhomie* seemed to return. Like a gaslight, it was turned back up. He had already decided. "Mmm, let us see. On the one hand, we have a need, no, perhaps rather a desire to inflict pain on Mr. Barela here and I shall be disappointed to renounce this desire. On the other hand, I wish to keep your loyalty and your services, which could be very useful to me. Now, which weighs heavier in the balance?" Barela continued squirming and groaning into the gag. "Of course, if you were to insist, Josh, you would have to go through Dutchy here. But no, let us not go down that road. I renounce. To please you. And to please Mr. Barela here, ha ha! Untie him, Dutchy. Let him sign the papers."

Josh waited till Barela was loosed, hastily signed the papers, and then fled from the room, then turned away, not hiding his disgust, and left Hoodoo's office. It was the moment he decided to bring Hoodoo down.

He did not know it, but it was also the moment that Hoodoo decided to do away with Josh.

***

New Mexico Chief Justice L. Bradford Prince of Santa Fe spoke slowly, almost ponderously, as if every word weighed him down. But there was a fire in him. He was an impressive figure, largely because of his expansive beard. It grew luxuriantly from his cheeks and chin, descending to cover cravat and shirt. The beard contrasted curiously, however, with the rest of his head for his skin was noticeably smooth and his hair was cut short and brushed back while his eyebrows were thin. All the better to notice his piercing gray eyes. He was angry.

Chief Justice L. Bradford Prince sat behind the desk up on the dais in the Las Vegas courthouse in a padded leather armchair. Beside him, not behind the desk but still on the dais, enough to make their solidarity evident, stood Marshal John S. Morrison. Marshal Morrison of West Las Vegas was no Joe Carson. Tall, erect, grim-faced, the man exuded probity and strength. He was thin faced. He wore a serge suit with a badge pinned to the vest. A pistol was discreetly worn high on the hip inside his coat and barely visible. But it was there. He remained silent; Chief Justice L. Bradford Prince did all the talking. Judge and marshal made a formidable pair.

Standing before them, uncomfortably, were some West Las Vegas police officers and deputies and the officers of East Las Vegas. The mayor, coroner and justice of the peace of the new precinct appeared relaxed and he often smiled but Josh reckoned it was a show. Joe Carson beside him looked unhappy and stood nervously playing with his hat in his hands, with his head slightly bowed, like some errant schoolboy before the headmaster. Dutchy and Josh stood a little further back and listened. You could read nothing on the face of either of them.

"Understand, gentlemen, this is not a hearing. I summon you to this courthouse as a convenient and large enough location but we are not in session. That does not mean, however, that what I am about to say to you has any less significance or authority. Indeed, you will defy my orders at your peril." The clear threat did not seem to disconcert Hoodoo at all. He smiled and bowed slightly in acceptance. Chief Justice L. Bradford Prince continued, "I have been informed in some detail of the violence and disorder that is besetting this town. All parts of this town. There has even been a lynching, which I absolutely will not tolerate. Much of this disorder is directly caused by the use of firearms. Now there is a clear ordinance to the effect that deadly weapons may not be carried by citizens or visitors within the town limits. Every difficulty that occurs in town grows out of a violation of this law, which should be strictly enforced, now that the influx of the population brought by the arrival of the railroad renders such difficulties particularly liable to occur." Chief Justice L. Bradford Prince could hardly have been clearer that he was laying the blame for crime directly at the door of Mayor, Coroner and Justice of the Peace Brown of East Las Vegas, who stood before him smiling. Hoodoo now spoke up.

"Your Honor, we understand completely and entirely agree with your analysis. We shall immediately do our utmost to enforce this ordinance and maintain a strict watch on the town to prevent infractions. Furthermore, Your Honor, I am at this very moment in the process of recruiting and swearing in a proper police force for Precinct 29. You may rest assured, sir, that peace and order shall reign over East Las Vegas and that all its officers will enforce it."

Chief Justice L. Bradford Prince looked distinctly skeptical but grunted his assent, and, forgetting perhaps that court was not in session, banged his gavel and barked, "Dismissed."

***

"Well, we will have to be more careful, boys. I don't too much like the look of this Chief Justice L. Bradford Prince. I do not want him spoiling things here. Just when we have got them set up so well. So hearken: no shootings for a week or so. Take pistols away from drovers and railroad men. Keep the whores more discreet for a bit. Let's just keep things battened down for a while. No excesses. Alright?"

Close and Paterson themselves and the assembled hangers on at Close & Paterson's saloon nodded their understanding and dispersed. "Josh," Hoodoo said when most of them had gone, "we need reinforcements. Some men we can rely on who can be sworn in as deputies. Now I want some Kansas boys. Any ideas? I thought of Dave Mather and that fellow Will Hardcastle, maybe. Someone with a bit of grit. But still, how shall I put it, comprehending."

"Well, I just been up in Colorado with a few of those boys at that little railroad war and yes, one or two might could be available. Not Will. He's marshal of some hick town up there now. But Mysterious Dave, yes, why not. He's been a good lawman off and on and is surely handy with a gun."

"Why is he called 'Mysterious'?"

"Well, for one thing he don't say much. He's a bit like Dutchy in that regard. I think he likes it to be thought that he is descended from Cotton Mather, the divine, and is an intellectual and all. But he don't say nothing about it, one way or the other. Then there's Dave Rudabaugh of course. He's always game for anything. But he has, shall we say, exercised his functions on both sides of the law. In fact, I was on a posse that arrested him in January last year after a train robbery. But he's tough, honest in a crooked sort of way and a good gun. In fact, they say he taught Doc Holliday how to use a gun and in return Doc taught Dave how to cheat at cards. But it don't seem very likely to me."

"Does not this Dave have a nickname?"

"Well, he do if the truth be told, though it ain't exactly flattering. They call him Dirty Dave."

Hoodoo raised his eyebrows interrogatively.

"Well, it's partially on account of his being not all that fond of soap and water. But I must admit that it's also because of certain other habits."

Hoodoo raised his eyebrows again. "Right, they sound ideal. Wire off to Dodge right away. I want all Daves, whether dirty, mysterious or dignified by any other epithet." Josh nodded. "Oh, and Josh, I want you to go down to Doc's and make clear to him what I said here. I don't rely upon that fellow to keep the peace. Speak to Wyatt. He'll keep Doc on a leash for a bit."

Josh doubted that but said he would go.

***

James A. Morehead, a large traveling salesman for several St. Louis firms, arrived on the train and checked in to the St. Nicholas Hotel in the new town, ready and eager to do business. He could smell business. New hotels and new stores were going up everywhere. All would need airtights and linen and crockery. It would all come crated, shipped down the line from St. Louis in a twinkling. He tapped the order book in his breast pocket affectionately. It was his oldest friend. There were those who said it was his only friend. A forty-year-old bachelor, Jim Morehead was not a person to waste business time cultivating worthless acquaintances.

He did however like the finer things of life, a good dinner, a glass of wine if he could get it, a cigar. In most of his travels, these were exotic luxuries to be dreamed of but completely inaccessible. But the more he followed the railroads, the more he found such items were becoming available. And he insisted upon good service.

The only, and therefore overworked, waiter so far hired by the management of the St. Nicholas Hotel was not, it was fair to say, the acme of charm and polished service. Jack Allen, a runty, oily-haired figure, had run a slightly less than salubrious saloon on Harrison Avenue in Leadville but had drunk much of his own profits, gone broke then drifted southwards. He did not shave quite as often as he might have done but he had already gained something of a reputation for other uses of a straight razor.

Morehead sat down at a corner table, brushed crumbs off the cloth with fastidious distaste and summoned the waiter with an imperious click of his fingers. "I shall take some fried eggs."

Allen looked at him, wiping his hands on his greasy apron. "It's past supper time. And we ain't got eggs on the menu."

"Nevertheless, I shall have eggs. Order the chef to prepare some."

"Chef?"

"The cook, you dolt."

Allen looked at him again. Then he shuffled off.

Morehead, waiting, became tetchy. Neither waiter nor eggs had appeared. He called, "Waiter!" Then, more loudly, "Waiter!"

Allen came up to his table. "What?"

"Where are my eggs?"

"Cook says he ain't got time to do eggs. You'll have to have what's on the menu."

This was most unsatisfactory. Morehead rose and went out to seek a more amenable dining establishment.

Next morning, he arrived late for breakfast. Allen asked him, "What do you want?"

"Why, breakfast, of course. What do you think I want in a hotel dining room in the morning, for goodness' sake? I shall have fried eggs if you please."

Allen came back. "Cook says you're too late for breakfast. He's already preparing dinner. He ain't got time to do eggs."

Morning and evening, for the next few days, Allen's irritation grew as Morehead presented himself late for meals and demanded eggs.

"Look, mister, you can have as many eggs as you want if you would just damn well get here in time."

"Now see here, my man, that is no way to talk to a client. I happen to be very partial to fried eggs and I do not see that it should be beyond the powers of a hotel to provide me with some."

Allen could take no more. "I do not care to hear any more about you and your damned eggs. I got other tables to serve and I got work to do. If you want eggs, go elsewhere, or come here at the proper times. If you don't like it, you can complain to the proprietor." He turned on his heel, thought of something and smirked. "The proprietor lives in Santa Fe," he added.

"You needn't get up on your left ear about it."

"Your constant racket about eggs is enough to put anybody on his ear."

"Please go to hell."

"I don't care to. But you can go as quick as you want to."

Morehead stood and rolled up his sleeves. "If you want anything out of me, you can get it."

Allen rushed him. They rolled over onto the table as they clinched, spilling glassware and cutlery. Morehead picked Allen up bodily and carried him across the room. It seemed his intention to defenestrate the waiter. But he fell over a chair and crashed to the floor, pinning Allen beneath him. Some diners managed to separate the struggling combatants and Allen rushed to the bar where he picked up a substantial beer bottle and rushed at Morehead once again. Morehead put his hand behind him.

"Oh, so that's how it is, it?" Allen dropped the bottle and rushed into the kitchen, where he borrowed a revolver from a dishwasher. He reappeared in the dining room, gun in hand. "You apologize, damn you."

"I shall apologize to you the day hell freezes over." Morehead advanced slowly on Allen.

The waiter backed off, step by step retreating to the kitchen. "You stand there. Stand, I say. If you do not stop, I shall shoot."

"Shoot? You do not have the courage. You are a despicable Irish tinker. Fie on you!" He continued his advance.

Allen pulled the trigger.

James Morehead died at ten o'clock that night. The passage of Allen's bullet had been slowed by his fat order-book but not sufficiently, for the ball had then entered a lung.

In his office, Hoodoo was furious. "Shit. Damn. This is just what we did not need. The very day after Chief Justice L. Bradford Prince's warning. Well, we must act firmly. As coroner I do hereby certify that James Morehead came to his death by a pistol shot fired by Jack Allen and the killing was willful, malicious and felonious murder, and without justification or provocation whatsoever. Apart from the eggs. Allen will be committed to jail to await trial where he will be found guilty and sentenced to hang. I do so find. Bring me a drink."

She drew her finger downwards from the nape of his neck tracing an imaginary line down his back. "Well now," she murmured. "This is a nice strong back. I do like a nice strong back." There was little more than a grunt in response. She sighed and looked along the big brass bed towards the ornate mahogany-framed mirror and was flattered by what she saw there. Her fair hair was charmingly tousled. The burgundy-colored velvet ribbon round her neck set off its whiteness. Her breasts were smooth and milky. She turned back to him.

"Look, we must do something or it will all go wrong. It is perfectly within the powers of Chief Justice L. Bradford Prince to have you removed and replaced."

Hoodoo sat up.

"That got your attention, didn't it! Well, I'm right. They could have you replaced as J.P. and coroner and then your authority would be confined to that of a so-far unelected mayor. We need to get a grip on this situation, Hyman, and instill a bit of law-and-order round here. Till things quiet down. You know in any case that the truly profitable business is not done with shootings and gunfights. And all that is so vulgar. How did you get on with Barela?"

"Oh, he signed over his properties. I've sent for someone up in Kansas who will ensure that Mr. Barela has an unfortunate accident. I don't want him blabbing round the town and I can't ask Dutchy or your husband."

"No indeed. What about this new fellow Webb? Wouldn't he do it?"

"Don't trust him enough yet. If I ever will."

"Barela signed the deed for the store over to me, I hope?"

"As agreed, my dear Mrs. Carson, as agreed." He rubbed his eyes. "What else do you suggest we do to keep the lid on things?"

"Well, no stage robberies for one thing. My years with the Pinkertons taught me just how easy it is to trace those responsible for robberies if you really want to. The average stage robber is hardly the soul of discretion or a master of crime. And they are inclined, when arrested, to give away the names of those of a higher station as it were. And I wouldn't put it past Holliday to have a go at this new train."

"Doc Holliday is a wild card. He seems ungovernable. And those Earps kind of think it's amusing and egg him on. I've sent word for them all to behave for the moment but there's no guarantee that they will."

"Hyman Neill, who's running this town, you or them? Put your foot down. If Holliday won't toe the line, well, run him out of town."

"You try."

"Well, use one of your assassins from Kansas then. We can't afford to have a very nice little set-up ruined by a crazed dentist." She softened. "A big strong man like you should be able to handle that. Come here, strong man."

The sleep fell all at once away from Hoodoo's eyes.

***

Saturday the 26th of July. The new clock on the depot said 3.10. The whole place was shimmering with heat. Two men descended from the train in from Raton, one small, dark, slender, frock-coated, his shirt collar done up with a stud but loose around his neck; the other full of face and collarless (for it would have been hard for any collar to circumnavigate his bull-like neck) and in a terrible baggy tweed suit bulging at every pocket. Both sported handlebar mustaches of a rather dashing cut. The slender fellow held a smart valise while his larger partner slung a bedroll across his shoulder, the butt of a Winchester repeating rifle sticking out of it.

"Well, here we are, Dave. The wild and woolly west, if I am not mistaken." It was the larger Dave who spoke.

In reply, the other Dave simply jerked his head towards the depot under construction and walked towards it.

"Oh, come on, Dave. You ain't said a darn word the whole way down. Surely it wouldn't hurt you to indulge in a bit of civilized conversation now and then."

The other Dave turned. "If it pleases you, Dave, I shall speak." As he paused, the big Dave smiled. But the smile soon faded for all the small Dave came out with was, "This way." And he turned again and set off. Dave Rudabaugh sighed, shook his head and followed.

They walked parallel to the tracks along Railroad Avenue searching for Close & Paterson's. The road was now closely lined with buildings of all kinds, wood and adobe but as yet no brick, including a great number of saloons and dance halls. But there were also low stores, a forge, a Chinese laundry, a livery stable and the usual inharmonious mixture of other commercial properties, though few if any residential ones. Everywhere there was building and work going on and the street was crowded with laborers and painters and carpenters, carrying ladders and buckets and saws, and loaded wagons and buggies and horses were trying to thread their way through them along the road.

They found a saloon with an ornate hoarding on its false front. In curly letters of many colors, the legend EVERYBODY ENTERTAINED IN THE BEST POSSIBLE MANNER was inscribed. "Good!" declared Dave.

"We'll see," answered Dave.

Below it, another sign, rather more home-made, advertised 'Close & Paterson's Variety Hall. Tonight: Deadshot Dick, King of the Pistoleers'. Two loud gunshots were heard from inside. The smaller Dave looked quizzical. "Do you think that's Deadshot practicing or are we home?" The bigger Dave smiled. It was evident which answer he preferred. In any case, they had arrived.

Chapter Three

"Well, I am very pleased to meet you, Daves. I hope you will be comfortable here. Tomorrow you will be sworn in as police officers of Precinct 29. But tonight, boys, is a big one. Tonight is the grand opening of this new town, and every saloon and gin mill and dance hall and gambling room and palace of pleasure is throwing a party. People have come from far and wide to be here. Ordinary farmers and workers of all kinds, certainly, but also personages of note, I do assure you. So you have arrived on the happiest of days. And I hope you have a whale of a time!" He smiled broadly and slapped both Daves on a shoulder.

Hoodoo was right. All day, farmers and ranchers from miles around, enticed by newspaper advertisements and street posters, many paid for by Hoodoo himself, had been streaming into town on horseback, in wagons, buckboards, buggies and carriages or on foot. Many had left their wives behind. Every building was decked out in bunting and flags and evergreen boughs. Stalls were set up selling every kind of food. Children ran and hollered. The heat was ignored. By the time night fell, the party was in full swing. The *Weekly New Mexican* a day or two later would report, "The halls were brilliantly lighted, music was furnished by excellent string bands for the dancers, glasses jingled in time with the music." It would add that, "The women who did the dancing were Americans and Mexicans ranging through nearly all grades of good and bad looks." Mrs. Carson would then throw down the paper with scorn. "No one comments upon the ugliness or beauty of the men," she would say tartly).

The Daves couldn't believe their luck. "Boy, Dave, this town do swing!"

"Quite, Dave."

***

Mike Gordon had started his celebrations early. In fact, he had started three days before. By dusk on the Saturday, any notion of sobriety had been left well

45

behind him. Gordon was looking for trouble. He liked trouble. To him, part and parcel of having a good time was trouble: fists and knives and guns. In addition, he intended to shoot the dick off Doc Holliday. It would be good sport. That would teach Holliday to mess around with Dolores. In Close & Paterson's, he had joyfully threatened to shoot out all the lights. He had always wanted to do that. "Shoot out the lights!" However, after another drink he had decided that there were too many lights and he was not prepared to work so hard. He left and passed on to another establishment. He decided instead to go see his woman.

Mike Gordon was not the handsomest of men. Put another way, he was plug ugly. Even before his disfigurement he had been bullet-headed, which a very short hair crop accentuated rather than softened. Dolores had tried to persuade him to grow his hair but he said it was harder to care for on the trail and he always had his head shaved—even though he had not been on the trail for many a year. His glory days as a scout for the 5th Cavalry were long gone. Fourteen years he'd served with the 5th. Rescued whole families from the Kiowa. Now he passed his days drinking in Las Vegas saloons and sometimes, to earn the money to drink there, working as a freighter. He had been in and out of jail. The beauty of his bullet head was not enhanced by the narrow, close-together eyes, into which, if you stared, as you could not really help doing, you noticed a distinct squint. But all this rather unAdonis-like pulchritude was outshone, as it were, by his nose. Or rather his lack of a nose. Mike Gordon was noseless. A gambler had bitten it off. The fellow had been irritated at losing. Some people are sore losers. The fellow had accused him of cheating. Well, it depended on what you mean by cheating. No one played poker straight up, did they? At any rate, this slimy dude, from Denver or Chicago or somewhere, had taken umbrage. Of course, had Mike been even halfway sober at the time, he would have had no trouble at all dealing with this weakling. But he had been drinking for a day or two, he had to admit, and the dude had got the better of him. Launched hisself across the table. Grabbed Mike's ears, one in each hand. A grip of fucking steel. Then bit. Bit! Like a girl! But this guy had no girl's strength. He was implacable. Like a bulldog. Those teeth just dug in and dug in. Boy, you'd think he'd break a tooth! But no. He just bit. And sure enough, eventually the flesh and gristle came away in the man's mouth. Mike's nose was gone.

When it healed up a bit, Mike didn't think it looked so very bad. Not really. But everyone else reared when they saw him. Some even covered their faces with handkerchiefs and turned away. Shits. Who needs a nose anyway? He was only sorry the gambler had got away. Once he'd sobered up, he'd done his utmost to find the fellow and kill him. But it was too late. The coward had left town. Anyway, noselessness is not a happy state but Gordon did not really seem to mind. He still managed to smell. In the sense of detect odors. He also smelled in the sense of emitting them. But, hell, so what. The extraordinary thing about it all, when you came to think about it, and admittedly thinking about it was not really Mike Gordon's strong point, was that women still found him attractive. Or at least Dolores did. Or was he making it up? He'd go and see Dolores.

She worked at a joint on Center Street. Some sorry dive. "Hey, Doloresh, come here."

Dolores looked at him with despair. How could you have such a man? She must do something to get rid of him. And now here he was, on the busiest night of the year, expecting her to go off with him. "*Idiota*." He hadn't got a brain in his head. "*Anda muchacho, ya largate. ¿Que no ves que estoy trabajando?*" Couldn't he see she was working? "*De hecho ya debérias estar en la cama. Necesitas un coyotito. Estás más briago que otra cosa. ¡Estupido¡ ¡No puedo acompañarte, claro que no!*" Of course, she couldn't come with him. "*¡Ora, lagarte! ¡Dejáme en paz!*" Leave me in peace! "*¡Ay Dios mio que lata!*"

Mike Gordon understood about half of what she said but enough to realize that Dolores was not going to go with him. He stumbled back out into the night. Well, then, he would start on his second plan for the evening. What was that again? Oh yes, shooting Doc Holliday's dick off.

Center Street. Now Holliday's place is somewhere here. He drew a pistol from under his coat and tried to check the loads. It wasn't all too clear. Well, no doubt it would fire. He stumbled over the step up to the boardwalk from the street. The gun nearly went off. This is the place. He looked in. No sign of Holliday. He must be here. There was a loud report. Gordon looked down at his gun and it was smoking. A Mexican on the sidewalk yelped. The bullet had passed through his pants leg.

The barman inside cried out, "Fuck!" The bullet had imbedded itself just in front of his bar.

Gordon smiled stupidly.

There were three rapid shots. They came from the sidewalk, just at the corner beside the saloon. Gordon staggered and fell.

Wyatt and James Earp appeared at the door of the saloon. "What's going on?"

"Someone shot the scout!"

"Where?"

But when they looked, no body was to be found. Only a trace of blood on the dirt. Wyatt looked at James and they went back in.

"Oh, Doc," James enquired, "where have you been? There's been a shooting outside."

"Really? Shall we play poker?"

A clerk heard the groaning and found Gordon thirty or forty yards away. He was leaking blood. They called for his girl and Dolores came running. She got him to her place up by the courthouse and nursed him. She cried. But it was no good. He died at six o'clock next morning. The last coherent thing he said was, "Fucking Holliday."

***

Down at Close & Paterson's, the celebrations in full swing, Mrs. Carson was being engaged in conversation by a quiet stranger in a discreet dark suit. Meanwhile, in a back room, Hoodoo was talking to Joe Carson.

***

"Why, Mr. Howard. It is a pleasure to meet a gentleman of manners in this rather wild town."

"The pleasure is all mine, I do assure you, Mrs. Carson."

"Won't you be seated?"

"Why, thank you, ma'am."

"Where are you from, Mr. Howard?"

"From the fine and noble state of Tennessee, ma'am."

"Tennessee? My, that is a long way from here. Are you traveling on business?"

48

"You might say so. I am looking around for a quiet place to live. Maybe a ranch. I'm staying at the Montezuma Springs. Just thought I'd come into town and enjoy the festivities tonight. And I am glad I did."

Mrs. Carson smiled and fluttered her eyelashes and her fan. "And so I am I, sir."

***

"Joe, I was talking to Mrs. Carson. To your wife, that is."

"Yes."

"Well, we were thinking that we need to keep a tight lid on this town for a bit. You remember, I was saying the other day."

Carson looked steadily at Hoodoo. "Talk often to my wife, do you?"

"Oh well, you know, just now and then. As the occasion warrants."

"Quite."

"Well, the thing is, what with this celebration and all, a lot of liquor around, I don't want any excesses. Especially no shooting. I'm a bit worried about certain establishments on Center Street."

"You mean Holliday's."

"Well, yes. I wonder if you could keep a particularly close eye on it."

"Yes."

"Right. Good."

"So my wife will be satisfied?"

"Excuse me?"

"You said you had been talking to my wife. You implied that she wanted the town kept quiet."

"Did I? No, I didn't mean to suggest...Look, Joe, I don't want any awkwardness here. We are quite well set up as we are, one way and another, aren't we?"

Carson looked stolidly at him. "In some ways."

"Yes, well. Exactly. So let's not rock any boats, eh? What is that about sleeping dogs?"

Carson stared at him, paused for quite a long time, then said, "Sleeping dogs lie, isn't it?"

He turned his back and went out.

"If you cared to come out to the Springs, Mrs. Carson, I should be delighted to entertain you there. It really is quite a good hotel. And I know the owners well, Mr. and Mrs. Scott Moore. Please do come. And your husband, of course. Tomorrow is Sunday. That might be a good moment."

"Why, Mr. Howard, that sounds delightful. I will ask my husband. Of course, with all his duties as a police officer he may not be able to come. But perhaps Mr. Brown might accompany me, or Mr. Webb."

"Well, I do hope so. It will be an enormous pleasure for me."

He rose, bowed and took his hat. "Till tomorrow, then, I hope. Good evening." He walked quietly out.

From a gaming table at the side, Josh observed all of this encounter with a pang of jealousy.

***

Carson appeared at the door of Doc's saloon. He looked around, saw Holliday and the Earps.

"Why, Marshal Carson. What a pleasure. What can we do for you?"

Carson looked at him steadily. "There's been a shooting, Mr. Holliday. Last night."

"So I understand. Who was it, do you know?"

"Yes, I know. Someone shot Mike Gordon. Someone shot him from here or near here."

"Well, well, I wonder who that could have been. Still, the rogue had it coming, eh?"

Carson set his face hard. "One of the shots was in the groin."

"Dear, dear, that must have hurt."

"Yes. He died this morning. So it's a murder charge."

"Murder, eh? Well, yes, I suppose it would be."

Wyatt looked uncomfortable. "Mr. Earp, did you witness anything?"

"No, Marshal. James and I went out when we heard the shots but saw nothing. Gordon was not there and we assumed he had left."

"I see."

"Yes."

"There were however several witnesses outside. Mr. Holliday, I may need to talk further with you. I would be grateful if you would not leave town for the moment."

Holliday looked Carson in the eyes. Suddenly his demeanor changed. "Fuck you, Carson. I shall leave or not leave whenever I damn well please. You go fuck yourself. Who the hell do you think you are? Some bought and paid for little sheriff with no guts at all, that's what you are. Run back to your boss and tell him you hadn't the courage to arrest me. For you haven't, have you?"

Carson looked at Holliday for a long time. Then he looked sadly at Wyatt, turned on his heel and left.

Doc went to the bar and downed a whiskey. Then he started laughing.

***

Josh knew pretty much all there was to know about wagons. Freighters do. He had ridden shotgun many times on a stage as well and not infrequently he had handled a buckboard. So he knew wheeled conveyances well. But he was a stranger to the carriage. This one's leather seats were soft, as were the springs. There were curtains at the windows, drawn against the sun. He felt a little seasick.

"It is good of you to accompany me, Mr. Webb."

"Joshua, please."

"Yes, of course, Joshua."

"Well, it is a pleasure."

Mrs. Carson smiled modestly.

The hot springs lie about five miles to the north of Las Vegas in a very pleasant spot about seven thousand feet up. Legend says Montezuma came there for the waters. The climate is good and the air healthy. They had built there the very presentable Adobe House Hotel, large, with substantial ornamental gardens in front. A central fountain played. The trail was quite an easy one and doubtless they would soon be building a spur of the railroad. It was accessible and attractive.

The Adobe House was owned and run by a couple, Mr. and Mrs. W. Scott Moore. The Scott Moores were evidently well off and they rather enjoyed being expansive hosts, especially if their guests were well known. He wore expensive suits from Denver and smoked fine cigars, so much that they had begun to yellow his gray beard and mustaches. She was a lady of ample proportions, one might even be tempted to say, were one not so gallant, very ample. Unfortunately, she did herself no favors by wearing tight silk or satin dresses which accentuated her rather un-hourglass-like silhouette. She had not always been a lady. In fact, Mr. Scott Moore had met her in a dance hall in St. Louis where he was working as a railroad engineer at the time. But now she was a lady.

When the black carriage drew to a halt on the gravel, the horses fidgeting and sweating a little from the climb, Josh and Mrs. Carson emerged to a truly splendid day, with bright blue sky, slightly cooler air, and a balmy breeze to welcome them. They both smiled. They could not help it. To the east, great yellow plains rolled out and to the west, tinged in pink, loomed the mountains which were named for the bloodlike tint they took on of an evening, the Sangre de Cristo range. As Josh gazed at them, they seemed indeed bloody, bloody in the sense of presaging bloodshed. His happy mood dissipated in a second. He shook his head to free himself of the absurd fancy but he could sense that, as if to negate all the daylight and sunshine and beauty around him, one of his black moods was just hovering somewhere near and waiting to descend upon him. He had felt that way since he got to Las Vegas. He must fight it. Not let the darkness engulf him. Those periods were too terrible. And getting worse. And longer. The next time he might not get out. He turned back to his companion and found her looking strangely at him. He offered her his arm briskly and with a smile invited her to accompany him inside.

When Mr. Scott Moore ushered them in, they were surprised, and perhaps in Mrs. Carson's case even unpleasantly surprised, to see Wyatt, James and Doc all assembled there and mingling among the other guests in the grand reception room which acted as antechamber to the dining hall. Josh recognized Henry Hoyt also, the young barman from the Exchange Hotel. He looked more like a guest now. The Holliday-Earp party seemed, however, on their best behavior, well dressed, clean-shaven and tidy, and sober in behavior also. Josh amiably gave them his trademark little wave, more of a flip of the hand to his shoulder, and Mrs. Carson gave them the slightest nod of her head and an even slighter smile. It was certainly impressive inside, with fancy drapes, fine mahogany and rosewood furniture, large crystal chandeliers and a very deep plush carpet. Prints of Scottish stags and English hunting scenes adorned the walls. French champagne was served.

Josh could see Mrs. Carson's eyes searching here and there for someone. He didn't have to guess very hard who that might be.

But for the moment the man before her was the hotel's owner. "Mrs. Carson, dear Mrs. Carson, what a pleasure to see you here. Allow me to present you to some of our more noteworthy guests." Mr. W. Scott Moore was the charming host. A fat ass, Josh thought him. But that's as maybe.

"I particularly would like to introduce you to my good and old friend from Tennessee, Mr., ahem, Howard. Mr. Howard has expressed an especial desire to meet you, my dear Mrs. Carson, and I do so hope that you will accommodate this laudable request. I may add that he is a very parfait gentle knight, if I may quote our dear Geoffrey Chaucer, ha ha!"

"Oh, we have already been introduced, sir. It would be a pleasure to renew Mr. Howard's acquaintance."

"Excellent, excellent! Come, come, my very dear lady, come with me. Mr. Howard is in a little retiring room yonder, with a certain Mr., ahem, McCarty. Follow me, if you please."

The 'little retiring room' turned out to be a huge ballroom or lobby. Wyatt, James and Doc had somehow infiltrated it and with them Josh noticed immediately the man who had descended from the train with him back on the fourth, the one who called himself Howard. The only other inhabitant of the room was a boy. He looked about seventeen or eighteen at most and had smooth, unwrinkled (and probably infrequently shaven) skin and a slight, youthful, even girlish frame. He had small hands. He was wearing a rather baggy but still presentable brown suit with a lighter colored vest. His shirt was buttoned to the neck but he wore no tie. He remained silent, standing beside a round table which bore a vase of flowers, with one hand resting on the polished surface. It looked almost as though he were waiting for a ferrotype to be made.

Josh shook hands with Howard and then left him to Mrs. Carson, who was already fluttering her fan with pleasure, discomforting thereby Mrs. Scott Moore, who probably felt rather proprietorial towards the handsome Tennessee man. Josh made his over to the youth. "Josh Webb," he said, holding out his hand.

"Henry McCarty." The boy then remembered something and added, "Your servant, sir."

My, fancy talk. Where had he learned that? When the lad spoke, he smiled at the same time. Josh saw he had buck teeth. "Taking the waters, Mr. McCarty?"

The smile again. "Yes, just visiting. I have come to see my friends the Moores."

Josh nodded. Why did he think that both Mr. McCarty and Mr. Howard were there for other reasons? A waiter approached with a tray and Josh took two glasses, offering one to the youth.

"No, thank you, I don't drink."

Wyatt and James approached. James tapped Josh on the shoulder, and took the second glass from his hand, downing its contents in one. "I see you have met Billy."

The youth looked at James sharply.

"It's alright, Billy. Josh is one of us. He probably knows who you are anyway."

Billy? The penny suddenly dropped. Oh, that Billy! No wonder discretion was called for. Suddenly his Adams detective job tugged at Josh's mind. A good thing Wyatt or James don't know about it. No, nor Hoodoo either. A rash of robberies…But no, he thought immediately, armed robbery wasn't in Billy's line at all. Rustling, range wars, all that, but not holding up trains. He weren't no Jesse James. But what was the notorious boy outlaw doing here?

Josh turned to James. "You know each other?"

"Nope, just met today. Mr. Scott Moore introduced us. Me and Doc and Wyatt have been enjoying a chat with Billy and with our other distinguished guest over there."

Josh turned and saw Mrs. Carson standing quite close now to the frock-coated man Howard. Who could it be, now? If he is in the same league as the Kid, then he will be famous indeed, and not necessarily for reasons that were noble, upright and true. Josh looked interrogatively at Wyatt, who replied,

"Come, I'll present you."

***

After their grand lunch, the men gathered in a smoking room. Scott Moore passed round a box of Cubans, then with a glass of brandy stood apart by a window talking earnestly but quietly to Henry Hoyt. It looked like business.

Josh sat with Wyatt, James and Doc while across a large coffee table from them, the Kid sat with Jesse.

Jesse was the first to speak. He had a distinct Missouri drawl. "Mrs. Carson wanted to accompany us in for a smoke, by God. She seems to have rather advanced ideas."

Did Josh detect a slight relief on his part to be free of her for a while?

"I don't see why a woman shouldn't smoke." The Kid was lively, alert. Possibly because he was the only one who had not taken champagne, red wine and cognac.

"A woman, Billy, maybe. But never a lady. Anyway, I am glad to have a little peace. Some ladies sure ask a good number of questions. It's pleasant now and then just to have male company."

James piped up. "It must be hard for you, Jesse, and Billy too, being wanted and all. I mean, the whole United States been searching for you since Medalia." The way he talked you'd think it was fun being hunted. "And I think General Hatch and the whole Union army is looking for the Kid, probably with the Governor hisself riding with them, after you just walked out on them, Billy!"

"Well, the Governor did not keep his word. And I detest that in a man."

"I do too," offered Jesse.

"The secret, though, is simply never to give it." Doc's contribution was, as ever, ironic or flippant.

A footman came in and handed a note to Josh. He read it, refolded it and put it in a pocket then excused himself.

"Duty calls, gentlemen. Will you forgive me?"

He wanted to stay longer and see what the two desperadoes were plotting. But they would probably not have been specific with him there. And the content of the note had been especially inviting. He found her out front by the carriage.

"I am sorry to drag you away from your tobacco smoke and masculine conversation, Joshua." There was a hint of mockery in her tone. "But I have had enough of this for today and would like to return to town, if you would be so kind."

"Of course, Mrs. Carson, of course. Allow me." And he opened the carriage door and handed her in.

The clop-clopping, the swaying and the heat made him drowsy. But he thought it was impolite to start nodding and so he began to speak. "Mr. Howard said you wanted to join us in the smoking room." It was said as an inconsequential conversational remark.

"You find that amusing?"

"Oh no. It's just that ladies don't usually—"

"Have you any idea what life is like for 'ladies' as you call them in these end-of-track towns and mining camps?"

"Well, no, I—"

"No, you don't. It is an entirely masculine society. There are far more men than women and the women fulfill roles of servants and those who, to put it bluntly, satisfy the needs of men. I am one of these. Do you think it is fine or pleasant? Try to imagine it. But no, you cannot. How could you? You are a man." She turned away from him.

"I'm sorry. Now that you explain it, I understand you have a difficult life. And yes, I suppose it is a male world. The qualities that are prized here are not gentle maternity or nurture but rather courage and manliness and strength."

She looked at him. "I misjudged you. That is very perceptive of you. Even if what you term 'courage, manliness and strength' I shall call arrogance, drunken bravado and mindless violence."

Later, as the carriage rolled down into town, she added, "You know, I know a woman, she writes me often, whose husband, a rather unsuccessful engineer, left her alone so much that the societal barriers that divided her from her maid so broke down that they became friends. They were the same age. In fact," and Mrs. Carson appeared to take a breath, "they became lovers."

Josh was shocked.

"But don't you understand? Left alone in a mining camp in Colorado, no feminine comforts at all, isolated, far from her family and friends in the east, of course she drew close to another poor lost soul." It grew hotter as they descended into West Las Vegas. It was palpable. "The only thing is, I could never share so much with another woman, never mind if she were a servant or a duchess. I need a man. Often."

Josh gulped.

***

56

That damn mahogany-framed mirror again. Why did it have to be there, at the end of the bed? Well, there might be a reason. He turned uncomfortably over. She stirred. Then she looked at him and asked, "Why do you hate him?"

"Who?"

"Hyman."

"I don't hate anyone."

"Or like anyone."

"Wait up. You make it sound as if 'like' is the opposite of 'hate'."

"It isn't?"

"No, 'like' is the opposite of 'dislike'. 'Love' is the opposite of 'hate'."

"So you love no one?"

"Ah, love. Well, it is given to mortal man, or woman also, I guess, to love but few if any. As for me, I loved my mother; my father less, it must be said; I loved my brothers and sisters, especially one; and one other person."

"Other person?"

"Yes."

Mrs. Carson was now silent.

"However, I am not really prepared to talk about that. Unless…"

"Unless?"

"Unless we became lovers. Then I would tell you everything and more."

"Everything and more, well, my, that's a lot!"

"Yes, ma'am."

Josh thought for a moment and looked at her. "What about him? Do you love him? Do you even like him?"

"Hoodoo is a strong man. A winner. He can give me what I want."

"I didn't mean Hoodoo."

"Oh, I see. Well, now we have entered very difficult territory. Indian territory. Dangerous, unpredictable."

"He seems to me a good man."

"I'm surprised you say that. Most people think he's just a cheap crooked sheriff. But you are right, he is a good man. There is no doubt of that."

"Reluctantly corrupt, one might say."

"I don't think he's corrupt at all."

"No, you are right. Not corrupt. But somehow weak. No, broken."

"Yes."

"Why?"

Now it was Mrs. Carson's turn to pause and think. She almost couldn't say it. She spoke in a whisper. "It was me. I did it."

"I see." Josh said no more. He understood.

"Let's fuck now."

"That's a very coarse expression, Mrs. Carson."

"Yes, but let's."

"Yes, let's."

The crumpled note she had sent him at the Hot Springs lay forgotten on the dresser under the mahogany mirror. It simply said, *We should be in bed.*

***

While Josh and Mrs. Carson lay in her large bed, at about five o'clock in the afternoon, out on the trail a dozen or so miles south of Las Vegas on the Santa Fe Trail, a man sat on a log. He had a big twelve-gauge shotgun across his knees. It was rather an aristocratic weapon, with 42" barrels, walnut stock and some English scrolling on the plate. One might have wondered where such a ruffian had obtained it. For the man was poorly dressed in ragged pants, a checkered shirt out at the elbows and the sorriest hat you ever saw. However, curiously in view of the heat, he wore over this ensemble a long yellow slicker that reached almost to the ground. He was unshaven. A central tooth was missing from its appointed place and the others were unattractively grimed. He had a beaky nose and his eyes were close set. He was not a handsome man. He was bored. He picked his pointed nose.

When he heard the stagecoach coming up the *puertocito,* he remained sitting but pulled a bandanna up almost to his eyes and jammed his sorry hat down almost to meet it. This man did not want to be recognized. Only when the Concord rolled into view did he rise. He calmly held out the shotgun, not aiming it but kept it pointing upwards for the driver and guard to see, and held up his other hand in a signal to halt.

Eric Bartels had been driving stagecoaches for a long time, despite his youth. He had been born and bred to them. He knew every spring and rivet and he managed his team with consummate skill. He was no stranger to road agents either. And he had learned that if you did what you were told you would probably get away unscathed. Beside him on the box sat his habitual messenger, Stocky Bob. Bob knew very well what was what. He looked at Eric

58

then took the Wells, Fargo ten-gauge that stood in the footwell and threw it down into the dirt and held up his hands. Eric nodded, brushed his moustaches, right and left, with his gloved hand then reined the horses in.

Eric was just beginning to wonder where the hold-up man's fellows were. You don't hold up stages alone and on foot. Not unless you are Black Bart. But his question was soon answered for two other masked men came out, one from each side of the trail, both holding Winchesters. The fellow in the yellow slicker, evidently the leader, gruffly told his accomplices to get the passengers down.

The coach contained three voyagers.

Belle, a saloon girl on her way from Santa Fe to find work in the new dance halls in East Las Vegas, was unafraid and looked even bored. She was first to descend and addressed the bandits simply. "You can have anything I got, boys, and much good will it do you. 'Cause I'm broke. Ain't got a bean." She attempted to chuck one man humorously beneath the chin but he angrily struck her hand down. Perhaps he was afraid of being unmasked. Belle shrugged, said, "Temper, temper," and moved away.

She was followed by a stout, gray-suited man who had earlier introduced himself to his fellow passengers as John H. Strahan of New York. He wore wire-rimmed spectacles on a florid face and he puffed as he got in a position to descend. As he got down, he tried surreptitiously to remove his watch chain, thrusting the timepiece into a trouser pocket. But it didn't escape the attention of the man in the yellow slicker.

Neither of these two passengers, however, prepared the man in the slicker for W. F. M. Arny. W. F. M. Arny came out shouting. "How dare you! How dare you!" About sixty-five or sixty-six years old, tall, thin, W. F. M. Arny clearly modeled himself on Abe Lincoln and indeed did look rather like him. Thin faced, with that fringe of beard, heavily suited and in an overcoat despite the heat, with a high-top hat, he exuded force and energy. He was a Virginia evangelist and Virginia evangelists are not noted for their reticence. He had also, since his arrival in New Mexico during the war, served as Indian agent, territorial secretary and once even as acting Governor. In short, W. F. M. Arny was not a man to be trifled with.

"I shall sit down," he retorted to the leader's order to sit on the log, "if and only if I choose to. And I do not choose to. I have been sitting long enough.

Furthermore, by perambulating I shall observe more and perhaps gather enough evidence to hang you when you are caught."

Slap-Jack Nicholson, in his slicker, smiled behind the mask. Now here was a feisty old gentleman. He turned to his friend Mullen, whose pock-marked skin was plainly visible above the bandanna—you couldn't hide skin like that—and told him to hold his rifle on the two seated passengers and W. F. M. Arny. He then signaled to the third member of the party, Bull-Shit Jack Pierce, to keep the driver and guard covered while he himself vaulted up to the box, threw the two mail sacks down, and then jumped back down himself. He took out his knife and slit the sacks open, spilling out the mail. He began ripping the letters open, looking for currency.

"Look at that wanton destruction. Shame on you for the villain you are!" W. F. M. Arny was in full voice.

Mullen stabbed his Winchester toward Arny and told him to shut up. Arny went on uninterruptedly. He was used to continuous discourse. "Why can you not open the envelopes more carefully and preserve their contents? That is the U.S. Mail you are tampering with."

Slap-Jack looked up at him, shrugged, then did as he was bid, carefully opening the end of each envelope and looking inside for banknotes. By the end, he probably had about two hundred dollars. "Now, let's see what our travelers have." And he approached the passengers.

Belle opened her arms cheerfully and said, "Search, Jack. Search away. It'll be a pleasure."

Slap-Jack started at the use of his name. Had she recognized him? But no, she was just using a name, any name. He growled, "My name ain't Jack," and snatched her purse. She was right. It contained nothing of value except a powder case which looked as if it might be valuable. But what did he know about powder cases? He handed it roughly back to her and turned his attention to Strahan while the Pock-Marked Kid went through the pockets of W. F. M. Arny. Slap-Jack came up with two hundred dollars from Mr. John H. Strahan of New York, not bad at all. Two hundred dollars and a watch. Gold, too.

He turned to the Pock-Marked Kid. "What you find on him?"

"Nothing. He ain't got nothing."

"Course he do. Search him again."

"I done searched him twice."

"Well search that antediluvian gentleman again. And this time find his money." 'Antediluvian' was Slap-Jack's favorite word and was probably the longest one he knew. "Antediluvian. That means old," he added, for the benefit of Mullen.

While Mullen was going through the protesting preacher's pockets again, this time finding a wallet, the old man suddenly lunged at Slap-Jack and grabbed his shotgun. Nicholson wrestled it back from the old fool's grasp but Arny managed to claw at his face mask meanwhile and pull it partially down. "Aha!" he cried triumphantly. "Now I shall be able to identify you!"

Belle looked at Strahan in alarm and Eric looked at Bob. This was foolishness indeed. They might all suffer for it.

Slap-Jack hastily readjusted his bandanna and raised the shotgun to the preacher's head. But then he stopped. Gunman he might be, and robber and thief, but he did not want to have any truck with wholesale slaughter. If he killed Arny, he would have to kill them all. He turned the gun and used its butt to club the fellow on the side of the head, not too hard but enough to make him tumble in the dirt. "Old fool!" He picked up the man's fallen wallet and rifled through it, finding a goodly sum in banknotes, which he stuffed into his own pocket. Then he turned to the driver. "Unhitch them horses."

Eric sighed. He was going to lose his best team. And Mabel his favorite too.

In fact, they left Mabel and rode off on the other three. So all in all, as Eric and Bob debated if one of them should ride Mabel into town for help or whether they all ought to set out on foot, Eric Bartels reckoned he had gotten off lightly. Again. And he still had his watch.

***

In Joe Carson's new office in East Las Vegas, near the depot, Detective Charles Cole of the Post Office Investigation Department, who looked about twelve, faced W.F.M. Arny.

"Mr. Arny, I have, as you probably know, recently arrived in this town, with express orders to investigate a particular felony at which, I understand, you, sir, assisted."

Arny looked up. This bantam had almost as flowery a turn of phrase as he did himself.

"It was, sir," Cole continued, "a heinous assault upon both the liberties of our citizens, including your esteemed self, and furthermore—even worse, one might conjecture—an assault upon the dignity and integrity of the United States of America." No one bothered to contradict him, even if all knew they were not in the U.S.A. at all. But, as if forestalling this unexpressed criticism, Cole went on, "For of course, while New Mexico Territory does not, or does not yet at least, constitute a part of the United States of America, technically speaking, nevertheless we are all aware that the mail carried on this coach was the U.S. Mail, sent by honest American citizens who confidently expected it to arrive. Who placed a profound trust in us, sir, to ensure that it was delivered. You may imagine, therefore, my—"

"Cut the crap, boy, what do you want to know?"

Detective Cole looked up, shocked, at W.F.M. Arny. "Sir?"

"Yes, yes, all that rigmarole. But what do you want to know specifically? I want these bandits arrested, in short order. This century, preferably. All your windbaggery and verbiage is taking up valuable time. What do you need to know?"

W.F.M. Arny's elocutionary style had suddenly adapted itself, faced with the more ornate one of his interlocutor, so like that which he was used to employ himself. "Get on with it."

"Yes, sir. Quite! Well, put simply, we need to arrest the stage robbers."

"Brilliant." Arny looked at Carson. "The boy's a genius." He turned back to Cole. "When did you get out of short pants, sonny?"

"But, Mr. Arny, Marshal, I have leads. Yes, leads."

"Leads." Arny's eyes rolled up in his head.

Joe Carson intervened. "You suspect someone?"

"Well, yes. I have made inquiries. I have talked to various people in town. And I have narrowed the hunt down to some clear suspects."

"And who might they be?"

"Well, let me see." He pulled out a notebook. "There is this fellow William Clancy. Clancy is a railroad worker. In the know about the mails, you see. And disreputable. Disreputable."

Carson looked skeptical.

"And then there is Antonio Lopez. Now Lopez is a known associate of Clancy's. He is a Chilean of bold appearance."

"A Chilean of bold appearance."

"Yessir."

Arny could hide his impatience no longer. "Oh, for goodness' sake."

Cole tapped his notebook. "And lastly a fellow here called Elijio Perea."

Carson: "So two of them were Spanish, is that what you are saying?"

Arny: "None of them was Spanish. None of them! They were American hoodlums. American!"

Carson looked at Arny closely. "What do you mean, 'hoodlum'?"

"It's what they call villains and rogues and bad men in San Francisco street slang."

"It is?" Carson was surprised at Arny's knowledge of the vernacular. He turned back to Cole. "You say you spoke to people in town. To whom did you speak?"

"Oh, well, I spoke to a couple of lawmen. One was called David Rudabaugh. And the other, let me see, Mr. Mather."

Carson sighed.

"And Mr. Brown vouched for them. Mr. Brown is Justice of the Peace. No, I don't think there's any doubt about it. None. I think we should bring these men in, Marshal. I do really."

"Well, let's have a look at them," suggested tiredly W. F. M. Arny.

***

Josh and Dave Rudabaugh accompanied the manacled suspects to the marshal's office. Josh and Dave were getting along better. Josh liked the straightforwardness of the man. He was straightforward even in wrongdoing. There was no side to him. He did what he did and if it was one side of the law or the other, he just shrugged and smiled. They found Clancy down at the roundhouse and the other two playing keno in a bordello on Railroad. The two Mexicans looked genuinely surprised to be arrested. Clancy was a shifty customer who obviously thought he had been caught for some misdeed. He tried to bluff it out but they could see in his eyes that he was guilty of something.

The extraordinary thing was that once they got the men to the marshal's office W. F. M. Arny took one look at Clancy and said, "That's the man. No doubt about it. That's the culprit."

"You sure?"

"Certainly, I am sure, Mr. Carson. I got a good look at the fellow, remember. And he is of the same build. And his voice is that of the leader of the bandits. It is he."

"Who the hell is this?" asked Clancy.

"You know very well who I am, sir. And I told you that you would be caught. And hang."

Clancy turned round to Josh and Dave. "I never saw this old vulture before in my life. What is he accusing me of?"

"Stage robbery."

"Stage robbery? You are joking."

The other two suspects were not following all the talk but they understood enough and began to remonstrate.

Carson shook his head then said, "Alright boys. Get in that cell. You got a case to answer."

Josh shook his head too. If these men were guilty, he was Billy the Kid.

Chapter Four

Bob Paul and Eric Bartels were riding in their customary fashion, side by side on the northbound stage out of Santa Fe. They had grown used to each other's ways. Stocky Bob didn't say too much because Eric was inclined to do all the talking. Anecdotes and tales and jokes flowed from him like a mountain spring. Bob was a taciturn sort of fellow but quite liked other people to talk. Like many solitary and quiet folk, he was a good listener.

"So I was driving one day, see, and this fellow up behind me—we had twelve people aboard that day—well, he was a drummer of some kind. What was it now? Oh yes, I believe it was ladies' corsets. Because I laughed when he said he traveled in ladies' corsets. Anyway, he was recounting this story of what happened to him down in some border town, I forget where it was, might of been Bisbee, and he said there was this fellow there, some old drunk, who dropped dead in the street, pop!, like that, and everyone passed by and stepped over him and ignored it till this drummer could stand it no more and routed out the undertaker and slapped a five-dollar piece in his hand to bury the poor man up in Boot Hill." Eric paused, for breath and to throw a couple of pebbles at Mabel's rump to help her up the incline. "But the thing was, see, that the townsfolk wouldn't allow it 'cause this dead fellow was an Indian, and the corpses up there in Boot Hill, well, they may of been ne'er-do-wells and vagabonds and the like, but they was white, see? And the undertaker wasn't prepared to risk his new hearse. It was a thousand-dollar hearse from Denver, see. And he was afraid that it might get shot up. And his driver quit and no one would drive it. But then two gunmen, they was real gunnies, stepped out and said—"

"Hold!"

Two gunmen stood in the road. One was holding up a long shotgun and wearing a long yellow slicker.

"Oh shit," said Bob. "Not again."

***

"And I tell you, Marshal, I'm gettin' mighty tired of it. Exactly one week after the last one. And you can depend upon it, the same men. The very same. Yellow slicker, English shotgun. They went through the mail and searched the passengers. Allowed each one to keep fifty cents for something to eat. 'Cept old Ben Stoop. We picked him up and gave him a lift. Shouldna done. Against company regulations. But Ben only had fifteen cents on him anyway. He asked the robbers for thirty-five cents to make it up to the fifty. And they did. I might of thought that was kinda generous of them 'cept that it was the other passengers' money they was giving Ben. Took the horses just like before. We walked in. Only difference I could see was they was five of them this time, two back in the bushes in a buggy. They must of been a high class of robber, I reckon. Any buggies gone missing from town lately, Marshal, or been rented?"

Carson bowed his head and was silent a moment before answering. "Well, we shall inquire. But one thing is clear. If you are absolutely positive that it was the same men who robbed you both times, with exactly the same modus operandi, that means I have sent the wrong men to Santa Fe for trial for the first robbery."

"Yessir. I reckon you did."

"Well, thank you, Bartels. I'll need a signed statement from you and Bob. You can dictate it all to Dave Mather. Don't miss out any details, no matter how small. And get that old timer Ben Stoop in too, for what his evidence is worth. I'm going off to see the justice of the peace and then down to Santa Fe to get those other men out of jail."

"Yessir. Only it's got to stop, Marshal. I mean, next time me and Bob might not ec-scape."

Walking over to Close & Paterson's later, Joe Carson looked pensive. He met Josh in the street on the way and smiled in greeting. Josh said, "Joe," and fell in beside him. They found Hoodoo, angry at a table with Billy Paterson and George Close.

"Carson! Come here! Dammit, Carson, I said keep a lid on it here for a while. Let's keep our heads down, I said. Be good boys and girls for a bit. Or at least pretend to be. And what have we had since Chief Justice L. Bradford Prince's shot across the bows less than a month ago? We've had two fatal shootings and two stage robberies, that's what. Jesus, Carson, what the hell do I pay you for?"

"Now hold on a minute, Mr. Brown. Just hold your horses a moment. It wasn't me who fingered Clancy, Lopez and Perea for that first robbery. In fact, it was plain it wasn't them. That fool detective Close said it was you and Mather and Rudabaugh who put him on to Clancy & Co. If you ask me, the real guilty parties are men working for Holliday. Charlie up at the livery stable tells me that one of those ruffians who hang out at his saloon rented a buggy and brought it back with the horse lathered right after the robbery. I reckon it was those three gunmen of his who held that stage up, the ugly ones with the dumb nicknames they are so proud of, and I wouldn't be surprised if this time Holliday and Earp were out there with them. As for the murder of Gordon, that was Holliday too. I'm sure of it. Shot him from ambush and won't admit it. That's Holliday's style alright. And Holliday and Earp and the others are supposed to be part of the Kansas clique here in this town, Mr. Brown, the Kansas men who do your bidding. So I really don't think you can justifiably lay the blame all on me."

Josh was impressed when Carson added, "Although some of it is mine, yes." He was also impressed at the impassive and stoical way the man withstood the ensuing storm of abuse that lashed him. Like a great tree. When Hoodoo's foul language and temper were spent, the marshal said, "Well, if that is all, I will get back to my duties," turned and left. Carson was going up in Josh's estimation, even if his own relationship with the marshal was complicated by his relationship with the man's wife. As Carson left, however, the sheer look of hatred and contempt on Hoodoo's face made Josh fear for Carson's safety.

***

"It's done, Mr. Brown."

"Discreetly, I hope."

"Yessir. We jumped him out on the open road up towards Mora. No one around."

"You disposed of the body? I can't afford any more corpses or crimes right now."

"We threw him down an abandoned mineshaft. He'll never be found. You have heard the last of Señor Barela."

Hoodoo nodded and bought the boys a drink.

Hoodoo Brown marched down to Center Street, Dutchy Schunderberger slightly behind but not much. It wasn't like Hoodoo to run his own errands but he wanted to confront the blackguards in their own lair.

There was a strong smell of baking from next door which Dutchy enjoyed but Hoodoo ignored as they pushed in through the rattly two-paned door into Holliday's miserable saloon. The narrow room was empty except for the three 'hoodlums' with the absurd nicknames who were attached to Holliday: what was it, Slapjack, Bullshit something, Pock-Marked Kid. They were only cheap gun hands. Not even good ones. They'd get away with a spot of rustling for a while or even a bank job, once, but sure enough they would be found out. They just hadn't the wit or skill. They weren't professionals. They would be barely passable for fixing the odd fight, doping a horse, that kind of thing. Nothing more.

"Where's Holliday?" he demanded of the one with bad skin.

"How the hell should I know?"

The slap across the face was hard, as well as unexpected. Hard enough to knock the man back painfully into the bar. Hoodoo had a short way with lack of respect and he had a boxer's shoulders. He followed up the slap with a sharp kick, striking the youth expertly on the side of the knee, causing a good deal of pain. Hoodoo was still an artist in a dirty fight. "I said, where is Holliday?"

"Out back. With Earp."

"Call them in."

The man looked at his companions.

"Now." Hoodoo's tone left no room for hesitation.

"Yessir."

Hoodoo looked at Dutchy and raised his hands to heaven. And these were the men Holliday was using. Dutchy shook his head in agreement.

Doc came in, followed by James and Wyatt. The Pock-Marked Kid, who had gone to get them, skulked off to join his mates at the bar. Doc sensed the atmosphere and did not even attempt friendliness or welcome. "What is it?"

"I need to talk to you."

Doc shrugged and signed him to take a seat.

"Now, look. I won't beat about the bush. You know very well that we are nicely set up here. Very nicely. You also know that the law has been looking at the situation here too closely for comfort and we have decided to be discreet for a while. Do what we want but behind closed doors as it were. For the time."

"You have decided, you mean."

"Alright then, yes, I have decided. But I am running things here and it's the right decision."

"Well, so?"

"Well, so your shooting army scouts in the street and holding up stages in broad daylight doesn't exactly fall into the category of 'behind closed doors', now does it?"

"Who are you accusing of murder and armed robbery?"

"Oh, cut it out, Holliday. I know you shot Gordon. Carson told me. I don't care about that. The ruffian had it coming. He threatened you; I know that. I have no problem whatsoever with that. But his body should be lying unnoticed at the bottom of some mineshaft, not stretched out in town for all to see. Jesus."

Holliday looked at Hoodoo right in the eyes. "Carson told you. Carson. I'm going to have that bastard. He won't see the week out."

"The hell you say. You will do no such thing. He is the appointed marshal in this precinct. Touch him and I'll run you out of town." Hoodoo went on, "And you know as well as I do that these sorry sons-a-bitches here held up the Santa Fe stage a week ago, and again yesterday. And I have reason to believe that you and Earp here were up there with them this time."

Doc smiled and took a drink. "Well, a bit of fun never hurt anybody. It was a lark."

"That's just what I mean. 'A lark'. Totally irresponsible. Well, let me put my cards on the table. You and Wyatt and the other Earp here—he indicated James, who clearly resented being referred to in such terms—will lie low from now on. Do what you want in here, cheat the customers, water the liquor, run poxy whores, do what you fucking want, but NO shooting and NO robberies. Is that clear? Because it's that or farewell, Holliday. I mean it." And with that he got up, took his hat back from Dutchy and left, slamming the rattly old door behind him with a clatter.

Doc looked at Wyatt. "I think our beloved mayor and his trusty marshal may be getting above themselves. And you know what can happen to people who get above themselves." Wyatt raised his eyebrows. Doc's however descended as his brow darkened, he took a deep drink and started to cough.

***

Hoodoo summoned George Close as if he were a messenger boy instead of owner of the saloon. "Here, I want you to send this telegram to Denver. Pay the clerk well. I don't want anyone blabbing its contents about town." Close looked a little offended to be treated so peremptorily but took it. Hoodoo looked up and added, "And that goes for you too."

***

It occurred to Josh that he had not seen Mr. and Mrs. Carson together. Not once. Not even talking. He blew cigar smoke at his bedroom ceiling. Of course you don't have to talk to love someone. Love transcends idle chatter. True lovers are happy sharing silences. Yet that was the point. These two didn't share silences. They had their own separate silences. They didn't share anything. Anything at all. Except a surname.

And yet Carson loved his wife. Josh could see it in the man's eyes. And in the pain with which he dealt with the knowledge that she was seeing Hoodoo. Josh wondered if he knew about him. He hoped not. Or her making up to Jesse James. She was an adulteress. It was not too strong a word. Yet he knew also that she still loved Carson. The bed partners didn't mean a thing. She still loved her husband. It was really very odd.

But it meant that Mrs. Carson was not for him. He must break it off.

***

On a humid, overcast and very hot Monday, the eleventh of August, the AT&SF train pulled out of the Las Vegas depot almost exactly on time at only a few minutes after noon. In view of the recent stage robberies and fearing that the train could be next, the *Las Vegas Gazette* had reported that "All employees on the train from La Junta to Las Vegas have been furnished with carbines and ammunition to protect the passengers and express from road agents. Men who know how to shoot and are experienced in the use of Winchester rifles at short range are being placed on the train." The brakeman and fireman had revolvers. Certain passengers most certainly were armed. And Detective George Cole had come down from Denver again, especially so that he could go back, riding the train to protect the mails. There were two Pinkerton's operatives aboard also.

Not far up the line, in a deep cut, five long-coated men sat their horses. They were masked in the approved fashion, with large kerchiefs tied at the nape and covering their noses. They had pistols at their belts and all held a Winchester or a shotgun, the butt seated on a thigh or saddle. The trunks of two piñon trees lay across the tracks and behind them a pile of stones for good measure.

"You'll see, Billy, it's a piece of cake. And as I said, you must rob at least one train in your life. Otherwise what kind of outlaw are you?" Jesse chuckled behind the mask.

The Kid grunted skeptically and wished he hadn't come. He liked Jesse and yes, this was rather a lark, but this really wasn't in his line of work. Furthermore, he disliked and distrusted Holliday and did not really care for the Daves, or at least the Mysterious one.

Still, it was too late now. And the five of them should not have too many problems. And Jesse was right in a way. Although there was no possibility of Billy's acceding to Jesse's suggestion to join forces when Jesse came 'out of retirement' and went back into business. Well, let's get this over with.

Dave Rudabaugh looked over to Dave Mather. "You ready, Dave?"

"I'm ready, Dave."

"Good." Dave nodded approvingly. Then he added, "'Cause I'm ready, Dave."

Mysterious Dave sighed. Intelligent conversation was always a challenge when Dirty Dave was around. He levered a round into the breech of his Winchester and let that suffice as a response.

Holliday's horse stood back. Doc had pulled his mask down and he yawned expansively before tucking a cheroot between his teeth and lighting it. Even the first inhalation was immediately followed by a fit of deep coughing. Mysterious Dave wondered why on earth he did it. He looked back at Doc who just smiled, took a silver flask from his pocket, swigged at it, then proffered it to Dave. Mysterious Dave shook his head. He could see Doc's trademark plated .38 tucked under his arm. He lightly slapped at his own long-barreled .45 in its holster just below his right hip. He considered that it was a more serious weapon.

Dirty Dave turned his head to see what Mysterious was looking at. Holliday offered him the flask too. Dirty Dave spat and turned back. Holliday shrugged at the rebuff.

The fierce afternoon heat shimmered the tracks and a buzzard wheeled overhead. Dirty Dave slapped at a horsefly. Otherwise they heard only the cicadas and Doc's occasional cough. They were all sweating beneath their long coats.

At first, Jesse thought it was one of the horses panting but it was the locomotive, grunting up the gradient. "Here we go, boys. Have fun!"

When the great black beast snorted to a halt, the driver and fireman looking out of the cab at the obstruction, both their mouths making an 'O' of surprise when they saw the masked horsemen, Jesse dug in his spurs and galloped down the track to come alongside the engine. "Drop any arms in the dirt and get those hands up, gentlemen, please!"

Billy had come up behind him, the others following, and Jesse waved them on to their allotted tasks. Dirty Dave swung up into the cab and covered the men there while Mysterious Dave and Doc, both well masked, mounted the first car and entered, guns at the ready, Doc ordering, "Church collection time! Watches, purses and wallets, ladies and gents, please. In this hat. Any holding back gets the person shot. Otherwise no one gets hurt. Please give generously." They made their way down the car and then entered the second. Meanwhile, Jesse and Billy rode straight to the express car.

Inside, alongside the strongbox, stood a rather anxious Detective George Cole of the Post Office. He didn't know why they had stopped. It was too soon out of the depot to take on water. He looked at the railroad employee beside him then opened a leather case to reveal a matched pair of shiny Smith & Wesson revolvers, which had never been used. He took one and broke it open but his fingers seemed inexplicably shaky and inserting the loads was quite an enterprise.

The railroad employee leaned over, took the pistol and in an extremely adroit maneuver in which he appeared to twist the wrist and insert all five bullets in one action, impressing Cole enormously, he snapped it shut, swung it round so that he was holding the barrel and offered the butt back to Cole.

"There ain't a safety," the railroad employee said.

"Safety. Yes, of course, no safety."

"Hola, inside! Open up!"

Cole looked startled. "Open up? Why, who is it?"

"Jesse James and Billy the Kid. Who do you think it is? We got Wild Bill Hickok and Black Bart here too, and Calamity Jane on the engine. Now open up."

"I most certainly shall not."

"Okay, as you wish. But know that the dynamite is already lit. You've got about twenty seconds, I would say, before you're all blown to hell. But have it your own way. We're going to draw back a little for a minute."

The door was hastily slid back.

"Jesse James and Billy the Kid, my foot. I don't know who you are, sirs, but I do know there will be no hiding place! We shall track you down, though it be to the ends of the earth."

"Shut up," grunted the Santa Fe employee. "'No hiding place', indeed. You sound like a durned illustrated paper. Give them the mail sacks."

"Give up the U.S. Mail?"

"Or be shot. You choose. Personally, I am for giving up the U.S. Mail."

"Admirably put," approved Jesse. "You heard the man; the choice is yours. Or Jesse here will shoot."

Billy joined in. "No, you're Jesse. I'm Billy."

"Oh yes, silly of me. Sorry. Well, either Billy or Jesse will shoot you."

The employee grabbed the sacks and heaved them out.

"Excellent! Jesse, go and get Wild Bill and the others."

"I done told you. I'm Billy."

"Whichever. Let's go."

When the five galloped off, the various officers hastened to free the engineer, who had been tied to his locomotive's wheels by Dave, to delay the departure of the train. A few aimed rifle and pistol shots at the receding horsemen but it was futile. Detective Cole put his head in his hands and sobbed.

***

They divided up the currency at a grove of cottonwoods about thirty minutes' fast ride from the train. Dirty Dave seemed to have hit it off with Billy and they were laughing and joking and digging each other in the ribs. Mysterious Dave and Doc were rather more bored with proceedings now that the action was over. They were passing Doc's flask to and fro. Then it seemed to Josh that Mysterious fastidiously wondered if he might be catching something contagious from Doc and refused the flask when it was offered again.

Jesse seemed enormously pleased with himself. "Boys, I'd forgotten how good it feels. Time I went back into business. Who's for joining me? What a gang we'd make, eh? Mind, a name would be a bit of a problem. The James-Younger Gang had a good ring to it. Even if Cole always did think it ought to have been the Younger-James gang. The James-Bonney-Doc-Daves Gang don't seem to do it somehow. We'll just have to call ourselves the Regulators or something. What do you say, Billy?"

Billy smiled. It had been an experience. "No thanks, Jesse. I got enough on my plate right now. Half of New Mexico chasing me, arrest warrants right and left. I got to get all this sorted out 'fore I start out in another profession, as it were. I got to write to Governor Wallace again and see about this pardon. Also, I have a certain Spanish girl waiting for me down in Roswell."

"Doc?"

"Quite fun, now and then, but no. I think I'll stick to pulling teeth."

"Daves?"

Dirty Dave took some time thinking about this. You could see he was considering it. He looked across at his friend. "Dave?"

"No, Dave, I don't think so. Right now we have a good berth as lawmen. And we don't really want this little escapade to get advertised just now, do we? Maybe next year. But now, I think we should get back to Las Vegas."

Dirty Dave looked over at Jesse and shrugged. "You got your answer, Jesse. Thanks anyway. And good luck."

Jesse laughed. "I better be off. Might go into California and see what's what. Ride with me just a little along the way, Billy?"

"Just a ways, alright."

They mounted up and said goodbye. In parting, Billy said to Dave Rudabaugh, "Look me up if you are ever in my area, Dave!" Mysterious Dave noticed that the offer was not extended to him and he began to sulk. Doc and the Daves rode back to town.

***

Two legal sessions were convened six days later. The first was in the Las Vegas Court House and was presided over by Chief Justice L. Bradford Prince.

"The court is in session." Chief Justice L. Bradford Prince banged his gavel. He seemed to enjoy doing it. "We have charges here lodged by Mr. G. W. Cole. Is he here?"

Detective Cole rose. "I am, Your Honor."

"You have preferred charges against two citizens of Las Vegas, Mr. David Rudabaugh and Mr. David A. Mather. Are they present?"

The Daves stood. Mysterious Dave replied for them both. "We are, Your Honor."

"The charges relate to a felony committed on the eleventh instant, namely the assault upon the Las Vegas to Raton train at approximately twelve-thirty, eight miles north of Las Vegas. Is that right?"

Cole rose again. "Yes, sir."

"Well, tell us, Mr. Cole. Why do you think that these two gentlemen, who are both, you know, sworn officers of this town, had any part in this robbery?"

"Well, sir, it is upon the say-so of three gentlemen whom I interviewed in connection with another robbery, one upon the Santa Fe stage. They informed me that—"

"Wait a minute. Three men accused Rudabaugh and Mather, is that what you are saying?"

"In a way, Your Honor. You see they—"

"Well, where are they?"

"Ah, they have, unfortunately, left town, sir."

"They have left town."

"Yes, sir."

"Mr. Cole. Are you familiar with the legal concept of hearsay?"

"Yes, I am, Your Honor. But—"

"Well, you'd better explain."

"Thank you, sir. Well, these three, named Nicholson, Pierce and Mullen, were, I believe, responsible for a recent robbery on the stage. So I suspected them of involvement in the attack upon the train. They seemed likely culprits, as it were. They denied complicity and were able to furnish alibis. They had been with known persons in town at the exact time of the train robbery. However, they indicated to me when I spoke to them that Mather and Rudabaugh were, they believed, members of the gang that held up the train.

75

They said they had been told this but would not divulge by whom. However, inquiries on my part into the past of Messrs Mather and Rudabaugh do lead me to believe that it is more than possible that they were involved. Mr. Rudabaugh was in fact arrested in Kansas for train robbery last year while—"

"Mr. Cole. You say, 'They said they had been told this but would not divulge by whom.' You understand that it is a very weak case you are presenting so far?"

"Well, perhaps in some respects, Your Honor, but I do honestly feel that—"

"Mr. Mather, Mr. Rudabaugh, what do you have to say?"

Once again, Mysterious did the talking. "Your Honor, this is a complete fabrication and a lot of nonsense. Of course we held up no train. We are sworn deputies and responsible for the maintenance of law and order in East Las Vegas. Clearly malicious tongues are at work here. But there is not a shred of evidence. Furthermore, we too can provide clear and irrefutable alibis that we were nowhere near the scene of the crime at the moment it was committed."

"Go on."

"We were both, Your Honor, eating dinner with Mr. Hyman G. Neill, Justice of the Peace, Coroner and Mayor, and with Joseph Carson, Marshal. I have here," and he withdrew a paper from his pocket, "a statement to that effect signed by both those gentlemen."

"Mr. Neill. Or Brown. Whichever it is. That gentleman." He sighed and rubbed his eyes. "Mr. Cole. Is it not the case that you arrested three men for a robbery recently who turned out, after the justice system of this territory had been put too much bother and expense, to be totally innocent?"

"Oh, well, yes, sir, it is. However, I—"

"Mmm. Well, I think we do not have enough here to commit these gentlemen to trial for robbing a train." He raised his voice. "In fact, we do not have enough here to accuse them of jaywalking or spitting on the sidewalk! Come back to me if and when you have what we in the legal profession like technically to call evidence. Case dismissed." The gavel was once more pressed into action and the Daves walked happily free, though not before they had cast black looks at Detective George Cole. As for Cole, he sat once more with his head in his hands. He was thinking of taking up another profession.

***

The second official exercise of the laws of New Mexico Territory occurred concurrently with that presided over by Chief Justice L. Bradford Prince but in the bar of Close & Paterson's Dance Hall on Railroad Avenue. The East Las Vegas Justice of the Peace addressed the patrons. "I got to do a wedding tomorrow. It's my first. I don't know how to do them. I must practice. Dutchy, come here, you're going to get married."

"I am?"

"Yes, to Joe here. Stand up, you two."

There were hoots of laughter.

"Joe can't marry Dutchy, Hoodoo," said Wyatt.

"Why not?"

"Well, he's already married. It'd be bigamy."

"Yes, you have a point there. But they must get the license first and that's when they check that one of them ain't already wed. So we'll imagine for the sake of argument here that they are bachelor and spinster. Now, let me see." He opened a black book and read, "We are assembled here at this time to join—name man, it says, well, Joe Carson then—and—name woman, Dutchy Schunderberger—in marriage according to the laws of the Territory of New Mexico. Stand closer there. It is our firm belief that those who enter this relationship do cherish a mutual esteem and love—is that right, you too? Good—and do promise to bear with each other's infirmities and weaknesses—well you both got plenty of those—to comfort each other in sickness, trouble and sorrow; in honesty and industry to provide for each other and for their household—mm, honesty and industry, eh? Well, we'll skip that bit—and to be mindful always that marriage is designed for the happiness and welfare of mankind and therefore to be entered into advisedly and discreetly and in good faith.

So then, will you, Carson, have this woman to be your wife, and will you love her, comfort her, honor and keep her in sickness and in health, and, forsaking all others, keep only unto her as long as you both shall live? It says here that the man shall answer, I will. So go on then."

Carson looked around. "I feel foolish."

"Well you look foolish. So what? Get on with it. I got to practice this and get it right."

"I will."

"Right. Now, Then the magistrate shall say to the woman, so, you, Dutchy Schunderberger, will you have this man—wait a minute. You can't really be named Dutchy. That's just what we call you. To be married you got to use your true given name. What is it?"

"I prefer just Dutchy."

"So you may. That's not the point. This here is a legal civil ceremony."

"If it's a legal civil ceremony, I will legally be married to Joe."

"Never mind about that. I'll divorce you tomorrow. What's your name?"

Dutchy sighed. "John."

"John, eh? Okay then. Will you, John, have this man, Carson, to be your husband, and will you love him, comfort him, blah, blah, blah, as long as you both shall live? The woman shall answer I will." He looked at Dutchy.

"I will."

"Right, Joe, take her hand."

"What?"

"Take her hand. You have to put the ring on her. Who's got a ring, anyone? Come on, come on. Josh, grab one of them curtain rings. Now you say, This ring I give you, in token and pledge of my constant faith and abiding love. Go on."

"This ring I give you, in token and pledge of my constant faith and abiding love."

"Good. That's that part done. Now then, what next? Oh yes, By the authority committed to me as a Justice of the Peace of the Territory of New Mexico, I declare that Marshal Carson here and John-Dutchy Schunderberger are now husband and wife. You may kiss the bride."

"The hell I will."

"The hell you won't. I have to get this right. The groom will want to kiss the bride."

Dutchy offered Carson a chaste cheek. Joe pecked it at it.

"Well, that wasn't much good. I suppose it'll do for the form though. Right, get lost." He snapped the book shut and turned to the bar.

James and Wyatt started up.

"Where are you going for the honeymoon, boys?"

"Dutchy, throw your bouquet. We'll see who catches it."

"Got the rice, Josh?"

Carson took it in good part. "Do you want to hit them, Dutchy, or shall I?"

Dutchy smiled and offered Joe a drink.

Wyatt came up and stood between them. "Allow me, fellows. I think you're both going to need a few before the wedding night."

**

Dirty Dave and Josh were having a drink. Or in fact they were having more than one. They were having a good evening. It was in the back of Josh's mind that it was his duty to resolve these robberies and bring the guilty parties to book. It was what he was being paid for, and either he should perform his duties or resign. He had more than a suspicion that Doc was involved. The trouble was he had a shrewd idea that his friends were too. The Daves, Wyatt, James. What was he going to do, turn them in? No. But then he must tender his resignation to the Adams Express Company. He would do it tomorrow. Meanwhile, why not an evening of fun? He thrust the thoughts out of his mind and turned to Dave. He liked Dave. There was nothing complicated about him.

"Have a drink, Dave."

"Why, thank you, Josh, don't mind if I do. You probably know this about whiskey, but if you always stand up to drink it, it don't make you drunk."

"What? I didn't know that."

"That's because it ain't true. You can get as drunk standing as sitting. Cheers."

"Idiot. Anyway, what do you know about being drunk? You've been as sober as a temperance lady all your life."

"Aye, I have that. You're right there. Never touched a drop." He threw another whiskey down.

"So what do you think, Dave? We going to stick around for a bit?"

"Sure, why not. We ain't gonna find much of a better berth around for a while. Maybe if this Lincoln County war flares up again or something we could get some work of that kind but right now I prefer it here. Hoodoo's organizing a prize fight. Wyatt's going to referee it. And we have a pretty good idea," and he tapped the side of his nose, "who might win it. Now the odds are still to be had so I reckon it's worth stopping here for a bit, eh?"

"And Wyatt says he wants to organize a racetrack. He's got some invincible piece of horseflesh that's going to make all the others look like donkeys. There might be some betting to be had there too."

79

"Oh, good, I didn't know that. I do like a day at the races."

"As long as we don't all get shut down."

"What do you mean?"

"Well, Dave, you know, the good days at these end-of-track towns don't last long. They get law and religion and temperance movements. Before you know it, there are more churches than saloons. Citizens committees and fourth-of-July picnics. You know. Things are already a bit too lively here and it wouldn't take much for them to appoint a new mayor and a new police force."

"That would be a pity. It's all arranged pretty sweet right now. Listen, there's a new place opened up on Grand Avenue. Why don't we take a walk and go see what it's like?"

"Why not? The next ones are on you."

They walked together down Railroad, where men were already laying red bricks to pave the roadway. The bricks had come down by train from Colorado because they had the word TRINIDAD molded in them. They'd started work on a brick railroad depot too, and there was talk of streetcars.

As they approached the new saloon, a couple of men came barging out of it. One was a teamster, by the look of him, or maybe a railroad man. The other was a soldier, but in the filthiest uniform you ever saw. Both were drunk and shouting. It was difficult to make out in their rage if they were arguing over whores or a horse. The soldier had drawn a long pistol from its flapped scabbard and the other man had produced a mule man's knife. Dave did not hesitate. "Work, Josh." He addressed them both. "Now, boys, we been told to make sure that no deadly weapons are waved about in the streets. Put up that gun and knife, would you, please?"

The soldier snarled at Dave, "Go to hell. In fact, maybe I'll send you there before I deal with this vermin." And he cocked his pistol.

Dave was not one for fine manners. He pulled his own revolver from a pocket and immediately shot the soldier. The man was hit in the arm and staggered backwards but did not drop his gun so Dave shot him again. Then the knife man tried to get in on the act and cut the soldier's throat but Josh pulled him off while Dave kicked the soldier's gun away and asked him if he wanted another bullet.

"You shot my thumb off, you bastard, you shot my thumb off. And I'm hit here too." He clutched his upper arm.

"Yes, you could die from wounds like that. Wounds like that can prove fatal. What a pity. Why don't you get off to Doc Shout and see what can be done? I'll look after your pistol for you." And he picked it up and thrust it in his belt. Then he looked once at the other fellow and slugged him a huge blow on the jaw, laying him out flat and totally unconscious. "There," he said to Josh, "that's that done. Let's go and get that drink."

"Dave, don't you think we should take these fellows off to jail?"

Dave considered for a moment. "Nah. They been punished and it would mean all that writing up reports and such. Can't be bothered. I want a drink." And he walked inside, leaving the two men lying in the street.

***

It was about half past ten and the evening had grown cooler. The streets were quieter too although there seemed to be some disturbance just outside McKay's restaurant. Here was a crowd in a circle watching a fight. They were railroad workers. Quite a party of them had come into town earlier that day and had been visiting the saloons freely. Some fellow, one of them, it seemed, was trying to part them.

"Come on, boys, this won't do. Break it up!"

But the crowd was enjoying the spectacle and someone called out, "Can it, Castello, leave them be," and someone else said, "Get out of the way!" They kept urging the fighters on. The fisticuffs were in fact quite expert, both men clearly having had some experience in the pugilistic arts, and people began to lay bets. But the fellow endeavoring to keep order kept trying to disperse the crowd.

"Please, move along, men. There is nothing to be gained by staying here. We are employees of the Santa Fe and do not wish to bring the company into disrepute. Please now, go along."

Finally, the sober man, Castello, drew a pistol and addressed the fighters. "Now stop. That is an order. This has gone far enough. And you men," and here he waved the gun in the direction of the crowd, "you get off to your lodgings." The crowd recoiled and one of them also produced a revolver. It didn't look good.

Mysterious Dave was walking towards a rendezvous with a Mexican lady he had come to know. He was even more carefully dressed than usual, for he liked to make a good impression, and had spent some time brushing his hat and cleaning his boots and pomading his hair. Turning the corner upon which McKay's stood, he was suddenly faced with an ugly crowd and two men holding guns. He recoiled. But Mysterious Dave was no stranger to dangerous moments. "Put up those guns immediately. There has been far too much trouble of late." And he walked towards them. It was a brave action. Joe Castello, telegraph operator, self-appointed constable and except for Dave probably the only sober man present, was surprised and he panicked. He pointed his gun at Dave and told him to get back. It was a very grave mistake. You should never point a pistol at a man like Dave, either Dave really, unless you immediately use it. In town, Dave kept his .45 in a shoulder harness under his coat and he was very proficient with it. Rather like his namesake an hour earlier, he simply drew his pistol and fired. It was how he had stayed alive and gained a reputation as a law officer. You tell them to put up their weapons but if they aim one at you, you shoot them. The bullet entered Castello's body on the left side below the ribs, penetrating the lung, passed downward though the stomach and into the liver. The man was carried into Hoodoo's office where Dr. Russell Shout was called but of course he could do nothing. Castello expired at six o'clock the next morning after a night of considerable pain.

The soldier shot by Dirty Dave was also in a bad way. The first shot had taken him very badly and by early morning he was running a high fever. Doc Shout did not rate his chances highly.

Hoodoo was furious. He could see his whole empire dissolving before his eyes. But Mysterious Dave was calm and clear.

"Look, Mr. Brown, you are expecting too much. Law and order do not descend upon a town like this simply because you wish it to be well-behaved for a week or two. Occurrences like this happen because violent men drink and lose money gambling and share women and are armed. It is hot. They are by nature combative. What do you expect? Both these shootings tonight occurred exactly because we carried out your orders and disarmed men who were breaking the ordinance against carrying deadly weapons. If we ourselves, Dave, and I, had previously been freely shooting up cowboys or something, then that could have been stopped at your orders. But we weren't. And we aren't. Whether Dave and I had been on the scene or not, there would have been fatalities tonight. In fact, they probably would have been worse. You must just accept it. If it's a problem for you politically, well then you must solve it politically."

It was such a reasoned and reasonable discourse that Hoodoo had nothing to say and it was greeted by silence.

The coroner's jury found that Castello had met his death at the hands of an officer in discharge of his duties; that said shooting was justifiable and in self-protection. The names of the jurymen who signed it followed. Paterson, Close, Schunderberger, and so on, the usual list.

***

Later, in bed, Mrs. Carson said to Hoodoo, "It's all going wrong, Hyman. Best make plans. We will have to leave."

Hoodoo grunted and turned over. "Not yet, we won't. Damned if I am going yet. I have a particular project to bring to a conclusion first." He went to sleep.

***

Governor's Mansion, Santa Fe.
1st September 1879.

Dear Prince,

It is now abundantly clear that things are out of control in Las Vegas. Killings seem to be a nightly occurrence, stages and a train are robbed and the U.S. Mail abused. There have been lynchings and disappearances, including that of a substantial property owner, Jesus Barela. I believe we will have to consider martial law.

From what you have told me, part of the trouble, if not its root cause, is the fact that an inappropriate person has installed himself in offices whose function is to preserve the peace yet this person is exploiting these offices for pecuniary gain. I have met this man and think you may well be right. I instruct you to gather evidence for a case against him. As soon as you are convinced that you have sufficient grounds, he should be immediately replaced, at least from those offices that are appointed rather than elected. New police officers should be enlisted, ones who are reliable and sound. I rely upon you to accomplish this in the shortest time possible.

New Mexico Territory has, as you know, suffered for several years from violence and criminality on a scale not formerly known. It is my absolute and convinced determination to restore order and law to this territory. I know I can count upon the Territory's Chief Justice to aid me in this. Let us deal swiftly and firmly with the situation in Las Vegas first.

Sincerely,
Lew. Wallace.

Part II

Chapter Five

The Denver police were as enthusiastic at beating Chinese as the roughnecks and rowdies were. On the corner of Arapahoe and 14th, the officers were laying their nightsticks about them with gusto. Some were to be seen in upper windows throwing furniture and possessions down to the street. Other policemen were happily looting stores. They expected first choice before the common boys came in. This day's effort was what the constables referred to as 'a first-class riot'. It only took some rumor, usually maliciously spread and untrue, that a Chinaman had robbed someone or was planning to. 1880 was a good year for it. Chinese merchants, laborers and laundrymen were running wildly, trying to escape the flailing fists, the boots lashing out and in one case, a bullwhip. There was the sound of smashing glass, of splintering doors, of deep thuds, gunshots, and barking dogs, and above all there was the high-pitched wailing of the suffering Celestials, men, women and children. A washhouse had taken fire and the noise and confusion was added to by a careering, bell-ringing fire engine charging to the spot, its thundering horses snorting and neighing.

Michael Kelliher watched the scene with amusement, idly rubbing the white, wrinkled scar that rose from his forehead up into the hairline. It was a habit he had. He didn't even know he was doing it. He hated Chinese with a passion and was pleased to see them getting what they deserved. He did consider joining in and was fond of a fight. He had been a policeman in Chicago once and had enjoyed that part of the work. He fingered the small cudgel he always carried in his coat pocket. But this wasn't a proper fight. Anyone could beat a Chinaman. Anyway, he was eager to continue to profit further from his current run of luck at the tables and so he just smiled again and moved on, back to the hotel. Horace would be waiting.

Kelliher thought that Lieutenant-Governor H.A.W. Tabor, the richest man in Denver, the richest in Colorado come to that, was an interesting figure. He had made his fortune in silver mines up at Leadville, become mayor there, provided the town at his own expense with a fire brigade and an opera house and now he was lavishing his wealth on Denver too. He had invested all over, from Mexico to Chicago, in railroads, mines and telephones. He was said to be worth eight or ten million dollars. He already owned heaven knew how many lots in Denver and had built the Tabor block on 16th and Larimer. He was planning another, vastly greater opera house. He was also a less than permanent consort to his wife and was said to be besotted with someone else Kelliher knew, Baby Doe McCourt. Not surprising, that. Baby Doe was a corker. She was a prize worth competing for. Outstandingly beautiful, sparkling, witty and vivacious, Baby Doe had them waiting in line to woo her. She could have had her pick. Yet she chose dear, old, married Horace! Horace was an amiable enough chap but no handsome man and he was twenty-five years her senior. Of course having eight million in the bank does help somewhat against the competition.

But best of all, from Kelliher's point of view, Tabor loved to gamble. And he thought nothing of losing ten thousand dollars in an evening's play. Losing was something he got plenty of practice at. Amiable fellows do not always make good poker players.

"Horace, my good fellow! How are you?"

"Well, Michael, well. And yourself?"

"Fine, fine."

Tabor took the arm of a man standing beside him. "Allow me, Michael, to introduce you to Dr. Harold McKenna. Dr. McKenna is an eminent surgeon from New York, out here in the wild and woolly west sampling frontier life, ha ha! Dr. McKenna likes the occasional game of cards too."

Kelliher saw a portly, middle-aged fellow in a well-tailored coat. He wore a curious single eyeglass, attached to the coat by a silk thread. The glass would occasionally pop out and be polished before being replaced. The glass had the unfortunate effect for observers of magnifying the eyeball behind it, giving McKenna an almost cyclopic appearance. The doctor sat down and invited Kelliher to join him with a gesture of the hand, almost a proprietorial one.

Tabor also sat down, fastidiously pinching up his trousers above the knee to prevent them bagging but forgetting to flap out his coat tails so that his not inconsiderable posterior pinned them to the chair, causing him to wriggle and squirm to free them. He seemed not to want to rise again once he had gone to the effort of sitting. Then he realized he was still holding his silk hat and had no one to hand it to. He placed it on the carpet beside his chair, then turned brusquely to call a waiter and knocked the hat over.

Horace was, of course, immaculately dressed in a finely tailored coat and vest and a lilac silk necktie which was centered by a diamond pin which could by no stretch of the imagination be called discreet. His hair was glossy, wavy, pomaded and trimmed and it contrasted with Kelliher's own, cropped brutally short, almost shaved. While Kelliher was clean-shaven, Tabor wore a luxuriant mustache, grown to conceal a weakish chin but only really serving to accentuate it. At least according to Kelliher. The whiskers protruded from beneath his nose and descended, covering his mouth and finally curling in two waxed points just above the lilac necktie.

Kelliher had never wasted time or money on such foppishness as neckties and pins and pomaded locks. What he had earned by his business dealings or at the tables was to be kept, preferably in a good safe at the ranch rather than in some crooked bank, or, better still, invested in land and cattle. With all the cattle-rich acres that he now owned, stretching across Colorado into Wyoming and the Dakotas, and all the cash he held now, some in banks, but most in safes and in bags he carried about with him, he was indeed a rich man. Not in Tabor's class, of course, but even had he been a millionaire like Tabor, he would not have wasted his wealth on such unmanly fripperies. A sound, long-wearing suit, good boots and a broad-brimmed hat against the sun and rain were enough for him. He liked to keep his hat on. His wife had once had the effrontery to suggest that it was to hide the scar that disfigured his upper head. He had reacted properly to that impertinence and she would not say it again. She had earned her own adornment to her upper head, he thought with amusement, which had taken several weeks to disappear.

"Well, gentlemen, shall we begin? I feel lucky tonight."

"What, again?" Tabor laughed good-naturedly. "Well, I'm sorry to hear that!"

As the game progressed, and Kelliher was pleased to see the pile of chips diminishing in front of both his opponents, there was some discussion of the riot. Kelliher disapproved of discussion of any kind during the rite of poker and only joined in with a rare, laconic observation such as, "Damned Chinese. They are not a race like us. Underdeveloped."

The New Yorker evidently had other views. "Well, I have performed autopsies upon white men and Chinamen and Indians and Negroes. And I can

89

tell you that apart from a slight difference in the pigmentation, they are all pretty much the same. Same lungs and livers and lights. And the same room inside for a soul. Though it must also be said that in all my operations I never did find a soul yet. As for being underdeveloped, I find it curious that a white man whose father arrived on the continent yesterday can talk to a member of a race as old as Israel and yet the white man looks down at the Chinaman with a superior contempt. The same is true of Indians, of course."

Kelliher was a man of discipline, and the discipline he imposed on others, but he had never been a man able to control his anger. It flared up in him unbidden and he could no more extinguish the flame than fly to the moon. The preposterous rubbish this man was spouting made him suddenly furious. But as he spat out his contempt and scorn for the surgeon's views, he realized that it was affecting his game. He was concentrating less, making rash decisions on calls and cards. With a supreme effort, he brought himself back under control, took some deep breaths and drank a glass of water, then resumed his steely, clinical play.

***

Kelliher sat at the table in his hotel room, neatly stacking hundred-dollar banknotes into piles, the easier to count them. He topped off the last pile with Tabor's diamond pin.

"Come!"

Williams hesitated before entering, putting his head round the door. Experience had taught him to be wary of what mood his boss was in.

"Come in, come in. Don't just stand there, for God's sake."

Williams was an Englishman. He had once dared to contradict Kelliher and claim he was a Welshman. It was different, he said. Stupid man. He never really liked the English. Just because they ruled half the world, they thought it made them in some way superior.

"Get me that leather satchel." Williams looked around and saw none. "Over there, you idiot. Come on, hurry up."

Once the newly-won money was neatly stacked inside and added to the already substantial contents, Kelliher heaved the case into the bottom of the closet.

"Don't you want me to take that to the bank?"

"What for? You think someone would dare to steal it from me? He wouldn't live long if he tried." Kelliher looked him hard in the eye as if warning him off trying.

"No, I just meant that it's a lot of money and—"

"Stop fussing and listen." Kelliher pulled towards him a folder of papers and extracted a telegram form. "Now, we need cattle. A lot of cattle. The new sections I have need to be properly used. Cattle are still cheap in New Mexico, even if they are mangy beasts. Well, my Colorado grass will fatten them up. And this new railroad will let me ship them back north. But we must act fast. The railroad is already influencing stock prices. You will accompany me to Santa Fe where we will put some of this cash to good use."

"Oh, but Mrs. Williams is expecting, you know, I told you, and I don't think I—"

"Shut up and stop whining. You are supposed to be a foreman, not a midwife. She will give birth perfectly well without your help. Or die without it."

Williams winced as if hit. Kelliher did not seem to notice.

"I want to stop at Las Vegas in New Mexico Territory." He tapped the cable. "There's a man I know there. I can buy cattle there too. And I have some other business."

He fell silent and a black cloud appeared to cross the window, darkening his face. He gently rubbed his scar.

"Now, listen. Get out and go find me a jeweler. Someone who will give a good price for this pin. Better find two and let them compete. And I also want someone to bring me a pocket derringer, a Remington. Well, what are you waiting for, you shiftless English weakling? I pay you good money and all you can do is stand there with your mouth open like a fish. Get going before I fire you and find someone who actually has a backbone." If he had been standing and on the foreman's side of the table, he would have given him a good kick. But the man finally understood and left. Kelliher deemed the people around him fools and weaklings. He was surrounded by fools and weaklings.

***

He joined his wife and daughters in the dining room. Kitty Kelliher sat straight, a small, trim woman with a hard face and gray hair drawn back tightly in a bun. She had once been a beauty and that hair had been a flashing red but years of toil had washed the beauty and fire away. The eyes which once had glittered now had a lackluster paleness about them. She was careful not to speak unless spoken to and not in any way to incite her husband's wrath. She took pains to ensure that her daughters also took such care and glanced sternly at them now that their father was approaching. She need not have for they sat mute, hands in laps and eyes downcast.

Now twenty-five and twenty-two, Lucy and Maria Kelliher were well-dressed, neat, groomed and totally silent. They looked at the tablecloth. Lucy was tall, even gangly, and she had developed a stoop, as if self-effacingly to try to make herself smaller. Her younger sister Maria showed some of the color her mother had once displayed but none of the fire or vivacity. None of the women showed any vivacity nor had they done for some time. They had been beaten and browbeaten too long.

Kelliher showed no apparent interest in them and did not ask any of them how they had spent their day. But he looked at them. He ought not to think it probably but the fact remained that the women were a drag on him. Why could the girls not find a man? Marry some farmer and set up home elsewhere. But no young men ever came courting. Yet the girls were not displeasing to look at, he supposed, and of course not poor either. And why could not one of them have been another son, to replace Harry? As strong as Harry but more obedient. He shook his head as if to free himself from memory and gave one of his small snorts, somewhere between a sigh and a clearing of the throat, a habitual expression of general and universal dissatisfaction. He ran a hand across his scar and bristly hair and looked across at Kitty. At least, his wife was a decent woman, respectful and keeping house properly, even if she was too extravagant and far too soft with the servants.

"You will return to the ranch tomorrow. Some of the men will be waiting for you at the station. Here are the tickets."

They knew better than to ask where he was going or when he might return. Kitty simply reached over and put the tickets in her purse, then raised a hand to summon the waiter who ran immediately across, stood, and waited to be abused, as usual, by Mr. Kelliher.

***

Will Hardcastle did not come often to Denver. Not that he disliked it but it did not really offer him too much now. Very occasionally he came to see the manager of his business affairs, Mr. Clarence Shoesmith, and he had indeed profited from this visit to see him, but more usually it was lawman's duties that drew him to the state capital, as was the case this time. He had seen the judge and signed the papers and could return to Dolencia tomorrow. But he had bumped into Horace Tabor and had promised to join him for a drink later. He liked Tabor. Horace was an essentially generous man, generous with his wealth and also generous of spirit. There were those who accused him of munificence as a means of climbing the greasy pole to political power but Will knew it was not that; he had bought that fire engine from San Francisco and built that opera house for the good of Leadville and to improve Colorado. He meant it. Will was not really a social person and would not have sought an invitation from Tabor but he also liked the man and was not going to be rude enough to refuse one.

Horace had invited him to sit down at the gaming table but those days were gone for Will. Tabor had been rather chagrined. "Well, you might give me the chance to win back that fifty thousand." Will had reminded him that it was ten thousand, not fifty, and had told him that he was now a poor marshal in a small town and not in a position to gamble as he once had. This was not strictly true, else he would not have been visiting Mr. Shoesmith to discuss his investments, but nevertheless his gambling days, which he associated with an unregretted past, were over. Tabor had started reminiscing about the 'glory days' in Leadville and Will let him run on. He had agreed anyway to join him for a drink this evening. It would be champagne, knowing Horace.

When Will reached the hotel, Tabor was in conversation with two men, one of them a bullet-headed, stocky man, about fifty, who looked like an ex-prizefighter. Not neck enough to hang. Then Will wondered why such an odd idea had come to him. The fellow kept stabbing a finger at Tabor's vest, not angrily but ramming home some point or other. He was one of those naturally aggressive speakers. Horace smiled blandly in response. When Will approached, the man turned and looked at him almost contemptuously and Will smelt the whiskey on his breath. But it was Horace who spoke.

"William, my dear chap. Welcome. How nice to see you again. A fellow citizen of dear old Leadville, eh? Allow me to introduce you to Mr. Harold McKenna, surgeon, of New York and Mr. Michael Kelliher, rancher, one of the most substantial denizens of the most substantial state of the Union, our own dear Colorado." Horace was doing his politician's act. He wanted to be a Senator. Will extended his hand and said, "Hardcastle." Kelliher ignored the hand and turned back to his conversation. Or rather monologue.

Will had heard of Kelliher. Some admired him for the fortune he had built up and for his grit and courage. He had certainly achieved great things. Others detested the man for his brutality and callousness. In particular, the fellow had an unpleasant reputation, justified or not Will did not know, for making his first significant money when he had been an Indian agent up on the Platte by cheating the Oglala Sioux, selling government supplies destined for them and giving them instead rotten food and miserable blankets. But mostly Will remembered that once, a couple of years ago in Dodge, must have been '77, his friend Josh Webb had so far unburdened himself to tell of a man who had cheated him and whom he had killed in Cheyenne. He wondered if Josh knew now that the man had survived. Well, he wasn't going to bring that subject up here.

"No one ever, ever, asked me about this scar!"

"No, well, Michael, you forget, I didn't ask you either." Horace had at least the gumption to resist. "I mean, you brought the subject up. I'm not really interes—"

Kelliher had not heard him. He was not used to listening to interlocutors. "I got this scar, if you really want to know, from a skunk, a cur, a low-down snake..." Will always disliked absurdly mixed metaphors, especially ones which attributed human deficiencies to animals, but he kept silent. "...who shot me when I was down, on the floor, and he shot me. What kind of cur is that? He just pulled a pistol and fired it at my head. While I lay, defenseless, on the ground. All my life since, all my life, I have vowed that I will find that snake and kill him, crush him, squash him, wipe him off the face of the earth where he does not deserve to exist, to—"

"Dear Mr. Kelliher, I was rather hoping that we might sit down to a game of cards. I—"

"Webb, his name was, Webb. Some cheap teamster, I don't know. Claimed I owed him money. It was a lie. I—what did you say?"

"Oh, er, I just suggested that we might play—"

"Yes, yes, of course." Kelliher paused, rubbed his head, composed himself. "Yes, let's play. Yes. Let's play."

Will thought that the time had come to excuse himself. "Horace, I must be going. Please give my—"

"Yes, well, go then, begone." Kelliher could not muster even the minimum of courtesy. Will had had enough. He turned his body full on to Kelliher and threw him a steely look.

"Please do not interrupt." Then he turned back to Tabor. "Horace, as I was saying, I must go but I have appreciated this opportunity to meet you again. Please give my regards to Mrs. Governor…That is to say, your family. My very best wishes." He shook Tabor's hand, bowed to the New York surgeon, gave the curtest of nods to Kelliher, turned his back and began to walk out.

Kelliher turned, strained, thought of punishing such insolence, but was too keen to get his lamb to the slaughter. "Horace, my dear friend, would you like to break this new deck, or shall I?"

***

"I would like this to be sent for the personal attention of Mr. J.J. Webb, Las Vegas, New Mexico Territory."

"Yes, Marshal, right away."

The telegraph clerk began to tap at his key. KELLIHER ALIVE AND WANTS TO KILL YOU STOP IN DENVER NOW BUT COMING SOUTH STOP WATCH YOUR BACK STOP WILL.

***

The three shiftless hoodlums were lined up, looking for all the world to Hoodoo like boys who had been caught playing hooky before the schoolmaster, though they would not have felt this themselves, none of them ever having graced a schoolroom when young, if we except Slap-Jack Nicholson's brief stays before once being expelled for a knife fight in the schoolyard and again at the next establishment for an improper suggestion to the schoolma'am's daughter. The schoolboy image was not very appropriate either because schoolteachers do not usually address their charges in the bar of a dance hall-cum-bordello. But Hoodoo still felt that they had the bearing of naughty pupils and were holding their dirty sombreros just as if they were scholars' caps.

95

"Look, I know you work for Holliday and that's okay by me. I have no problem with that. But enterprising fellows like you ought to be able to see that Holliday's days are numbered in this town, whereas with me you will find stability and good pay. Just now I want someone to undertake a mission for me." The flattery of calling them 'enterprising fellows' and the use of phrases like 'undertake a mission' were already having an effect. The louts stood a little more upright and a faint gleam of interest could be seen in their faces. "You probably know that we are staging a prize fight here in Las Vegas. We have been trying to get Sullivan but he won't do it. It looks now like Joe Goss versus Paddy Ryan. Now you are to look after Goss and take care of him and get him everything he wants. I want everyone to know he is our man. In reality, of course, Ryan is going to win it and I will instruct you later how to administer the soporific to Goss."

Hoodoo knew very well that these three imbeciles would not understand half of his discourse. But he also knew well that they were incapable of keeping such a secret, because of both their stupidity and guile, so that it was inevitable that the money would go on Ryan, which was what he wanted.

"At any rate, I want you to install yourselves here at Close's. If Holliday objects, tell him to come see me. I will have other jobs for you. Some of them will require more than just fixing a fight. I presume you have no problem with actions which may not, strictly speaking, be considered entirely legal?"

Mullen and Pierce looked completely baffled and stared at Nicholson for assistance with the question, Pierce wiping a filthy sleeve under his nose and Mullen picking at his pock-marked face. Nicholson understood. "Not if the pay's good enough."

"Good, because in this territory murder and theft are not considered entirely legal. Here," and he handed each a sheaf of banknotes, waving them as if to send the schoolboys away, doubtless to commit further outrages. These men were entirely without worth but would serve his needs.

***

Dirty Dave and Slap-Jack Nicholson stood at the bar of Close & Paterson's. They hadn't exactly become friends but there was enough of a similarity between them to make their occasional companionship understandable. For one thing, although Nicholson did not bear a nickname such as 'Dirty', personal hygiene was not exactly his forte, and the two men were probably equally strangers to the bar of soap and the washbasin. True, Slap-Jack had never acted on the side of the law, but then Dirty Dave was not precisely a paragon of probity as far as that was concerned. They both were handy in a fight. Both now worked for Hoodoo. Dave Rudabaugh didn't exactly like Bill Nicholson but he didn't actively dislike him either, and he was prepared to have a drink with him. They also shared an interest in prizefighting.

It had not taken Slap-Jack long to blurt out Hoodoo's 'secret' and tell Dave that Ryan was Hoodoo's favorite in the forthcoming match. "But you're not to tell no one, Dave, you understand. This is between us so you can get a bit of the action. Get some money down on Ryan while the odds are good. But it's a secret, see?"

"Don't you worry. I can keep a secret. And thanks for the tip."

"You're welcome." Nicholson drew a sleeve across his snotty nose.

Josh came in and up to the bar. Nicholson glanced at him, downed his drink, wiped his sleeve across his face again and shuffled off to join Pierce and Mullen.

"I don't know why you hang around with Nicholson, Dave. He's no good."

"Oh well, he ain't so bad. He's no saint, I dare say, but then we ain't no Sunday-school boys, are we? Anyway, he tells me that the money's going on Goss but in fact Ryan's the man."

"Yes, well if I were you, I would wait to hear that direct from Hoodoo before you place a bet. And even then, I'd hesitate."

Dirty Dave finished his drink. "Yes, you could be right there."

***

Governor Wallace, when he wrote, and Chief Justice L. Bradford Prince, when he received the letter, were not to know that in fact the recent flurry of violence and misdemeanor had reached a climax and that Las Vegas, New Mexico Territory, was entering on a period of relative calm and tranquility. Whether it was the march of civilization and the growth of urban values that the town was espousing or simply that the heat of the summer had burned itself out and the fall was about to give way to winter; whether it was that the railroad was moving on, down towards Santa Fe; or whether it was simply plain happenstance; whatever may have been the reason, as 1879 became 1880, no fatal shootings occurred in the street, no trains or stages were held up and no bodies were found in unexplained circumstances.

This did not mean, of course, that Las Vegas, New Mexico Territory became overnight a paradise of goodness and brotherly love. All the usual drinking and whoring and gambling and cheating went on, but it went on behind closed doors and without, for the moment, provoking much beyond the odd fistfight in a saloon.

In fact, all the news was about the resumption of the career of Jesse James back east. He had held up and robbed a train at Glendale, Missouri and got away, it was said, with six thousand dollars. The newspapers were full of it and it monopolized the talk in the saloons.

The new-found relative peace and decorum in Las Vegas, New Mexico Territory did not stop Chief Justice L. Bradford Prince from planning to remove Hoodoo Brown from office. And Marshal John Morrison was the Chief Justice's chosen weapon.

Marshal Morrison was sometimes thought of as a grim, humorless man. He was not. He was a loving husband and caring father who believed in the future of a law-abiding New Mexico. Yet he certainly was steely, determined and strong-minded and he was equally certainly loyal to Chief Justice L. Bradford Prince. He stood now before the worthy judge, upright and unsmiling as ever, but those very few who knew him well, and the Chief Justice was numbered among these, might have seen a glint in his eye.

"John, it will soon be time to move. When I have my case ready, I shall depend upon you to arrest Mr. Brown, or Neill, or whatever his damned name is, and, if necessary, those Kansas renegades of his also. I know it won't be easy for they are reputedly dexterous and unscrupulous gun hands, but I will back you up with all the support you need, swearing in officers if need be. The Governor has even discussed using the army but this is to be avoided unless absolutely necessary. I know you have the strength of character to carry out the instructions."

Morrison looked him in the eyes. "Your Honor, you don't have to worry about that," was all he said and it was enough. Chief Justice L. Bradford Prince nodded and returned to his writing and Marshal John Morrison put his hat back on and left.

***

Since he had known him, Josh would never have compared Joe Carson to John Morrison. Morrison was a strong, upright, decent officer. Carson was a weak, cuckolded hireling. But the more Josh got to know Carson, the more he detected the hidden depths in the man. And a deep sadness. And an inner decency.

So he was not as surprised as some when Joe Carson came into Holliday's gin mill and quietly handed him a paper which summoned him before the Chief Justice (and not the local Justice of the Peace) to answer charges of keeping an unruly house and permitting unlicensed gambling.

Holliday's vituperative response and foul-mouthed shouts of abuse were also to be expected but Carson's calm dignity impressed Josh and maybe also Wyatt and James. Carson simply repeated, "Well, Mr. Holliday, you shall appear for if you do not you will be arrested and imprisoned. I suggest you make ready to pay a fine, perhaps a substantial fine. Good day." And he tipped his hat like a gentleman and walked calmly out.

Holliday's wrath at losing his three hired thugs to Hoodoo was now compounded. He had never looked so poisonous and vicious. Holliday caught Josh's glance. "What the hell are you looking at?" His voice was a snarl. "Get out of here, fuck off, all of you. I have a murder to plan."

***

Carson's next port of call was Close & Paterson's.

"I want Nicholson, Mullen and Pierce."

"What do you mean, you want them?"

"I want to arrest them. I am sure they carried out one or both of the stage robberies, and that under Holliday's orders."

Hoodoo looked at him as if he were mad. "And so?"

"And so I shall arrest them."

"The hell you will. They are working for me now."

"Even so."

"Carson, I don't know what's got into you lately. You are behaving almost as if you were a lawman." Carson looked at him steadily. "Instead of a hired lackey who will do as he is bid." Carson still said nothing but gazed at Hoodoo straight in the eye. "A weak, spineless flunky." Hoodoo saw the goading was getting him nowhere and changed tack. "Look, Carson, what is it? You want more money? You want more of a say in what goes on around here? Well, alright, I can give you both. We have a good arrangement here. It would be a tragedy to break it up over some foolishness."

Both men knew to what the 'foolishness' referred but neither spoke.

"Look, those gunmen will be arrested. Shortly. I just need them for a couple of jobs. In fact, I can guarantee that they will be arrested."

Joe Carson thought for a moment, then accepted the terms. With no farewell, he simply turned on his heel and went out.

The look on Hoodoo's face as Carson left was one to have been clearly understood by anyone in the saloon bar, had anyone been present.

***

"I want to send this cable to a Mr. Michael Kelliher at the Alvord House Hotel, 18th, and Larimer in Denver. And as usual, I depend upon your discretion."

"Yessir, Mr. Brown, you know you can rely on me."

"I do." The look that Hoodoo gave the telegraph clerk which accompanied the proffered banknote left no room for doubt in the clerk's mind that the threat was at least as compelling as the bribe.

"And, um, Mr. Brown, you know you asked me to inform you of any incoming or outgoing wires that might—"

"What of it?"

"Well, sir, this one came in about an hour ago. It's addressed to your associate, Mr. J. J. Webb."

"Give." Hoodoo read the cable, looked grim, then changed his mind and smiled slightly. He handed the clerk another five dollars, raised the glass globe of an oil lamp, thrust the telegram into the flame and used it as a spill to light a cigar.

***

You could see your breath. The intense, stifling heat that had greeted Josh's arrival in New Mexico seemed a distant memory. He turned up the collar of his range jacket and slapped his arms against his body. He wanted some coffee, as strong and bitter as possible, to ward off the chill. He'd get some at the marshal's office.

"Joe." Josh flipped his hand up by his ear.

"Morning, Josh. Coffee?"

"Oh, well, yes, why not?"

As he poured some from the pot on the stove, the marshal looked at Josh. "I'm going to be making some arrests shortly and I might need some help."

Josh nodded.

"But tell me, Josh, how come you have never officially been sworn in?"

"That's a good question. Hoodoo always said he would get round to it but never has."

It was Carson's turn to nod. "Well, I think you should be. I can only have you backing me up if you have a badge, Josh. Wouldn't be legal otherwise."

"Legal. Right."

"Yes, legal. I want it legal. Is that so surprising for a sworn officer of the law?"

"No, of course not. Not at all. It's just that…"

"Just that what?"

"Just that, you know Hoodoo and—"

"Yes, well, things have changed round here, Josh. East Las Vegas now has a peace officer who intends to keep the peace."

There was silence between them.

Josh drank down the last of the coffee and rose to his feet. "Right. Good. I'm glad. I'll go down to Close's right now and tell Hoodoo that he must either swear me in or no longer count on my services. Then I'll be pleased to back you up."

Carson nodded again. Josh flipped his hand in another of his small waves and went out into the bracing air.

***

At the bar in Close & Paterson's, despite the early hour, Nicholson, Mullen and Pierce were drinking whiskey. Josh walked past them addressing a question to their backs. "Anyone seen Hoodoo?"

For reply, the Pock-Marked Kid spat expertly into a spittoon. Josh ignored them and headed for the stairs. He had gotten to the third or fourth step when

Pierce said, "He said he ain't to be disturbed." The ruffian dug Nicholson in the ribs and added, "And we all know what that means!" and they all gave suggestive sniggers.

Josh hesitated, then came back down. He had a shrewd idea of what that meant too. He would come back later in the day.

Back in his own room, Josh had an uneasy feeling. Something was brewing but he didn't know what it was. The 'law and order' that prevailed seemed too brittle to last. Joe Carson's laudable efforts had contributed to it but might also be the cause of its downfall. Josh feared a new descent into lawlessness and killing. He had to see Hoodoo now. He had been putting off too many things for too long. He must get sworn in or break with Brown. And he must resign from Adams. And he must formally break it off with Mrs. Carson. He hadn't been to bed with her for over a month but that was not good enough. He must tell her. In a fit of decisiveness, he strapped on his gun belt, put his jacket back on, jammed his hat on his head, and went downstairs into the street.

***

Josh was about a hundred yards from Close & Paterson's when he saw Joe Carson open one of the glass outer doors and step inside the dance hall. Josh felt an unaccountable urgency and quickened his pace, his hand falling to rest on his gun as he walked.

When Josh entered, Carson was at the bar drinking coffee and the three layabouts hired by Hoodoo were at the other end of the counter in a close huddle, whispering something to each other. Josh thought he heard, "Let's do it, then."

Josh stood beside Carson, looked at the barman and also asked for coffee.

"Did you get sworn in?"

"Not yet, no. I came to do it but Hoodoo was, er, engaged."

Carson looked up at him sharply. He clearly understood very well with what Hoodoo had been engaged. Josh sipped some coffee and added, "But I'm going to see him now. I have certain other things to do, too."

"Well, I'll wait a bit. I'm not going to arrest those three just now anyway."

"Arrest them?"

"Oh, yes, I'm going to arrest them alright. As soon as I have seen Hoodoo."

102

Josh raised his eyebrows, then said, "I won't be long" and moved over to the stairs again. It was time to get sworn in. As he got to the top of the first flight, however, he heard Slap-Jack Nicholson speak up. His voice contained an even more sneering tone than usual. "Well, well, look here, our brave Joe. The law in town. Keeps the peace."

Carson looked over at him. "Careful, Nicholson, if you go on talking like that you may even use a word of two syllables."

"What?"

"It doesn't matter."

Pierce stepped forward. "Ain't you gonna tell us to check in our guns, Marshal? You see we are wearing guns. I thought there was a town ordinance about wearing guns?"

Carson gritted his teeth. "There is. Take 'em off."

"And supposin' we don't care to?"

"I said, take them off."

Mullen ostentatiously took out his gun and turned the cylinder, then put another round in a chamber. From above, Josh could clearly hear a slight sigh from Carson and he saw a setting of the shoulders as the marshal turned to face the men. Josh wondered if he should go back down but then paused. If there were to be trouble, he would be just as effective from here. More so.

Carson walked slowly the length of the bar to close the gap between them, then stood with his hands on his hips and said, "Well?"

Josh saw a look of uncertainty pass over Nicholson's face. Pierce and Mullen were too stupid to understand that they were at risk. Suddenly, Nicholson reached down and snatched at the gun on his hip. Carson lashed out with a fist and caught Nicholson full in the mouth. Josh clearly saw a tooth fly out. He would have a bigger gap now.

Carson did not wait but swung the weight of his body round, jerking the point of an elbow into the face of Mullen and then he swung round again to hit Pierce. Josh admired his technique. But Pierce had drawn his pistol and as Carson faced him, he discharged it. In his haste, Pierce had not aimed and the bullet struck Carson in the foot. He staggered but did not fall and drew out his own gun.

Josh saw Nicholson on the floor, his mouth now bleeding profusely, pull his pistol too. "Look out, Joe!"

Nicholson fired into Carson's body from behind. Josh aimed two-handed from the balustrade and shot Nicholson through the leg, then again in the upper arm.

Pandemonium ensued with everyone shooting, most shots going wide in the panic but several striking Carson and one hitting Mullen's ear. Josh felt a round go through his coat and wondered if he had been shot but kept on firing till his Colt's was empty, then hastily tried to reload, snatching bullets from the loops in his gun belt and ramming them home. The few other people in the bar had backed to the walls and a woman screamed.

Then there was a pause. Carson lay motionless on the saloon floor and Nicholson lay groaning beside him, his pistol discarded for his gun hand was clenched over the wound in his arm that Josh had given him. Mullen was trying desperately to staunch the flow of blood from his ear. Pierce held his empty gun downwards, still smoking, and stuttered that he was going to get horses.

Nicholson cried out, "Make it a wagon." Pierce rushed out and Mullen helped Nicholson to his feet.

Josh had his Colt's reloaded and called out, "Hold!"

Nicholson pulled a second pistol from a pocket and fired immediately. It was a very good shot and for a second time, Josh felt a bullet whip through his coat. He ducked down and when he came back up for another shot, the two were at the door. This time it was Mullen who fired but the shot went wide and struck an unlit lamp on the wall beside Josh. Then they were out. Josh rushed downstairs and over to Carson just as both Daves came running in from the back, guns drawn, darting looks everywhere. Then they saw Josh leaning over Carson and backed over, very professionally, covering the whole room between them.

It was immediately clear to Josh that Joe Carson was dead.

"You okay, Josh?"

Dave Rudabaugh said with a grim smile, "Old Josh is bullet proof!" but Josh himself was more circumspect:

"I think so. Get out there after them. They are trying to get a wagon."

In fact, Nicholson had staggered about twenty yards then flopped to the sidewalk. Mullen helped him sit up while Pierce ran on to the Lewelling and Olds Corral where, no wagon or buggy being found, he leveled his gun at Charlie Olds, who was not to know that it was empty, and took three horses. Mounting the first and towing the others behind him, Pierce raced back to

Nicholson and Mullen. They got Nicholson sprawled over a saddle and finally the three of them made it out of town, Dave Rudabaugh catching sight of them as they turned a corner and firing a desperate last shot with his handgun, wishing he had his Winchester but he had not.

From within the saloon behind him, Dirty Dave heard a banshee screech. As he went back in, he saw Mrs. Carson, hardly fully dressed, rushing down the stairs and pushing everyone aside as she forced her way over to her fallen husband. She threw herself upon him, almost knocking Josh over, and covered his body with her wailing and her long, undone hair and her tears. Josh tried to pull her away but she angrily brushed off his hand and resumed her keening. The noise was painful and shocking, so completely without control was it.

Dave Mather was picking men out and calling for guns. Dave Rudabaugh started helping and sent a man out for horses. Josh stood bemused, then happened to look up. There was Hoodoo Brown, standing just where Josh had been, upstairs, hands on the banister, looking down over the confusion. His face looked blank. There was no feeling displayed. Then Josh detected the barest hint of a smile began to form. It was a split second only, then the face returned to glacial expressionlessness and Hoodoo promptly turned his back and disappeared again into a room.

Chapter Six

Two weeks passed. The posse had failed. Joe Carson was buried, his widow inconsolable. Josh was astonished to learn that the Carsons had a fourteen-year-old daughter attending school in Nashville, Tennessee. No word of the miscreants was heard. Hoodoo continued to rule the roost like an increasingly irritating bantam cock. Josh found that his dissatisfaction with the status quo was shared by the Daves. They too had come to revise their opinion of Carson, in his favor, and of Hoodoo Brown, in the reverse direction. But Mysterious Dave thought he would sit it out for a bit and Dirty Dave went along, although he mentioned Billy quite often.

Josh had failed in his mission to be sworn in. Hoodoo was clever. He didn't say no. He said yes. He just had such-and-such to do, then they would perform a ceremony. But it never happened and Josh knew it was never going to happen. Why? Why was it in Hoodoo's interest that Josh not be a sworn deputy?

But he had two other missions to complete. The first was simple. He wrote a letter to the Adams Express Company in Boston resigning his services as their agent. It was short and polite but left no room for doubt. He sealed the envelope and put it in his pocket. He would mail it the next time he passed the post office.

But the second…That was more delicate. He was pondering the question in his room when there was the slightest of knocks at the door, more like the brushing of a gloved hand. Careful, he went to the door and then pulled it open suddenly. Mrs. Carson stood there, in her widow's weeds, her face under the veil clearly pale and drawn. Josh opened the door wider and said, "Come in, please" although he was not sure as to the propriety of such an invitation. His only room was his bedroom. He installed her in the armchair and took her parasol. He asked her if she would like some tea to be sent up.

"No, I only want to go to bed with you."

Josh must have looked as if he had been slapped. "I…I…"

"Come, now," and she rose, crushing her black dress against him. Josh recoiled. "What is the matter?"

"The matter? Why, I…"

She began urgently unbuttoning his shirt and snatching at his belt.

"Mrs. Carson, I can't, I…"

She suddenly stopped and was cold. "Why?"

"Mrs. Carson, please. You in your mourning dress. I…"

"You think I am no longer a woman?"

"No, of course not but…"

Then he knew. And he added, "It is out of respect for Joe."

It was Mrs. Carson's turn to look as though she had been struck. Then she turned on him in fury. "How dare you! How dare you!" She flung her gloves down. "Do you think I love my husband the less now that he has been heartlessly and brutally slain? How dare you! I despise you!" She snatched up her parasol and lashed out at him with it. He fended off the blow with an arm. Suddenly he could no longer bear to call her 'Mrs. Carson'. It was ridiculous.

"What is your name?"

"What?"

"Your name, what is your name? I can't call you forever 'Mrs. Carson'. It is absurd."

"It was good enough for you when you were rutting with me in my husband's bed."

The savagery was palpable. He didn't understand it. She had loved her husband yet continually betrayed him. Now she came in her black to betray him again. "Mrs. Carson, I am sorry but I do not wish to see you again. I mean, not in the sense of…"

"You coward, you worthless worm, I spit on you." She turned and swept from the room. Josh gazed at the slammed door then sat heavily down on the chair. His eyes fell upon the fallen gloves.

***

Charlie Olds never did accept the loss of his livery's horses and when it was suggested to him that the pistol Bull-Shit Jack Pierce had aimed at him was unloaded, he was angrier still. Charlie spent two weeks searching all over the territory. At the beginning of February, he returned with his stock and the news that Pierce, Mullen and Nicholson were hiding out in a farmhouse up near Mora, about thirty miles to the north-west. Nicholson was said to be in a bad way.

Josh felt good that now was the time for straightforward action. No doubts or equivocations. They would ride out and apprehend Carson's killers. He remembered another posse he had ridden on back in Kansas. Bat had led it and Josh and Prairie-Dog Morrow and Will Hardcastle had been his companions. Whatever had happened to Will? He would like to hear from him some time. Among those they had arrested for train robbery had been Dave Rudabaugh. It seemed a lifetime ago. Now Dave was by his side.

"You okay about going after these men, Dave?"

"Sure I am. Why not?"

"Well, you were kind of pally with Nicholson. I wouldn't want you to—"

"Listen, Josh. I got along okay with Nicholson, in a way, that's true. But he ain't no pal of mine. And him and his no-good pards done shot the marshal in the back. I'm with you on this trip and if need be, I'll shoot Nicholson or any of them."

Josh nodded. He'd guessed as much but it was good to know.

So early in the morning on the fifth of a bitterly cold month, a Friday, a wagon loaded with supplies and ammunition was led out by Josh, the Daves, Charlie Olds, George Close and Dutchy Schunderberger. Hoodoo had first said that Close and Dutchy should not go, indeed he seemed to be against the whole venture. "Let 'em rot, who cares," he had said. But Josh had the idea that Brown finally thought it better that Dutchy and Close should go. The members of his gang he could truly trust seemed to be getting fewer and his chief lieutenants ought to be there.

North-west out of Las Vegas, the trail climbed high. As they paused for a rest beside the ten-thousand-feet-high peak of the Sangre de Cristo Mountains which the Mexicans called Cerro el Teoclote and the Anglos Owl Peak, Charlie Olds told them the story of El Hermitano, a long-bearded Italian wanderer and mystic who had lived up there on a lonely ledge. The local peasants thought him to be John the Baptist. He had walked all over Spain and South America and Mexico and was eventually killed by Apaches in the Organ Mountains. Charlie had known him. "He used to come down to Vegas from time to time to see Jesus Barela, who fed him and gave him shelter and talked to him of philosophical matters. It was typical of Jesus; he was a good man. We never knew what happened to Jesus Barela, except people say Hoodoo Brown profited mightily from his disappearance." He looked darkly round at the members of the posse. "Anyway, Barela wanted to shower hospitality on him but El Hermitano would only accept cornmeal and sleep on the floor. He was a saintly fellow. Some said he was a healer."

Mysterious Dave looked bored. "Can we get on now?"

Charlie looked up and said, "Sure. Just trying to pass the time, friend."

"Time passes quite quickly enough as it is, thank you, and I was not aware that we were friends."

Charlie looked hurt. Then he shrugged, mounted up and led the way out. Josh cast a look of reproach at Mysterious and then followed with Dave Rudabaugh at his side. Dutchy and Close brought up the rear. As he rode silently on, trying to keep a slight distance between himself and Dirty Dave, who kept scratching and then pinching between his fingers the small critters he found about his person, Josh thought about this wandering, this inability to settle and the urge to roam which was typified by the old hermit. There were people like that and maybe Josh was one. Oh, he did not wander for religious reasons of course and no one certainly would ever accuse him of being a saint but he had the same desire to move on. More than a desire, it was a necessity. What was it?

"I must be gone and live or stay and die." Of course Romeo meant that in the sense that he wanted to stay but would be killed if he did. But words like that are also open to personal interpretation and for Josh they meant that to stay put, in one place, forever, was death, death of the mind and spirit, a way of suffocating. He had to go, to be free, to be on the move. That was life for him. Such as it was. And it would soon be time to move on from Las Vegas. Where? He didn't know. Down to El Paso maybe or over into Mexico. But he had some business to finish first.

They arrived in the town of Mora late in the evening. 'Town' was maybe a kind exaggeration. Despite being the county seat, it was one dirt street with a few low adobe and wooden buildings lining it. They checked in to Thomas Walton's Hotel (it was that or sleep in the wagon) and sat down to eat together and drink some whiskey against the cold. Or that was the reason several of them gave. Josh woke next morning with a thick head and by the look of his compadres he wasn't the only one. But they ate some eggs and drank some scalding coffee, checked their weapons and set off for the farmhouse out of town where Carson's assassins were said to be hiding. They were joined by a rancher named Daugherty, owner of the farm the villains had occupied and angry about it, and the County Sheriff, A. P. Branch, a mild little man who seemed to be there for the sake of the form but perfectly happy to leave everything to the Vegas lawmen. So the party was now eight in all, and all well-armed.

The farm was a squat, log-built place and it seemed to cringe in a tree-ringed hollow beneath a leaden sky. A miserable plume of smoke curled from the only chimney. There was nothing else moving apart from two spavined old long-suffering burros standing in the cold beside a broken-down wagon in a corral, but it was a close contest as whether the mules moved more than the wagon.

One thing the posse had not settled at all was who, officially, was in charge, and after a brief discussion it fell to Mysterious Dave because apart from Sheriff Branch, who was more than happy to defer to the Vegas men, Dave and his namesake were the only ones present to wear a badge and Dirty Dave always let Mysterious run things. In his usual laconic way, giving out an impression of great boredom which masked a ruthless efficiency, Mysterious Dave disposed the men about roughly two thirds of the rim of the hollow so that the house was as surrounded as was possible yet the men were in touch. Josh thought it was well done. By then, it was about ten o'clock of a Saturday morning, yet there was still no sign of life.

Mysterious Dave loaded a shotgun, snapped the barrels back and walked down, in the open, towards the cabin. "You boys in there!" He just waited patiently then again shouted, "Ho, you boys in there!" A shutter was partially closed by a hand. So they had heard. "Now listen. We have come to arrest you and take you back to Las Vegas for trial on the charge of the murder of Marshal Carson. Come out with your hands up." That was all he was going to say and so now he just waited.

It sounded like a pistol shot rather than a Winchester or a Henry and it ripped into the branches of a tree well above and to the right of Mysterious. He just shrugged, fired both barrels of his scattergun at the house, then calmly turned his back and walked slowly back up to his men as if he were strolling along to the barber's shop for a shave. "Okay, boys, let her rip."

The fusillade that followed lasted perhaps three minutes. Mostly at that range it was Winchesters and they can do a lot of damage. Bullets ripped into the door and through windows, smashing glass and ripping through flapping rags of curtains. It must have been very uncomfortable inside. After three minutes, Mysterious said, "That'll do" and when the guns had fallen silent and the smoke cleared, he stood clear of a tree and repeated his shout. "Well, there you are, boys. You haven't got much alternative. There's no way out of there so you surrender or die. Your choice."

"You rot in hell!" It was the voice of Bull-Shit Jack Pierce.

Mysterious shrugged and called back, "Are you sure that's what all of you think? Because I am not going to stand here all day discussing the matter. If you all think that, call out and we'll get to shooting. If any of you want to come out, do so now. We won't hurt you. One minute."

They could hear raised voices inside. Pierce seemed to be for fighting it out. Nicholson and Mullen seemed to be in favor of walking. Finally there was a thump and a crash from within and Nicholson's voice rang out. "Okay, Sheriff, we want to talk. Let me come and talk to you. But listen, I am wounded and can hardly walk. I'll be using my rifle as a crutch but that don't count as a weapon, alright? Here, I'm throwing out the other guns." Two pistols were tossed through a broken window.

"What about the others?"

"First, I talk. We want to negotiate terms."

"Negotiate? I think you have got hold of the wrong end of the stick, Mister. We aren't negotiating. It's come out or get shot to death. It isn't so complicated. We don't need fancy European diplomats to negotiate an international treaty here."

"Mr. Mather, let me come out and talk to you. That's all I ask."

Dave sighed. "Come on, then."

The door opened tentatively and Nicholson's voice came up towards them again. "You sure you ain't going to shoot?"

"I told you. Now come on."

Nicholson hobbled out. He was using the butt of his Winchester as a low, uncomfortable crutch, the barrel digging into the earth. It wouldn't have fired anyway but they remained alert. As he got closer, it was clear that Nicholson was in a bad way. A dirty bandage was wrapped tightly round his upper left arm where Josh had shot him and it showed an alarming yellow-brown stain. The leg was in no better shape and he was clearly in pain. This man needed a doctor, and fast. He finally got up to Mysterious and when he started talking in response to Dave's 'Well, say your piece', the lack of front teeth was disconcerting and affected his speech.

"Look, Mr. Mather, we been talking. We are prepared to surrender to you. Go back to Vegas. We reckon that we're going to get a hearing and we could tell things in such a hearing. Maybe strike a deal. Plus, I need a doctor, bad. So we will come quietly with you. But—"

"But what?"

"Mr. Mather, you know what Las Vegas is like. That damned windmill. We want guarantees that no lynch mob is going to do away with us before we get to trial."

"Guarantees, eh? Well, I will give you my word that while you are in my charge no one will lynch you. Will that do as a guarantee?"

"And after?"

Mysterious grew tetchier. "Well, I can hardly promise to protect you when you are out of my keeping, now can I?"

"But-"

"But nothing. I'm tired of this. I am going to take you back to Las Vegas where you will be lodged in the jail to await trial. That's that. Come willingly or we'll get back to shooting it out. That's that, I say. Yes, or no?"

Josh knew that Mysterious Dave never favored talking at the best of times. This conversation was getting way too prolix for his liking. He turned his back on Nicholson, whose shoulders sagged. The hoodlum hopped round to face the house and shouted down for the others to come out. Mullen, a gross bandage half covering his pock-marked face, came out backwards, dragging an unconscious Pierce beneath the arms. George Close drove the wagon down and Dutchy hoisted the dead weight of Pierce up into it as if he were a light sack of dried hay, then helped Nicholson up. The party moved slowly out.

"Well, that's that done," announced Dave Rudabaugh. "I'm hungry."

"You're always hungry, Dave."

"And why not? Eating is one of the pleasures of life. Like drinking. And plump señoritas and a poker hand. We ain't on this earth for long, Josh. We got to have fun!"

"I know," Josh answered sadly.

***

With two of the culprits lodged in the town jail up in old Las Vegas (for it was stronger than the new one down by the railroad), and Nicholson in one of Doc Shout's bedrooms with an armed guard outside the door, Josh felt that a part of his work was concluded and he could begin to think about moving on. He wanted to be sure that the three had robbed those stages and he liked to think that they would get their deserts for the murder of Joe Carson but he wasn't necessarily going to stay around for that. He had broken with Mrs. Carson. Not in the way he would have wished, but still, it was done, and final. He had told Hoodoo Brown that he no longer worked in any way for him (though the man had hardly been listening and hadn't seemed to register much).

He wrote a letter back to Dodge, care of Prairie Dog Morrow, to see if anything was going on there, although he did not really care to go back. He never had cared to go back. And he wrote another to Will Hardcastle at the marshal's office in Dolencia, Colorado, asking him if there were scope for a man there, maybe mining or freighting or any other kind of action. He asked if the railroad war were truly over or if there might not be some possibility for a fellow in that regard. But he didn't really hold out much hope from either letter and his mind began to turn south. Go down through Santa Fe maybe, then across to Fort Sumner and Roswell and down to El Paso. He had heard tell that El Paso was a town with possibilities. Its border location tended to attract people for a variety of reasons. It might be worth a look.

All the same, he could not shake a feeling of—what was it? Impending doom, he believed it was called. Some menace gathering force and looming, ready to fall upon him. For some time now, he had thought it was one of his depressive fits hovering, coming back soon to grind him down and send him back into that black hole of self-loathing and pointlessness, the hole that had no exit door, only dark tunnels leading off it to worse depths, but now somehow, he sensed a more direct menace. It was something to do with Hoodoo, that he knew. Maybe he ought to stay around long enough to make sure Hoodoo Brown got what was indubitably coming to him. He'd like that. Well, he would wait just a week or two for any reply that might come to his letters and meanwhile he would go heeled and watch his back.

That night, Josh was drinking with the Daves. Mysterious was his usual taciturn self and seemed morose, gloomy. Dave Rudabaugh was cheery, drinking copiously and telling jokes but his eye kept straying to one of his 'plump señoritas' in the bar. They invited Dutchy to join them but he declined, saying he had business to do.

"He don't never get close, do he?" said Dirty Dave.

"He's Hoodoo's man," his namesake answered.

"Well, loyalty is a virtue" was Josh's contribution.

"Depends on who or what you are loyal to, doesn't it?"

"Yes, I suppose it does."

Dirty Dave was having none of that. "The hell it do. You give your word to a man, you stay with him. Fair weather or foul. Rain or shine. Sticking by a pard, that's what counts."

"Dave, you could hardly call Dutchy and Hoodoo pards."

"Maybe not, Dave, but anyways if a fellow signs up to be another fellow's sidekick, why, that's that. There's no third way."

"Well, I guess you and Dutchy think alike on that one."

"Anyone fancy a hand?" Josh brought out a deck.

As the night got late, Dirty Dave departed. His mind had not been on his cards and in truth even when it was, no one would ever describe him as a successful monte player. But he had disappeared upstairs with the saloon girl and Josh and Mysterious stopped playing, out of boredom, really.

Josh rubbed his brow. "Fancy a stroll? It's a nice night and not too cold."

"Where to? Up to Holliday's place?"

"Well, if you really wish but I must say that would not have been my first choice. Let's walk along to West Las Vegas and have a nightcap at the Exchange."

Mysterious stood and put on his hat for answer and under a cold moon they walked up Douglas and Sixth and turned onto Main Street heading for the river and the plaza.

"What about Hoodoo, Dave?"

"What do you mean?"

"Well, are you, as Dave said, Hoodoo's man, come rain or shine?"

"Are you?"

"No."

"No more am I." Mysterious lit a cigar. "And what's more, he's riding for a fall."

"Time to get out?"

"Not yet, no. Soon, but not quite yet. There's life in the town yet. And don't write off Hoodoo till the full count of ten. He's nobody's fool and gives no quarter. But yes, I am looking around. This honey pot is getting rather low. Dave has the same idea. He's thinking of joining Billy. You?"

Josh shrugged. "Might be dangerous to stay."

"Might be."

There was no more to be said.

Josh and Dave spent an hour in the bar of the Exchange, Henry Hoyt refilling the glasses unasked whenever they got empty. There was always more to Henry Hoyt than met the eye, in Josh's opinion. He seemed too, what was it, educated, or rather too knowing, for a barman. And he had a way of getting information out of people. But there he always was, just tending bar. Josh shrugged again. It was becoming a bad habit. "I'm tired. Think I'll hit the hay."

"Me too. Just once round the plaza maybe to finish this cigar. Coming?"

"Okay."

They walked out into the night. There were a lot of shadows flitting on the plaza and more people than one might have expected for what must be easily two o'clock by now. The shadows reminded him of a night he had once spent up in the San Juan mountains in Colorado when wolves had run silently here and there, never quite distinct enough to see yet undoubtedly there. Josh began to get a little uneasy. Mysterious sensed the same thing for he looked quickly about and quietly put his hand under his coat and put a reassuring grip on the pistol he kept there in its shoulder harness.

There was a ruckus over at the jail. A crash, as of a door being broken in and a single shot fired.

Josh understood right away. "They're lynching Mullen and Pierce."

Mysterious Dave was grim and clear. "Not with me here, they are not." Josh noted his habitual avoidance of the 'ain't'. Dave then drew the pistol and walked over towards the noise. Mysterious always walked. He never ran. Josh followed hastily and they arrived together to see a substantial crowd of men bringing out the prisoners. Mullen, in his new, cleaner bandage, looked scared and was being pushed and prodded forward, his hands tied before him with rope. Pierce was being carried again. Perhaps he had resisted too much. Someone grunted, "That Bull-Shit, he'd rather fight than eat." The party walked straight into Mysterious Dave, who had his pistol leveled at head height.

"Stop there."

The blow from a reversed shotgun that struck Dave from behind and laid him low might have cracked his skull, it was so hard. Josh was suddenly angry and drew his own gun, crying out, "He was only doing his duty!" but before he could do any more, a dozen pistols and rifles were aimed right at him and he was drowned out by the inharmonic concert of clicking hammers and breeched rounds. He looked around and thought about it, then with a black look he put the revolver back in his pocket and bent to help Dave. The men, some masked, some not bothering, dragged Mullen and Pierce out of the jail and over to the centre of the plaza where the windmill-gibbet loomed, casting a long, night-black shadow in the light of the icy moon.

They prodded Mullen up the ladder onto the platform and dragged a now conscious, but groggy, Pierce up after him. A noosed rope was thrown over one of the beams supporting the windmill and a man snarled out, "Say your prayers, boys, because you's about to be jerked to Jesus." Another man adjusted and tightened the noose about Mullen's neck and still a third asked if he had anything to say. He replied that his real name was William George Mackintosh and asked that somebody write to his parents, who were still living, Mr. and Mrs. Thomas Jefferson Mackintosh of Rome, Georgia. But then his courage began to fail him and he began to whimper. Bull-Shit Pierce, who had turned out to be the strongest of them, said from his crouched position on the platform waiting his turn, "Kid, be still and die like a man" and this did indeed seem to help Mullen regain his composure for he called out, "Boys, you are hanging a mighty good man and I go now to meet my Maker." They were fine words but he spoilt them by adding, "Please button up my pants." Then one fellow shoved him hard in the small of the back and another hauled on the rope and Mullen swung out into the night air, kicking horribly and emitting ghastly garbled sounds from his strangled throat.

The body was still writhing when Mrs. Carson fired the first rifle shot into it. Then she expertly levered another round and fired again, and then again. She had come to exact her revenge upon the men who had murdered her husband and there she was, cold, silent, the rifle butt pressed into the bodice of her elegant dress, pumping bullets into the corpse. When she was satisfied, she looked for the other murderer and saw him crouched on the platform and began firing at him. For a while, the onlookers were shocked at Mrs. Carson's actions and looked at her amazedly but then they liked what they saw and almost together began firing too. They brought out pistols and rifles and shotguns and blazed away. The hanging party on the top had scuttled off, almost falling down the ladder in their haste to get out of the line of fire, leaving Pierce there, his hands tied. Gunsmoke drifted white across the moon and a fusillade of bullets smacked into the windmill.

Pierce was shot, then again, then again. He crawled to the edge of the platform and cried out, "For God's sake shoot me again, shoot me in the head" and then, more by accident than good aim he got his wish and his body slumped suddenly to the boards and he was no more.

Only Mrs. Carson kept up her expert use of a Winchester '73, for she had reloaded it with some borrowed .44 Colt's ammunition and systematically pumped bullets into the corpses until Josh came up beside her and forced the barrel down. She looked at him fiercely then suddenly drooped, her shoulders sagging, and allowed Josh to take the rifle, which he did almost tenderly.

***

As the day dawned, those who had not attended the executions got to hear about them and many drifted to the plaza to see what might be seen, some idly picking up brass cartridge cases, most just talking. There was great excitement among the small boys of the town and several of them took to hanging dogs, pretending that any convenient beam or bar was the wind pump and the ragged mutts were desperadoes. Josh passed two or three of the poor creatures and cut them down. He wondered at the effect on the young of the town.

But it was in a sense the end. A petition was circulating rapidly all over town to have the windmill torn down. It had all gone too far. In a matter of hours, two carpenters had been recruited and, supervised by Marshal Morrison, they spent the day dismantling the pump and its macabre base. By the end of the day, when a coroner's jury found that the deaths of Mullen and Pierce had been caused by 'a mob unknown to this jury', the windmill was gone and the plaza empty.

Mysterious Dave was not seriously hurt and was confirmed as the successor to Joe Carson in East Las Vegas. Josh saw him on the other side of the plaza shaking hands with Marshal Morrison, something unlikely to have happened six months before. Josh was on his way to Doc Shout's.

Nicholson lay in a comfortable bed and was looking a lot better. The doctor said he had feared that the leg might have had to be amputated but was convinced now that it would no longer be necessary. Josh was glad. He would not wish to have been the cause of that, whatever the man had done. With the happenings of the night, the guard on the door had been doubled and two sheriff's deputies with carbines sat in the corridor.

"So you heard about the events last night then?"

Nicholson looked sour. Josh had the idea that he would have spat had he not been in such a respectable place. "Yeah, well."

"Well, I want to know what you are prepared to tell me."

"Why should I tell you anything?"

"Simple. Your friends were illegally executed but your fate will be very similar. Oh, you'll be hanged legal but you'll be hanged. You shot Joe Carson, a law officer in the exercise of his duties, in the back and in cold blood and then you fled, all before a whole roomful of witnesses, including me. They'll take you down to Santa Fe and there'll be a trial but I reckon the outcome is nigh on certain, don't you?"

"So what are you proposing?"

"Not much. But I reckon that if you tell me what you know, in front of Marshal Morrison, and I mean about the stage robberies as well as the murder, you could find that a few years in Yuma might be better than a legal rope in Santa Fe."

"What they call a plea bargain?"

"Of course, when you are better, and the Doc says that'll be soon, they'll remove you from here to the town jail."

"They wouldn't!"

"Why not? You're only here because of your wounds. As soon as you are able, they will put you where you belong. Of course, the lynch mob probably won't strike again but then again on the other hand…"

"Look, I'll tell you about the stage robberies. Killing Carson, well, you know that already."

"Not really, I don't. We'll get to the stages in a moment but first, who put you up to kill Carson?"

Nicholson looked shifty and undecided. "No one. We was drunk. You do things, you know, under the influence of whiskey that you come to regret when you're sober."

"I don't believe you. None of you had the nerve to do that on your own. You were put up to it. By whom?"

"Honest, I-"

"Holliday? Hoodoo Brown? Come on, out with it."

"Look, maybe I will talk to Marshal Morrison, or better yet the judge about that. Maybe. When the time comes. Right now, do you want to hear about the stage robberies or not?"

"I do."

"Well, we done them both. Robbed both them stages. Held 'em up."

"On your own."

"Course."

"Unprompted."

"What?"

"No one suggested you do it or paid you to do it or helped you do it?"

"You want to know more'n I'm prepared to tell, Mister. Anyways, far as I understand it, you ain't even got no badge. Why should I tell you anything?"

"In fact, I am employed as a detective by the Adams Express Company and have been charged to investigate attacks in this area upon its strong boxes and upon the U.S. Mails. So I am fully authorized to make these inquiries. But never mind, no problem. I'll be back in half an hour with Marshal Morrison. Don't go away."

Nicholson did not appreciate the joke.

***

"You did what?"

"I told John Morrison everything Nicholson told me. Morrison's with him now. I reckon he'll tell everything to escape the rope."

"For God's sake!"

"Why? What was wrong with that?"

"If you had to involve a lawman, why didn't you use Mather?"

"It was up in West Las Vegas, in Morrison's jurisdiction."

"So what? So what? Since when did you care about the niceties of legal jurisdictions?"

"Mr. Brown, you seem to forget that I do no longer work for you and am not, nor ever have been, a sworn officer of this precinct."

"The hell you don't work for me. I paid you good money, took you in, paid for your accommodations, gave you orders. Of course you work for me."

"Not anymore, not since you refused to swear me in. I told you."

"I did not refuse. Here, we'll do it now!"

"Too late, Mr. Brown, too late. I shall be leaving town shortly."

Hoodoo looked him sharply in the eye. "How shortly?"

"Oh, a few days, I guess. Maybe a week. Soon as I get the reply to a couple of letters."

"Now look, Josh. Sit down, please. Look, I am sure we can sort things out. Come to some arrangement. We Kansas boys got to stick together, no? Let me get you a drink."

"Thank you but I have some errands to do."

Hoodoo brought his fist down on the table, making shot glasses and playing cards jump. "Dammit! Dammit!"

"I wish you a good morning, Mr. Brown." And he tipped his hat, turned and left.

Outside, he met Wyatt and James. Both were agitated. They wanted to know about the events of the night and whether either of the men had talked.

"They didn't get the chance. But Nicholson'll talk alright. Sing like a canary. I'm sure of it."

Wyatt and James exchanged looks. Wyatt asked, "Walk along with us? We're going up to Doc's."

"Well, I'll walk along with you, be glad to, but I got to get up to the old town and do a few things so I won't be stopping at Doc's."

At Holliday's saloon, they parted. Josh walked slowly and thoughtfully on over the Gallinas Bridge and up Bridge Street. As he passed the post office, he suddenly remembered something and pulled a crumpled envelope out of his coat pocket. He finally mailed his too-long forgotten letter of resignation to the Adams Express Company. He was a free man.

***

The next day Josh ran into Wyatt and James again. They were hoisting a trunk and some valises onto the top of the stage.

"Josh, there you are, we been looking for you. Wanted to say goodbye."

"Goodbye?"

"Oh yes, we're off. This town's about played out, you know? Thought we might go down into Arizona and see if we can get us some of that silver."

"Holliday going too?"

"Oh, yes, Doc decided to join us. He has sold his place and I have sold my share too. Time to move on. You know how it is."

"Yeah. I know how it is."

"What about you? You staying?"

"No, not staying. Soon as I have settled some affairs I'll be going too. Thought I might take a look at El Paso."

Wyatt nodded and looked unhappy. "Josh…"

"What?"

"Oh, nothing. But good luck, okay? Look after yourself. Watch your back."

Holliday emerged, his prematurely gray head uncovered but wearing a large, long overcoat with a shoulder-cape. He held a silver-topped cane and if one hadn't known better one would have taken him for a gentleman. He was cheerful and effusive. "Ah, Josh, my boy, how fortunate to see you so that we may exchange our fond farewells!"

"Bye, Doc."

"Yes, the time has come for us no longer to tarry. We must be gone."

"Yes, I guess you must. Things being as they are."

"Things being as they are? I don't know to what you refer, my dear boy. No, no, it's just that men like us can never stay too long in one place, eh? We must be eternally on our way. 'I must be gone to live, stay and die.' Romeo and Juliet, Act 3, Scene 5."

Doc had misquoted slightly. "Yes, though I think that Romeo meant that if he stayed, he would be killed, so he had to go."

"Aha, so you know your Shakespeare, Josh, my friend. Hidden depths, I always thought it, hidden depths. Well, here's hoping we run into each other again one of these days. Come and see us if you are ever down Benson or Bisbee way." And he swung up into the coach.

Wyatt shook Josh's hand warmly and then James did the same. James said, "Look after yourself, Josh. Take care."

"Everyone is advising me to watch my back and take care. Do you know something I don't?"

"Oh no, it's just a figure of speech is all. Goodbye, Josh."

As the dust raised by the wheels subsided, Josh thought he may have been guilty of not facing the hard truth. Even dereliction of duty. He was sure that it would finally emerge that Holliday and the Earps had been involved in one or both of those stage robberies. But then he was no longer any kind of officer and Wyatt and James were his friends. Let them go. He would miss both, though. He didn't have so many friends that he could afford to lose two of them.

Chapter Seven

It was a leap year and Michael Kelliher arrived in Las Vegas, N.M.T. on 29th February. He installed himself in the Exchange Hotel and threw a heavy carpetbag, as was his custom, into the back of a closet. This time he thought he would use a bank. There was simply too much money there to leave lying in a bag in what would often be an empty hotel room. In Denver, he had counted over thirty-six thousand dollars, and more had been added since then. Some of that would go on the cattle purchase but far from all. The banks would be open tomorrow. He gave orders to his foreman, Williams, who had accompanied him, to go straight out in the morning and start prospecting around for cattle to buy. He himself had other business. He examined the two-shot under-and-over Remington derringer he had bought. Was it too womanly a weapon? No, gamblers used them. And the little guns did the business at close range over a gaming table, say, or across a small bar room.

Late in the evening, he stuffed wads of banknotes in his pockets and after a few restorative potions in the bar of the Exchange, he put on a long greatcoat and walked back the way a buggy had brought them earlier in the day, back towards the depot. He called in at Close & Paterson's and asked to see Mr. Hyman G. Neill.

Dave Mather saw them there, at a table in the corner, heads close together, discussing something earnestly for quite a time and he wondered who the close-cropped, stocky and muscular man with Hoodoo might be but was then distracted by a call for his services and walked out to do his duty in the maintenance of the peace in the saloon next door.

Later that night Dave saw Kelliher twice more, in different saloons, drinking hard and getting noisier. When they are drunk, some people talk more loudly, almost as some deaf people do. Kelliher's voice had a booming quality. At Goodlet & Robert's, Dave heard the man bellowing to Bill Goodlet behind the bar asking about some Indian war clubs up on the wall as decoration. He wanted to have them handed to him. He would show them all, he said, how to wield a war-club. He hadn't been a policeman in Chicago without learning how effectively to wield a club. You didn't need a gun when you had a good cudgel or club. But Goodlet wouldn't do it and Kelliher got angrier and louder. Mather cast a professional eye over the situation but decided it was all just braggadocio and the man was not seriously going to harm anyone or do damage, and he left on his rounds.

Meanwhile, Josh was packing his bags in his room. He had received a letter from Will Hardcastle in Colorado. It started by saying that he hoped Josh had gotten his telegram and was watching his back. Here it was again! He had received no telegram. But the letter went on to tell him that the Royal Gorge railroad war was well and truly over and settled but that there were openings for anyone willing to work hard, especially if they had something to invest. He himself was thinking of a small ranch and could use a partner. Freighting was a good line too, or would be anyway until the railroad had taken all the business.

There was nothing in the letter for Josh, though. It all sounded too safe and law-abiding. He hadn't received an answer from Dodge but didn't think it was worth waiting for. It was time to move on. He would make a round of calls tomorrow to say goodbye to a few folks and then would take the two o'clock stage. It felt good to be on the move again.

***

Monday morning, the first day of the new month, dawned bright and crisp and blue-skied. There was a smell of early spring in the air. Maybe it was that which was prompting him to be gone. He would have liked to have taken a horse and ridden out, for the sheer pleasure of it, maybe up to Montezuma Springs. On any other day, he would have done that but he had decided to leave town today and leave he would. No point in putting it off; no need to, either.

He walked briskly along to Close & Paterson's. He didn't really care to see Hoodoo again but he had to go back there to say goodbye to Dutchy and maybe find the Daves but in particular, he thought Mrs. Carson would be there and he didn't want to leave without saying adieu to her. It wouldn't be easy but he wanted to do it. He felt it would be almost cowardly just to leave without saying anything to her and let her find out by chance from another.

As luck would have it, none of those he wished to see was there. Only Hoodoo. Well, he would be polite at least.

"Mr. Brown, I have come to say goodbye. I am leaving on the afternoon stage."

"Josh, Josh, just the man I wanted to see." It was as if he hadn't heard what Josh had said. "Listen, I have something very urgent to tell you. It's very important. Come, sit down, here where we won't be disturbed."

"Now Mr. Brown, I told you. It's too late for that. I have made up my mind. I even have the Wells, Fargo ticket, see? No, I—"

"Never mind all that. Just wait till you hear what I have to say." Josh shrugged and sat down. Hoodoo poured him some coffee. "Now, listen."

And he proceeded to tell Josh that Michael Kelliher was in town and looking for him and armed, and that he had said he was going to shoot Josh on sight.

Josh did not at first believe it. What nonsense was this? Kelliher? That varmint was dead, long dead and buried. In Cheyenne, years ago, even before Dodge. Hoodoo sure could come out with crazy ideas. What was his point? Was he trying to get Josh to stay? And if so, why? But gradually, as Hoodoo expanded on the matter, Josh began to wonder if it might not be true. Had the man survived? It seemed unlikely. But people were shot in the head and lived. And certainly, Kelliher was such a man that if he had survived, he would have been prepared to devote the rest of his life to tracking down his assailant and murdering him. Josh looked over at Hoodoo.

"You got one of them telephones here, right?"

"Certainly."

"Is it connected with the Exchange Hotel? Can I speak to them there?"

"Of course. Here." And he ushered Josh to a hardwood box screwed to the wall which had two tubes hanging below it and a wooden or maybe bone piece on top which you spoke into.

"How does it work?"

"Here, just hold this to your ear and turn this handle. When the girl answers, you ask to be put through to the Exchange Hotel. You speak into this hole here."

"What do I say when the person answers?"

"Whatever you want, of course."

"No, I mean what do I say first? 'Good morning'?"

"Oh, well, we usually say 'Hello'. Some people say 'Ahoy'."

"Ahoy?"

"Yes, it sounds rather breezy and nautical, doesn't it?"

"I don't think I want to say 'ahoy'."

"Well, say 'hello' then. Go on!"

Josh turned the handle and jumped rather when a very clear voice said, "Which number, please?"

"Number? Oh, I mean, 'Hello'. What do you mean, Miss, number?"

"Who do you want to speak to?"

"Oh, the Exchange Hotel. I want to speak to them up there at the Exchange Hotel. But I don't know if they have a number."

"Twenty-three."

"Twenty-three, is it? Well, then, number twenty-three, please. Please call number twenty-three. It's Joshua Webb and I would like to speak to-"

"You can tell them that."

"Yes, ma'am, right. I will tell them who I am." He turned to Hoodoo. "I didn't think it would be so complicated."

"Hello?"

"Oh, yes, 'Hello'. Um, this here is Mr. J. J. Webb. I am down at Close & Paterson's here."

"Yes?"

"Oh well, I wanted to speak to Mr. Henry Hoyt. Your barman. Henry. Is he there?"

"Sure. Hold on."

"Yessir, I'll hold on all right. I'll wait right here." While he was waiting, he said to Hoodoo, "It's working alright!" But Hoodoo looked bored and wandered off towards the bar.

"Hello, Mr. Webb?"

"Oh yes, Henry. I mean, 'Hello'. Listen Henry, Can you hear me alright?"

"Yes, sure."

"Good. I can hear you too. I would like to know, has a Mr. Michael Kelliher checked in to your hotel?"

"Yes, he has."

"He has?"

"Yes, I was talking to him last night. He's here alright."

"Michael Kelliher from Cheyenne, Wyoming?"

"Yup. He has signed in 'Michael Kelliher, Denver', but he told me all about his ranch in Wyoming. He and his brother have part shares in a place in the Dakotas too. Up by Deadwood."

"Right. I understand. So he's there then."

"Well, he's not here right now, if that's what you mean. He's gone out."

"Quite. Gone out. But listen, Henry, he didn't mention my name at all, did he?"

"No, not specifically, no, he didn't. Do you know him?"

"Listen, Henry, do me a favor, will you? If my name comes up, you have never heard of me."

"If you say so, Mr. Webb. No problem."

"It's just that I am leaving town today and…Well, never mind. Thank you, Henry. Er, how do you, that is, say goodbye on these things?"

"Well, you say goodbye, sir."

"Of course, right, well, goodbye, Henry."

"Goodbye, Mr. Webb."

Josh was mightily relieved to replace the tube. He hadn't cared for the experience, all in all, and would try to avoid the telephone in future.

Hoodoo was back. "So, Josh, you know now."

"Yes."

"I don't want to know the old history and the wrongs and rights of it but let me tell you, Josh, that we are Kansas boys and we got to stick together and I will do everything I can to help you. But you should know that Kelliher is armed to the teeth and told me that he will shoot you on sight. He won't wait for a fair fight or anything like that. He said he gave you a fair fight before and you shot him in the back and that this time-"

"I never shot anyone in the back in all my life."

"No, of course you didn't. I said, you are a Kansas boy. But that's the way he sees it and, well, if I were you…"

"If you were me, you would what?"

"Well, I'd go heeled for one thing. But more than that, I'd look the fellow out, find him on a ground of my choosing and shoot him, right there where he stood. I wouldn't give him the option of an open duel or anything like that. Because, Josh, if you don't, that man is going to kill you. On sight. I mean it. He was quite clear about that. It's why he has come here. To kill you."

"You seem to be mighty carin' about my fate in this matter."

"I am, I am. I like you, Josh. I have always liked you. Not just because of Kansas. I appreciate your abilities and your worth. I know you are a good man and a brave one. I don't want to see you shot to death in a no-good end-of-track town like this one."

"Well, that's good of you. But to be honest, I don't aim to be shot to death here."

"No, of course not. But let me tell you, if you don't face this man down here, he will follow you all over the continent. He is implacable. Sooner or later, you will have to face him. Might it not be better here, on friendly ground, as it were? You know I will back you up. As Justice of the Peace." Josh did not answer. Hoodoo continued, "Well, I have had my say. I have done what I can. Just remember that Kelliher has come here expressly for you, he is armed, violent by nature and out to get you. If you see him, I implore you, do not wait. No fancy notions of a fair fight or a showdown in the street. That's the stuff of dime novels. If you see him, out with your piece and shoot the man down. It's the only way you will survive."

"Well, that's not really my—"

"Look, with the threats that man has uttered before witnesses and with my backing, you'll be clear with the law. Find him on your terms and shoot the man. Trust me, Josh, it's the only way."

***

The Governor's Mansion in Santa Fe was frankly a delightful house. It was low but large and surrounded by palms and shrubs. Small fountains played in its garden. Set in the heart of the old Spanish town, it's cool whitened walls and elegant colonnaded porticoes made it a refreshing and pleasant place to stroll, work or take one's dinner. Governor Wallace liked it very much and regretted the time he had to spend away from it, especially if the absence was caused by a visit to some infernal dirty town where law and order seemed to be unknown.

This evening, however, he was feeling well. He had had a productive day in his study immersed in ancient Rome and his head was still full of chariots and circuses and Mediterranean maidens. He could almost imagine himself now, in the cool of the evening, wearing a toga as he walked the atrium of his villa near the Temple of Marcellus overlooking the Tiber. But the servant announced his dinner guests and his daydream was rudely broken.

Chief Justice L. Bradford Prince was a regular visitor and Governor Wallace liked the man but the conversation was always and inevitably dominated by work. Lawlessness of every kind was rampant in the Chief Justice's territory and it was a constant battle to bring order and justice to its ungovernable lands. The wretched Bonney caused nothing but trouble, even in the newspapers of the east, and rustling and range war and murder were rife. Garrett seemed unable to find him. The boy needed to be caught and hanged or at the very least shut away in a penitentiary for life. And as for the town of Las Vegas, it was impossible. There, the so-called officers of the law were the problem and not its solution. A clean sweep was needed. The fellow Brown or Neill or whatever in tarnation his name was, must be removed along with all his cronies. The Governor sighed. An evening of conversation about the glory that was Rome must give way to hard talk of guns and posses and hangings.

At least, there was to be another guest and this man, whom the Governor did not know, was said to be a wealthy landowner from the north so perhaps he might have some civilization about him and some wider talk might be possible. Not that Prince was an uneducated man. Just that he was single-minded. Well, that was good.

The guests were shown in and Mr. Michael Kelliher was introduced to the Governor. He was, in Wallace's opinion, a tough, bull-necked rancher with not an ounce of flab about him and as he shook Kelliher's painfully hard hand, the Governor inwardly despaired of his evening's conversation. However, he was wrong, for Kelliher turned out to be charming. He talked of travels he had made to the east and to South America, with a knowledge and perceptiveness that impressed Wallace. They discoursed on the future of the western territories and the advance of progress. They discussed the Indian problem and railroads. It turned out to be a stimulating evening. Whenever Prince did turn the conversation around to the problems of Las Vegas, which Kelliher had just visited, Kelliher's contribution was sage and balanced, if firmly on the side of discipline and order.

"You know, Governor, I love this country. Its beauty and its potential. New Mexico will become one of the states of the union before we know it and one of the greatest states too. It has so much to offer. Once lawlessness is eliminated, settlers will come flocking in. My own dear wife and daughters— how I miss them when I travel for work like this and how they would love this beautiful land—would, I know, press me to settle here myself and exchange the Wyoming winters for these golden evenings."

"Oh but Mr. Kelliher, we do have winters here too, you know, and they can be fierce!"

"I have no doubt of that, Governor, no doubt at all. But I am quite sure that they would not be Wyoming winters. There, we are snowed in for months at a time and a winter is considered mild if we only lose hundreds of head frozen to death rather than thousands. If it weren't for my books…However, I am not considering a move for the moment. Rather, I wish to purchase cattle in New Mexico and ship them north on the new railroad. North-eastern Wyoming and the Dakotas are ripe for expansion and I need cattle for those lands. Your New Mexico cattle are sturdy and well-priced. I intend to make this a regular enterprise, Governor, from which New Mexico will gain enormously. This will profit me but will benefit this Territory in every way."

Later, when Kelliher had gone, Governor Wallace took Chief Justice L. Bradford Prince by the arm and they strolled through the garden, puffing on cigars.

"Good man, that Kelliher. The sort we need to encourage."

"Yes, Governor, yes. Surprisingly so."

"What do you mean?"

"Well, this evening he seemed, how can I say, softer. Up till now I had him down as a hard man, ruthless even. With no graces about him. Yet here he is, talking of books and his dear daughters and the golden New Mexico evenings…Unexpected, shall we say."

"Well, sometimes people take time to reveal their true selves."

"Yes," Prince replied. But there still seemed to be an element of hesitation in his voice. He shook his head as if shaking off doubts and put the subject behind him. Wallace was presented with an image of a large shaggy gundog shaking its coat free of water and could not resist a smile. But Chief Justice L. Bradford Prince was, as ever, in earnest. "Now, Governor, about the situation in Las Vegas…"

***

In Las Vegas, Joshua Webb was in a quandary. He had made up his mind to leave. It had taken a long time, too long probably, but he had finally decided.

Had the ticket, said his goodbyes. And now this. He hated these situations. A decision was a decision. You don't go back on them. On the other hand, it appeared that the man Kelliher, for years dead and buried and only a receding memory to Josh, was now not only alive but actively seeking vengeance. Josh was not afraid of him in the obvious sense. He did not wish to leave town simply to run away from the threat. But at the same time he did not relish staying and dealing with this implacable and intensely violent man. There would inevitably be blood and fury and even if he survived, probably arrest and a court case. What to do? But in fact he already knew what he had to do. Hoodoo was right: if he did not face Kelliher here, on this ground, it would be somewhere else, probably less favorable. There was no avoiding it. He would have to stay. At least, until this was dealt with. He sighed and unpacked his valise, then went down to tell the hotel clerk that he wanted his room for a few more days.

***

"What are you doing?"

"I am packing, Hyman, can't you see?"

"Packing?"

"Yes, I am leaving. I have told you and told you, it is time to go. If you can't see it, I am leaving alone."

"Look, if it's because of Carson…"

Mrs. Carson turned round and looked Hoodoo in the eye. She was silent for a moment then said, "If I thought you had anything at all to do with the death of my husband, I would kill you myself."

Hoodoo was shocked at the brutality and fire in her gaze and he blanched. Mrs. Carson resumed her packing.

Hoodoo tried again. "Listen. We will go. You are right, we must go. I have started winding up my affairs. But just give me a day or two more. That's all I need. A day or two. I have a large coup almost ready. It will give us all the money we need to travel wherever we like. New Orleans. San Francisco. Wherever you want. But I'm not quite ready yet. And I have just one or two loose ends to tie up."

"You mean people to get rid of."

"Well, I wouldn't put it like that. But you know, I like to leave a place tidy behind me."

Mrs. Carson looked penetratingly at him again, then turned and folded a blouse.

***

"Well, I am for toughing it out." Mysterious Dave was not a person to give up a profitable and comfortable situation without a fight. "You say it's all going to hell but I don't see it that way. We keep our heads down a bit, there is life in this town yet. The Governor isn't going to declare martial law. He can't afford to, not on top of all the Lincoln County problems. It would be the end of him. We should stay, at least a bit longer."

"He may not declare martial law but he is about to replace me in my functions here, I can feel it. And worse, there could be arrest warrants around. Prince and his sidekick Morrison are determined and they are about to strike. We need to pack up here and make ready to move out." Hoodoo seemed almost to be repeating the arguments given him by Mrs. Carson just half an hour ago when he had so opposed them. "I have already made various sales and realized several investments. I just need a day, at most two, to complete my arrangements and I am off. I strongly advise you to do the same."

Dutchy shook his huge head. He didn't say anything. He rarely did. But he wasn't happy. Perhaps he was of Dave's thinking. But there was no question: whatever Hoodoo said, he would do.

Dirty Dave was more sanguine about the end of the happy times. Good times always ended. He was ready to be on his way. They were all pulling out, it was clear. The Earps and Holliday had gone. That was no loss. He didn't care for them. It was only Mysterious who had detained him so far. He would ride off and find Billy. But he would still take his cue from Mysterious for the moment. If Dave said stay, he would stay. For now. He had no arrangements to make, no property to sell, no bank accounts to close. When Dave was ready and Hoodoo had left, he would just mount up one morning and be gone. He hoped Dave would come with him, or Josh if not. But if not, he would ride out alone. It wouldn't be the first time.

But it was clear to all of them that the time had pretty well come. Only George Close and Billy Paterson thought they might stay if they could manage to buy Hoodoo out reasonably. The saloon was making money and they had no place to go. They were unlikely to be arrested and could not be tied directly to any crime. But the Earps and Holliday were already gone and Josh Webb was soon to be on the stage out of town. Once Hoodoo and Dutchy left, the days of the Dodge City Gang in Las Vegas were clearly over.

***

Kelliher had been going from saloon to saloon most of the day. He had picked up some drinking and gambling companions along the way, men whose eyes had grown large at the huge sheaf of banknotes that Kelliher made no effort to be discreet about. The stocky rancher would peel off fifty dollars as if it meant nothing, paying for all drinks, leaving a pile of money on the table in front of him when at cards or when going outside to relieve himself, and carelessly stuffing the cash into pockets when it was time to move on. By two in the morning, now well into the second of March, they had arrived at Goodlet & Roberts, a well-known Dodge City Gang joint. Kelliher was at the bar, very drunk and, as always when in that condition, loud, aggressive and violent, enough for everyone else to be very careful what they said and did. The man exuded brute unpredictable force, like a loose floating mine.

Josh had prepared himself at the Exchange. He had stood motionless at the window looking out at the New Mexico evening until the darkness was such that he realized he was gazing now at his own reflection. He had then gone into action. He cleaned and oiled and reloaded his guns. There was a throwing knife in his boot. He was ready. He jammed his hat on, looked at the grim face that stared out at him from the mirror, did not care much for it and walked out slamming the door. He strode purposefully down towards the river, stopping in at various establishments, looking for Kelliher but not asking anyone if the man had been there. Sometimes he took a small drink at the bar. More usually he looked around, verified that his quarry was not present and moved on.

As he walked down the middle of the dusty street in the moonlight, he reflected on what he was about to do. He would shortly find Kelliher. He didn't know if Kelliher was actively seeking him out but it didn't matter. Las Vegas was a small place and very soon their paths would cross, probably at one of the joints down by the railroad. He knew full well that there could be no discussion, no reasoned debate. Kelliher would try immediately to kill him and he must forestall that. Josh knew how dangerous Kelliher was. Nevertheless, he was not going to shoot the man down without warning, whatever Hoodoo's advice was. He was most certainly not going to shoot the man in the back as Kelliher had done to him all those years ago, after Josh had beaten him in a fair fight. But he could afford no weakness, no half measures. He could not give the man the slightest advantage.

Josh had killed men before. Not many, but it had happened. He disliked the business but he was not sentimental about it. If someone was seriously trying to do him harm or take away his life, he would act, ferociously and first. He would do a lot to avoid getting into that situation, even at the cost of being thought a coward. He would not enter the arena willingly or at all if he reasonably had a way of avoiding it. But if he was obliged to, well, then he would be implacable. He had been and would be again. Now was such a time.

The air was fresh and clear. There was only a slight chill. The moon was brave and bright. It was a fine New Mexico night. Almost enough to make you want to stay. Almost.

He thought of looking out the Daves. A bit of support. But he had already decided that he needed to do this alone. It was a personal matter, not a law-enforcement one. He found he did not feel frightened or afraid of dying. He felt just quiet. He didn't want to do this but he needed to. He would try to accomplish what he needed to do. If he could, well. If not, well also. So be it.

The saloons still open threw out a yellow light to the street as he passed them. From them emerged the noise of laughter or a piano or a loud argument or on one occasion a señorita singing. The girl was singing a song Masie used to play on the piano. It was a sweet, delicate air Josh had always liked and it reminded him of her whenever he heard it.

He saw her now, sitting at the instrument, her long hair shining in the candlelight, her brow slightly furrowed with the concentration, her bottom lip ever so slightly protruding, the flush in her cheeks which at first had been so becoming. Then, when she was finished, that radiant look when she turned and realized he had been watching and she gave him a smile which lit the whole room. A distant gunshot followed by a dog's bark broke his reverie and he walked on down Main Street towards the railroad. The night seemed colder suddenly and he gave a slight shivering shrug and did up his coat tighter at the neck.

He found him at Goodlet & Roberts.

Chapter Eight

The bar was crowded. Three in the morning of a Tuesday and still business was good. Card players at all the tables. Saloon girls were wheedling drinks out of drunken store men and farm laborers (and neither farmhands nor shop assistants would be ready for work tomorrow at seven). A roulette wheel rattled. Josh noticed tired bunting on the balustrades, red, gray and blue, left over from the fourth of July last year. The smell of unwashed man and heavily scented woman mixed with that of spat tobacco and cheap whiskey. William Goodlet, one of the owners and another Hoodoo crony, stood at one end of the long bar and nodded at Josh then looked over at Kelliher.

Kelliher had his back to Josh and the door—not a position Josh would have adopted. The man was slumped low over the bar, fumbling for his glass. Josh put his hand on the gun butt in his coat and waited there, for all the world like a gentleman elegantly standing on a street corner waiting for his carriage with his hand in his pocket. He said nothing, just waited.

One of Kelliher's companions nudged him and indicated with a glance over towards where Josh was standing and Kelliher finally turned. Seeing Josh, the fog slowly cleared, then a look of real and intense hatred came over his face. Josh could see the man was if not drunk then at least the worse for wear. That was good. That would give Josh an edge. Kelliher uttered a low growl. It was animal in its sound and meaning. The man was clearly considering launching himself over to Josh and fighting him there but he thought better of it and his hand went to the side pocket of his coat.

"Hold! Don't do that! Throw up your hands!"

Kelliher hesitated but then resumed, digging into his pocket. Josh brought out his Colt's and aimed right at Kelliher's head. "Hold, I say, or I fire!"

Kelliher brought his right hand brusquely up. It got caught in the jacket and he tugged violently but it was too much movement for Josh and before he knew it, the Colt's fired. Kelliher staggered and blood spurted from his head. He fell back into the bar and a leg went out from under him but still he did not fall. Normally in such a situation Josh would have fired again, to the body, dropping his enemy definitively but he had not meant to shoot so. He was not ready and he hesitated. In any case, it was not necessary, for Kelliher swayed like a tree then crashed to the floor, his hand still in his coat.

The bar was silent with shock. The room smelled of gunpowder. Josh kept his gun in his hand, walked over and looked down at the fallen rancher. His bullet had struck the man high in the forehead, in the middle of the white scar caused by Josh's last attempt to shoot the man in the head. The man's eyes were still open but glazed. This time there was no doubt. Kelliher was dead.

Goodlet was the first to speak. "You all saw it. He went for his gun. It was a fair fight." Josh was grateful to him for that. But a man beside Kelliher said, "The hell you say! That was cold-blooded murder! This man was not armed!"

Another man leaned down and tugged Kelliher's hand free from the pocket. There was a sap in it, an ugly-looking weighted small bar-room club. But no gun. "See? I told you! Murder!"

"Nonsense!" A booming voice. Where did Hoodoo come from? He was on one knee examining the corpse. "We need to search the body carefully." Hoodoo went through Kelliher's pockets and came up with the sap, a cheap watch, and of course different sheaves of banknotes. "I am taking this money into custody. Goodlet, you will be my witness. We shall count it together. You men, get back. Lay this body out. I shall convene a coroner's hearing. Josh, get out. Put that gun away. I shall see you tomorrow." Josh walked dazedly out into the street and headed back up to West Las Vegas to his hotel. He needed to get back to his room and think. Kelliher was dead. Well, good. Had Josh done anything he should be ashamed of or afraid about? He didn't think so. But he needed to review it in his mind. The New Mexico night was colder.

**

Outside the office of the *Las Vegas Optic* at about nine the next morning, Josh, who had not slept in the intervening five or six hours, bought a copy of the morning paper, and read the article low on the front page.

Las Vegas, Wednesday 3rd March. About four o'clock this morning, Michael Kelliher, in company with William Brickley and another man, entered Goodlet & Roberts' Saloon and called for drinks. Michael Kelliher appeared to be the leader of the party and he, in violation of the law, had a pistol on his

136

person. This was noticed by an officer, who came through a rear door, and he requested that Kelliher lay aside his revolver. But he refused to do so, remarking, "I won't be disarmed—everything goes," immediately placing his hand on his pistol, no doubt intending to shoot. But Officer Webb was too quick for him. Kelliher was shot before he had time to use his weapon. He was shot once in the head and perished immediately. Kelliher had $1,090 on his person when killed.

It seemed to Josh to bear little resemblance to the actuality, though it certainly favored him, suggesting as it did that he was an officer of the law obliged to fire while carrying out his duties. How had they heard that Kelliher had a firearm? Josh had certainly believed the man to be armed but had seen no weapon and immediately after the shooting someone had said that Kelliher had no gun, only a sap. Kelliher had certainly not said in Josh's hearing that 'everything goes'. Nor had Josh come in through the back door. And what had the amount of money Kelliher had on him to do with it? Still, newspapers often got things wrong and by and large Josh thought that the report would do him no harm.

Then the lead article caught his attention. It foretold 'the impending collapse of the Dodge City Gang' and announced forthcoming murder indictments. Well, no wonder the Earps and Holliday had pulled out. He was surprised that Hoodoo was still in town. The Daves would certainly be on their way now. Then a thought struck him. Was he himself a member of 'the Dodge City Gang?' He supposed he was. And would he be expected to stay for a hearing or inquest into Kelliher's death that might be held? He doubted now that the East Las Vegas Coroner would be in town long enough to convene one. Perhaps Josh should get onto today's stage.

"Hello, Josh. Reading about the forthcoming end to the lawlessness and disorder in Las Vegas?"

Josh turned and saw Marshal Morrison. "Is that what it is?"

Morrison looked him in the eye and said, with an edge to his voice, "Yes. Yes, it is."

Josh shrugged. "Well, no bad thing."

"Josh, I have an unpleasant duty to perform."

Josh suddenly understood. "You have come to arrest me."

"I am sure I have no need for bracelets or the like but I am obliged to ask you, Josh, are you armed?"

"Nossir, I am not."

"Very well, let's go."

"You know, John, it was no murder. He had threatened me and was out to kill me. I gave him every chance not to draw on me. There were witnesses there who can vouch for that."

"Josh, that's for you to tell the judge. I am just carrying out my instructions. But one thing I know, and that is that you are not and never have been a sworn officer in this town and you were acting on your own account. And I am sorry to tell you that Kansas gunmen are not that popular round here right now."

Suddenly, and at long last, Josh understood. He had been so slow, so stupid. This was the way Hoodoo had always intended to bring him down. He was to be sentenced for the shooting down of an unarmed man carrying a great deal of money. He could hear the testimony of Hoodoo or his men now. He could hear the prosecuting attorney and his leading questions. He could see the judge with a member of the Dodge City Gang in the dock before him and he could see the jury of stolid townsmen determined to restore order and stamp out this plague of killing.

He would hang.

***

The two rigid brown leather valises, one tin trunk and a carpet bag sat together beside the tracks in the moonlight. Strapped incongruously to one of the valises was a frilly lilac parasol. Dutchy surveyed his master's luggage. He himself had only a gunny sack containing a few clothes, a pistol, and a photograph of his parents. Dutchy wondered why Mrs. Carson's parasol was with Mr. Brown's bags. But he was not about to ask.

"The train's late." Hoodoo was not exactly nervous or anxious but he awaited his departure from Las Vegas with impatience. And he did occasionally look round to see if anyone was approaching him with an official air. He turned to Dutchy. "Listen, Dutchy, as soon as the train arrives, you load on these bags and find us two good seats."

Dutchy said nothing but looked at Hoodoo interrogatively. Hoodoo went on, "Mrs. Carson will not be accompanying us." He lit a cigar. "Are you armed?" Dutchy nodded. "Not that I expect any tiresome resistance to or departure but it's as well to be ready."

The locomotive finally pulled the northbound express in from the roundhouse and snorted impatiently while the few passengers boarded. Hoodoo installed himself in a comfortable first-class seat and snapped open a copy of the *Las Vegas Optic*, while Dutchy remained at the entrance to the car, his huge bulk looming and dissuading any other from mounting there. The big man stayed in that position, immobile, until the train had pulled out and he gave a last look at the receding Las Vegas, New Mexico Territory, which he knew full well he was never going to see again. He still wondered about the parasol.

***

Back in a room at Close & Paterson's, another departure was being prepared. Mysterious Dave was meticulously folding shirts into a suitcase. Dirty Dave was watching him forlornly. "You mean you was just going to pull out, all alone, without telling me?"

"Of course I would have told you, Dave. I was just getting ready, that's all." He carefully placed a cravat on top of the shirts.

"But we never even discussed it. Where are we going?"

"Well, you may go where you please but I am heading back to Dodge."

Dirty Dave was clearly hurt at this. "Dodge? But I can't go back to Dodge. I'm kind of wanted there."

"Well, as I said, you may go where you please."

"But we always go together."

"Yes, well, we still can, if you choose to accompany me."

"But Dave, I done told you, I can't go to—"

"Look, Dave, I'm sorry but you are a grown man and must make your own decisions. I am returning to Kansas where I may resume my activities in the maintenance of law if they'll have me or I may indeed take up again the profession of saloon keeper. I have not yet decided. You may do what you choose."

Dirty Dave was silent for some time. Then he said, "It's not the splitting up that upsets me. It's the not talking about it first. If I hadn't happened along this evening, you'd of just pulled out. Wouldn't you?"

Mysterious Dave realized that this unusually perceptive if ungrammatical comment of his companion's was factually true and showed signs of a sensitivity which he didn't know that the man possessed. He felt uncomfortable. "Well, I am quite sure we'll keep in touch, Dave, and we shall certainly meet up again. I have a feeling that you might be headed to join up with Billy Bonney and you know, rustling and so forth, that's not my line. But look after yourself wherever you go. I shall miss you."

Dirty Dave nodded slowly and sighed. "Goodbye, Dave."

Mysterious Dave turned his back on his friend to straighten a shirt in the valise that was not quite to the vertical. Then he snapped the case shut and when he turned back, Dave had gone. He sat down on the bed. The room suddenly felt empty and bleak.

***

In the very early morning of Thursday, 4th March, at the small railroad halt of Otero, in Colfax County, up towards Raton, two men stood and watched the train disappear into the distance. It was cold and there was an ominous red sky. Hoodoo had judged it wiser to disembark and set off on horseback, fearing that an unpleasant welcome might have awaited him in Trinidad or further north if the telegraph wires had been buzzing. He had also decided that it would be better to travel alone. He would move east into Kansas and Dutchy would go south, maybe into Mexico. He held out a fistful of banknotes. "Here, Dutchy, you'll need some money. This is a hundred fifty dollars. That'll get you on your way." Dutchy Schunderberger looked at the proffered cash with distaste and did not move. Hoodoo resumed, "Look, Dutchy, it'd be dangerous to travel together. They will be looking for us. We'd much better go our separate ways. Take the money. You'll need it." He reached out, took Dutchy's huge hand, and stuffed the money into it. Then he strapped one of the valises, the one with the parasol, behind the saddle of his horse and mounted. Dutchy was still immobile. Hoodoo became impatient. "Come on, Dutchy, move out. I must go. Mount up." Hoodoo was used to Dutchy's taciturnity but became exasperated at this continued silence. "Well, I'm off. Look after yourself. Take care." Despairing of any reply, he wheeled his horse round and dug in his heels. When he took a last look back a few moments later, Dutchy hadn't moved.

***

The next morning, back in Las Vegas, a boxy, basic Bain wagon stood in the street outside Close & Paterson's in East Las Vegas. On its bed lay several cartons, three or four cases, and, under a tarpaulin, a long, thin wooden box. The horses waited patiently in the heat as two men loaded further items onto the wagon, including a birdcage with an alarmed fluttering sparrow in it, and not a few hatboxes.

When she was satisfied that all had been loaded and secured, Mrs. Carson hitched up her skirts and vaulted nimbly onto the sprung driver's seat. There she put a foot and shapely ankle onto the front board, which ankle was admired by the two lackeys, gave the whip a flick and expertly guided the wagon down the street towards the railroad station. The lackeys stared at the receding cloud of dust and looked at each other and nodded. They were nods of admiration and respect.

Mrs. Carson was a woman of presence and authority, as well as grace and charm, and she had no difficulty whatsoever in dragooning men to unload her wagon at the depot and put the cargo onto the train. She supervised the men with care, insisting that no hatbox be scuffed or suitcase dropped. She was especially solicitous of the large wooden box. Four men were detailed to carry it. "Careful there!" she commanded. "Treat that with respect. Put it down gently. My husband was a better law officer than you deserved in this Gomorrah." Mrs. Carson was leaving Las Vegas and her husband was accompanying her.

***

"The Grand Jury has indicted you. You are to come before Chief Justice L. Bradford Prince on Tuesday next. The charges are murder in the first degree and conspiracy to rob and murder. You know probably that under the law of New Mexico, a conviction for first degree murder automatically brings with it the death penalty. Neither judge nor jury has discretion in this."

"Conspiracy to rob? Look, it wasn't even murder and I most certainly did not rob anybody or conspire to do so."

The lawyer, Sidney Madison Barnes, a Civil War veteran, and U.S. Attorney from Santa Fe, looked compassionately at Josh but continued, "Mr.

141

Webb, you were known to consort with and, it is suggested, work for, Mr. Hyman Neill or Brown. Mr. Neill or Brown has disappeared, and, it appears, so has a very considerable sum of money. Not only the nearly two thousand dollars that the victim had on his person, declared by Mr. Brown at the time to be only little over a thousand but in reality, nearly double that amount, but also a much greater sum the man was alleged to have had in his hotel room. Many thousands of dollars, Mr. Webb. Now, you can understand that when, to all appearances, this man Kelliher was shot down by you and proved then to be holding no firearm and when your known friends and allies then disappear, for Brown is not the only one to have left rapidly, with moneys belonging to the victim, well then…"

"So you believe I killed Kelliher for his money."

"No, no, Mr. Webb, I most assuredly do not. I am your defense attorney, sir, and I will do my very utmost to disprove this theory and show it up for the calumny it is. But I only explain it to you now to show you in what danger, sir, you are and remain."

Josh stared at the white walls of his cell. Walls that had been white, at any rate. "Well, then. It looks bad."

"Yes, sir."

"But listen, Mr. Barnes, please understand the situation." And Josh proceeded to explain who Kelliher was and the history of the affair. He declared that he had not profited by one cent from Kelliher's death and that he had acted in self-defense.

"But not as a law officer pursuing his duties, Mr. Webb."

"No. Not as an officer. That is true. I was never sworn, though I often asked to be and was considered by all a policeman, but in this case, I was acting in my own account. That is so. I cannot and do not deny it."

"This is not good, sir. Not good. I will do my best. I assure you of that. I understand your position and will argue for you to the best of my ability."

The unspoken 'but' hung in the air as the disconsolate lawyer departed. Josh felt the whitened adobe walls turning to gray. Would they turn to black?

***

Monday 8th March. Parsons City, Kansas. The marshal's office. The marshal, a stocky, reliable individual in stout serge suit and narrow-brimmed

142

brown hat, looked up apparently incuriously when the boy came and placed a telegram on his desk. Had he been alone, he would probably have snatched up the envelope and eagerly read the message but in the presence of two of his deputies and his dear lady wife, who happened to be passing on her way to the whist drive, he preferred to glance at it casually, say 'Yes, very good' to the boy and go on discussing the proposed new town park without tearing open the telegram to see what it contained. He did not receive many telegrams. His wife eyed it, full of her own curiosity, and said, "A telegram, dear? Please do open it. I would hate to distract you from your duties." This allowed the marshal the even greater pleasure of saying, "Oh, routine, no doubt. I'll read it later. But about the park..." Of course, the moment she had left, he dismissed the deputies on paltry errands and fell upon the envelope.

ARREST HYMAN G NEILL ALIAS HOODOO BROWN ABOUT SIX FEET IN HEIGHT DARK FLOWING HAIR AND MUSTACHE WEIGHS ABOUT 140 SLIM AND ACTIVE BLUE EYES LAST SEEN DRESSED IN PLAID GRAY SUIT WAITING FOR A LADY ACCOMPANYING THE CORPSE OF HER HUSBAND STOP I HAVE A WARRANT FOR HIM STOP $200 FOR HIS CAPTURE GOVERNOR OF NEW MEXICO WILL UNDOUBTEDLY OFFER MORE STOP SIGNED JOHN MORRISON MARSHAL LAS VEGAS NMT.

This was an exciting telegram indeed, quite the most exciting that the marshal of Parsons, Ks. had ever received. It was all the marshal could do not to jump up and rush out into the street and tell everyone. But the dignity of his office enabled him to overcome this urge and instead he sat and quietly planned his course of action. The first thing was to visit all the hotels (this would not take long in Parsons) and identify this famous criminal. Then he would have to arrest and incarcerate the villain. This suddenly gave the marshal pause.

Marshal Clarence Naylor would not, ever, have defined himself as one of those frontier lawmen like Wild Bill Hickok or Jack Bridges, fast with a gun and handy with the fists. Parsons City had become a peaceful and law-abiding town and its marshal reflected that his dignity and weight and, well, no need for false modesty, authority had contributed largely to that. He considered himself more of an elected political official. He did not even carry a pistol and even if he had, he was not entirely sure of his proficiency with such a weapon. So now, suddenly, he was confronted with a murderous desperado, or so the telegram led him, reading between the lines, to believe, and he was somewhat nonplussed. He took a small revolver from a drawer and checked the loads, then he awaited the return of his deputies from their errands, for he felt more confident visiting the hotels in their company. Frank Harrison in particular inspired confidence as an extension of the arm of the law. Yes, Frank would know what to do.

The Belmont House Hotel was not perhaps the acme of luxury but it would do for Kansas. Hoodoo felt reasonably comfortable there and it was near the railroad station where he would shortly be meeting Mrs. Carson and her curious cargo. The dear widow was to arrive on the noon train. Hoodoo had enjoyed his eggs and coffee earlier and had smoked a cigar or two while leafing through the *Parsons Sun*, and rival *Parsons Eclipse*, neither of them perhaps the most riveting of journals.

Frank Harrison walked into the lobby of the Belmont House and pegged Neill right away. He checked dutifully with the register but although the clerk identified the guest as 'Henry Graham', Harrison was quite clear on the man's real identity. Tall, long-haired, and blue-eyed, the fellow sat comfortably smoking. Harrison had suggested to Naylor that he could handle this affair and proposed that the marshal remain in his office to 'coordinate the operation'. Marshal Naylor had gone through the motions of refusing but had allowed himself, finally, to be persuaded. "After all, Marshal," Harrison had argued, "it's one thing for a deputy to be injured or worse, but what would happen to the town if the marshal were..." He had left the sentence unfinished but it was enough for Naylor. "Quite, quite, you have a point there, Frank. You go and check those hotels and I'll, er, coordinate here."

"Mr. Neill?"

Hoodoo looked round. Who was this using his name, a name he did not himself use too often in any case? A badge glinted dully on the man's vest. Ah.

"Henry Graham, at your service."

"I rather think that you are Mr. Hyman G. Neill, alias Brown, known as 'Hoodoo'. And I must ask you to accompany me, sir, for you are under arrest."

"No, no, you are quite mistaken, and I fear that I am not in a position to accompany you anywhere for I must meet the noon train and it will be here in" (and here he consulted his watch) "thirteen minutes."

"Mr. Neill, it will be my honor to accompany you to the station, and thence to the marshal's office."

Hoodoo saw that he had little choice. He most certainly was not about to commence fisticuffs or gunplay and furthermore this lawman had a certain air about him. No, he would go with him.

Mrs. Carson descended from the train with her customary elegance and poise. Smiling sweetly, she approached Hoodoo and allowed him to peck her on the cheek. She gave quiet orders for her baggage to be stacked on the platform and for especial care to be taken with her husband's casket. Then she turned with slight, but only slight, curiosity to the man who accompanied Hoodoo. This man, rather handsome in a way, stepped forward and introduced himself. "Francis Harrison, ma'am, at your service."

Mrs. Carson smiled again and said, "Yes, well, Mr. Harrison, would you be so kind as to organize a conveyance for my luggage to the hotel—er, which hotel is it, my dear?"

Hoodoo answered, "The Belmont House, my…" but seemed unsure how, publicly, to address Mrs. Carson. "We shall be delighted to accompany you there but then I fear I have an appointment with Mr. Harrison here than I cannot, er, postpone. I shall join you at the hotel as soon as I possibly can but do, please make yourself comfortable until then."

Mrs. Carson looked mildly irritated but entered the carriage with good grace, giving orders for the casket to be guarded closely at the depot until she should come for it. Hoodoo felt uncomfortably that its contents would by now be no nosegay and wondered if she intended to have the box accompany them indefinitely.

**

Hoodoo remained in confinement for precisely two and a half hours. Having summoned the two most reputed (and costly) lawyers of Parsons to his cell as well as the local judge, he petitioned for a writ of *habeas corpus* and was released when the officers failed to show any legal authority for his detention beyond an unsubstantiated telegram from outside the United States. Hoodoo returned to the Belmont House, bathed, and changed, and by the next morning he and Mrs. Carson were on the M. K. & T. southwards and were never seen in Parsons again, rather to the relief of Marshal Naylor, who, however, felt that his courageous arrest of the desperado would redound to his credit come election time. Well, the courageous arrest by his staff under his coordination.

Hoodoo, as the train rattled south and thinking of the casket in the baggage car, felt that *habeat* rather too much *corpus* but there was nothing to be done about that for the moment. Mrs. Carson had her ways.

***

The same day, eight hundred and fifty or so miles away to the southwest, Dirty Dave Rudabaugh sat beside his horse in a gulch just outside Las Vegas and wondered where to go and what to do. He was alone and didn't like it. Soon after Mysterious had left town, he too had packed his bedroll, bought a horse, and left, riding east, with the idea of heading down to Roswell, where he remembered that Billy said he had a girl. But he hadn't gone far when he started worrying about Josh. He liked Josh a lot. In fact, it was extraordinary how a fellow could be on a posse to arrest you for something in Kansas and then grow to become such a friend in New Mexico in the space of hardly more than a year. But there it was. He liked Josh and he rather felt that Josh liked him. So could he simply abandon him in jail, on a charge of murder that they would likely hang him for? No, he didn't think that he could.

At the same time, what was he going to do about it? Bust in all on his own and break Josh out? That didn't seem too practical. This needed thought and thought was not really, Dave knew it, his strongest suit. But think it out he must.

Well, he could wait and see what the verdict was. That would be sensible anyway. No point risking a break-out if Josh was going to be acquitted anyway. Yes, that was one thing decided. Then, if Josh was to be found guilty and Dave was to attempt a rescue, he would definitely need help. That was sure. But who would help? Carson was dead and Dutchy and Hoodoo and Dave were all gone. Even Mrs. Carson. This wasn't easy. Heaven knew where Billy was, or even if he would help. Well, there was only one thing for it. He would have to go back into town. Go round the saloons. See which of the men he had run into there in the last few months might help him. There must be someone.

He turned his horse and headed back into town. He didn't like it, though. He didn't like it at all.

***

No one really knew where Slap-Jack Bill Nicholson had got his nickname. In fact, even Slap-Jack himself was not that sure. He thought someone had called him that in a poker game, as he slapped four jacks down on the table, but he had been so drunk he hadn't really taken it all in. He did remember shooting someone or other at that game, however, so he couldn't have been that drunk. Anyhow, the name stuck and he grew even to quite like it. It had a devil-may-care to ring to it, did it not? And after all, anyone on earth can be called Bill Nicholson. There must be dozens of Bill Nicholsons in New Mexico alone. But Slap-Jack Bill Nicholson, now there was only one of those.

Mr. Nicholson was not what you might call an honest and upstanding citizen. In fact, there were few crimes he had not committed at one time or another. Armed robbery was not the most heinous of these, even if it was the most common. Furthermore his standards of personal hygiene left something to be desired and he was not really an oil painting either. He had lacked one front tooth for some time and Marshal Carson, before going down, had succeeded in knocking out the other. This gap-toothedness affected Nicholson's speech thenceforth and he was on occasions barely intelligible. He dressed poorly, he didn't attend any church, he was unreliable, unpunctual, and unpleasant. Apart from a certain animal cunning, he lacked intelligence also. He drank and spat and gambled and fought. All in all, there was little good to say about Slap-Jack Bill Nicholson. He was also prepared to shoot honest lawmen in the back, and had proved it at Close & Paterson's on 22nd January. Shooting lawmen in the back is not normally considered a qualification of honest, upright citizenry. So Slap-Jack had rather forfeited his claim to that distinction.

As we know, he had been arrested for that crime, had been kept under guard at Doc Shout's until his wounds had healed sufficiently, and then, though perhaps we have not yet been apprised of this, he was sent down to Santa Fe, again under guard, there to face trial for the murder of Marshal Joe Carson.

But the law, if not an ass, certainly has its own ways, some of which are far from limpid to those not versed in them. One might have thought this an open-and-shut case. Nicholson had, after all, been caught *in flagrante delicto*.

There had been several witnesses. Marshal Carson's body was found to have a bullet in its back. Nicholson was a known criminal. It all added up to a swift trial and even swifter work for the hangman in Santa Fe. But, you see, all is not quite so straightforward in a court of law. Open-and-shut cases are rare, even unknown, and this description would honestly better be reserved for items of luggage. In a court of law, evidence and proof have to be offered up, and witnesses presented, and juries must be convinced. And if some of the witnesses in the saloon that day proved to be, shall we say, less than reliable? And say that others, who would have been very credible, had not been called? And if the science of forensics were not quite so advanced as to be able to identify the slug in Carson's back as one fired from Nicholson's gun? Imagine, also, that the defendant had been washed and dressed up in a decent suit and told to keep his mouth firmly closed wherever possible, so that he seemed quite presentable to the gentlemen of the jury. And, further, nay, above all, let us take account of the fact that this defendant had an extremely able and well-known defense attorney whose not inconsiderable fees had been paid by a certain person in Las Vegas before that certain person skedaddled on the northbound train...

In short, Bill Nicholson got off.

Now, why would a man who had, to be perfectly frank, "Got away with murder" immediately return to the scene of his crimes? Would that not be rather stupid? And to a place where his two accomplices had been lynched? Well, you could say that it was stupid but it is necessary to remember firstly that Bill Nicholson was no genius and secondly that in fact, having been acquitted of the murder of Marshal Carson, and no indictment having been advanced in the matter of stage robbery, there were no warrants out for his arrest in Las Vegas.

Furthermore, he knew his way around there, had a room to stay in and even a saloon girl who took more than a passing interest in his fine figure (as he saw it). So he went back to Las Vegas. And there he resumed his life of before, with its daily round of saloons, drinking, gambling, and ladies of the night to supplement his fiancée, all, of course, when he was able to finance this existence, that is irregularly and usually because of the minor criminality at which he was so adept. Slap-Jack was back.

Dirty Dave found him in Goodlet & Roberts on the evening of 9th March, the very saloon where Josh had shot Michael Kelliher exactly a week before.

***

At the very same moment that Dirty Dave met up again with Slap-Jack Nicholson in a less than salubrious drinking house, J. J. Webb was on trial for his life in the San Miguel County Court House in West Las Vegas. This trial, before the stately Chief Justice L. Bradford Prince, was very far removed from the judicial farce in Santa Fe that had resulted in the earlier acquittal of Dirty Dave's drinking partner.

The witnesses called to the stand were less than helpful to Josh's cause. William Brickley, the big Irishman who had accompanied Kelliher on that night, testified that Kelliher had not drawn a gun or even tried to, but that only a sap was in the pocket concerned; Morris Kelliher, brother of the victim, who had come down from McHenry County, Illinois to bring the body of his brother back to their grieving parents there, testified that Michael Kelliher was a decent, hard-working man who loved New Mexico and was here to purchase cattle; Bill Goodlet, the saloon keeper, followed the orders of Hoodoo, part owner of the saloon, orders given to him almost as the last thing Hoodoo had done in Las Vegas, and testified that Josh had told him that he had come expressly to kill Kelliher (this was the same Goodlet who, had it been known, had been generously 'recompensed' for 'damages' by Morris Kelliher); decent Marshal John Morrison testified that Mr. Webb had never been sworn as an officer in either East or West Las Vegas. Official books of the Justice of the Peace were produced that showed no record whatsoever of any such appointment.

Then there were other witnesses to talk of the large sum of money which had disappeared from Kelliher's room. Evan Williams, Kelliher's foreman, said that he had seen a large bag full of banknotes and that to his certain knowledge it contained thirty-five thousand dollars and possibly more. Furthermore, $1900 had been taken from Kelliher's body in the saloon but only $1090 declared.

Josh was called to the stand. He recounted the history of the affair as far as he was able, although Chief Justice L. Bradford Prince kept telling him only to answer the questions and not to expatiate. Josh was not entirely sure what expatiating was. He told how he had gone to the saloon to 'face' Kelliher but not expressly to kill him. This part of his testimony was music to the prosecuting attorney's ears for he kept asking what 'facing' a man meant if it did not mean to fight him. No one mentioned Josh's two shouted warnings to Kelliher.

The jury retired at about midnight and returned a verdict of first-degree murder three hours later. Josh's defense attorney immediately moved for a new trial but Chief Justice L. Bradford Prince, perhaps mindful of Governor Wallace's and his own determination to rid Las Vegas of the depredations of the Dodge City Gang and restore order, denied the motion and sentenced John Joshua Webb to be hanged by the neck until he be dead on Friday, April 9th. Josh looked blankly ahead as he listened to the sentence and meekly accompanied his jailer, Antonio Valdez, back to his cell where he hoped to get some sleep.

***

"You still around then?"

They asked the same question of each other at the same time, then laughed. Dave replied first.

"Yup. Although I wouldn't want everyone to know that. But I got some unfinished business. Kinda surprised to see you here, though. I heard you got off."

"Course I did. I was innocent, wasn't I? It just shows you how justice really works in this Territory. They wasn't going to hang a decent fellow like me."

"But you came back to Las Vegas?"

"Well, there ain't no warrants out against me here and I got a place and all."

Dave nodded and bought Nicholson a drink. The man wasn't ideal for what Dave had in mind but he would probably do. He kept to himself the thought that warrants or no, the man who had shot down Marshal Joe Carson and whose mates had been lynched for it wouldn't be all that popular in the streets of Las Vegas.

***

On March 15th, the *Las Vegas Optic* published a letter from Hoodoo Brown. It had been mailed from Muskogee, Indian Territory on March 11th and in it the fugitive justified himself and said he planned to return to Las Vegas to face all charges and prove them false. He had never acted, he said, in anything else except the best interests of the community of East Las Vegas of which he had been proud to be a leading citizen. He would never have left, he said, unless he had heard that, "There was going to be an indictment found against myself, Webb and Dave Mather, for killing someone, and that I would be arrested the next day and thrown in jail."

He was, of course, totally innocent of any such conspiracy. Indeed he had lost money as mayor of East Las Vegas, often financing civic improvements from his own pocket. He had most certainly not left the town with large sums or stolen money from the victim of the shooting—this was nonsense—and he would soon return to 'face the music' and prove his innocence.

Some read this letter in the *Optic* and shook their heads. Some muttered, "He had better not return here if he knowed what was good for him." Most said, "Hell, he'll never come."

Chapter Nine

Antonio Lino Valdez was a decent man and he worried about his prisoner. The man just stared at the wall. He seemed to do little else. It was hard to wake him up in the mornings and when he did get up, he seemed to be moving too slowly. Once, Valdez had caught him weeping. And whereas at the beginning he had been ready to converse, now he seemed morose and withdrawn. Such conversation as he had was jerky and even inarticulate. It was odd.

Valdez had watched over many prisoners, including those condemned to death or to life imprisonment, and he had never had one so, well, so strange as this. It appeared as though a glass wall separated Webb from the rest of the world. Valdez shoved the plate of food through the slot and waited for Webb to take it. It took an age and when the prisoner finally did, he placed it on the cot beside him and resumed staring at the wall.

Josh was unaware of all this. He was far away, in a sort of black pit. This pit had opened up before the trial and he had plunged into it as if losing his footing on an icy street and blacking out. It was black in the sense of a strange room at night when you wake up and do not know where you are and cannot find any light or door. Yet it was not entirely black. There was just the faintest distant gleam, enough to discern several dark tunnels leading off the pit. The mouths of these tunnels were just even blacker patches of blackness. He knew that if he were to slide down one of these tunnels in search of a way out, it would only lead to other tunnels and he would plumb lower and lower depths until there was no way out. Yet he felt compelled to enter one.

Sometimes, when he awoke in the morning with the light from the small window full in his face, he realized that the black pit had been a dream, a mirage, it was not real. But still he knew it was real and this morning, this cell, these bars were the illusory ones and they would soon disappear again to leave him back in the reality of his black hole. A Mexican man appeared, vaguely, and seemed to be proffering him something and he knew that this man was decent, was trying to help him, but he couldn't connect, he couldn't relate to this man, or indeed to anyone else. It was as if he were in some dense fog and groping.

He felt that he ought to acknowledge the kindness and he smiled. But his smiling muscles seemed frozen. Valdez—that was the man's name. He remembered now. He was the jailer. A good man. Hadn't he accompanied him back from the courthouse after the trial? Yes, he had. Valdez. Josh smiled again. There was a constrained smile in return. Josh sat back down and thought he would look at the wall.

It didn't really matter in any case because soon he was going to die and then he would enter the black pit forever.

Unknown to Josh, Valdez shook his head in pity and went out, closing the door.

***

Dave Rudabaugh came to visit Josh in his cell. Antonio Valdez recognized him and was uncertain because had not this big, rather fearful man been part of the disreputable Dodge City Gang? But he knew the man had been a policeman so as a kindness, he checked that the visitor was carrying no arms and let him in.

Dave waited patiently outside the bars until Josh acknowledged his presence. "Hey, Josh, how are you doing?" Dave was puzzled at the lack of reply but gradually Josh seemed to become more aware and eventually he answered.

"Hello, Dave. I'm fine. How are you?"

"Oh, well, I'm fine too. Yessir."

Josh looked back at the wall.

Dave seemed at a loss but gamely continued his rather one-sided conversation. "I was slightly unsure about hanging around, what with all these indictments and all but so far so good, as they say, and they haven't arrested me yet." He paused, then added, "Don't want to end up your neighbor in the next cell!"

The silence was becoming oppressive.

"Listen, Josh, um, I don't want to say too much but well, we mustn't give up hope, eh?" Another long pause. "Well, anyway, keep your spirits up. You never know what might happen, right?" Dave didn't know what else to say.

153

"Well, guess I better be off about my business. Look after yourself, Josh, okay?"

"Goodbye, Dave."

"Yes, goodbye. I'll drop by again and see you, okay? Okay then. See you, Josh. Bye."

When Dave had gone, the fog seemed to clear a little and he became aware that a friend had taken the trouble to visit him. It brought him back to the world. And it made him fumble around in an inner pocket and draw out an envelope containing a letter so battered and read so many times that it barely held together and could only just still be defined as a letter. Josh knew it by heart anyway but reading it was a reflex. He always did it when he was depressed or worried or sad. He looked at the lines rather than read them. His eyes followed the words and his lips silently mouthed the syllables.

My dearest Josh,

I write you this letter because I owe you at least that. I could not simply leave and say nothing. I don't write to excuse myself or even to ask forgiveness. I write to explain. Sam King and I are leaving for St. Louis. We have decided to be married and set up house there. Sam is sure that he can get a job in one of the big banks. You know, of course, that I do not really love Sam. Not in the way that I love you. You have always been and always will be the one love of my life. But Josh, Sam is a good man and a respectable one, one that will care for me, and you know that quite soon a lot of care will be needed. I don't think Sam is under any illusions. He knows I am not long for this world. My coughs and fevers get worse and worse. But he is a dear, dear man and he adores me. I feel safe with him and loved and cared for. Whereas you, Josh, well, you are never here. You are a wanderer. You are footloose. You are a strong man, and a brave one and deep down a good one, and although you never say it, I know you love me deeply. But you are never there when I need you. You are away for weeks at a time and you come back with scars and once even with a bullet wound and you say nothing. That is not the life for me, Josh. I know I have little time left and I want to spend that time in security, feeling safe in a furnished home, with a man who is always there and provides for me. Is that weakness? Perhaps it is. Perhaps I should follow my true heart and we should marry and wander the country together, no matter where and no matter how. But I can't, Josh, I just can't. So I am leaving. Should you wish to, you may reach me by addressing a letter to Mrs. Samuel King, at the Central Post Office, St. Louis. Who knows, perhaps we shall meet again. But even if we don't, my dearest Joshua, please accept all the love in the world from your dearest

Masie.

The letter slipped to the floor and Josh stared back at the wall.

***

Two men stepped out of a hired hack in front of the West Las Vegas jail at about two o'clock in the afternoon. The driver, Carl Caldwell, a stocky man, short and broad, waited with the reins loosely held in his hands. He was chewing something, probably tobacco. The other two entered the jail compound, a gated yard which housed the jail proper. One was tall, big, broad-faced with large handlebar mustaches and the other was a stumbling, dirty character with two front teeth missing.

Antonio Valdez looked askance at Bill Nicholson but had no problem with letting Dave Rudabaugh in. He knew him, though it had to be said he was slightly afraid of him too. So he unlocked the door and permitted the two to enter the inner *placita* where they walked across to Josh's cell. Dave smiled and handed Josh a newspaper through the bars. Josh took it mechanically but did not read any of it.

"We come to get you out, Josh."

"I see."

"Do you understand? You're leaving here."

Valdez looked startled and began, "Señor…"

Nicholson suddenly had a viciously tight grip on Valdez's arm and a pistol barrel tight against his chest. "Shut up, greaser. You heard the man. We're leaving, along with Mr. Webb here. Give us the keys."

"I cannot and will not, Señor." Valdez tore himself away and stepped back. He was unarmed and did not know how to act. He didn't have to wonder long because Nicholson shot him in the chest. Valdez went down and lay slumped in an uncomfortable pose as blood seeped out of his body into the sand. He was gasping for air and then blood appeared on his lips. Nicholson snatched up the fallen keys and threw them into Josh's cell. Dave cried out, "Hurry, Josh,

155

unlock the door, we'll be in the hack outside. Be quick!" And he and Nicholson ran back though the courtyard out into the street.

Josh stood motionless in the cell, with the fallen keys on the floor. He gazed into the middle distance.

Outside, Dave told Nicholson and the driver Caldwell to wait and he ran back in. "Come on, Josh, for God's sake! Let yourself out!"

Josh did not move. The keys were now inside the cell and Dave could not reach them. "At least, give me the keys, Josh, and I'll open the door. Come on!" In the courtyard, he heard voices and running footsteps. "Christ! This is your last and only chance, Josh! Move!"

Josh spoke. "Is Mr. Valdez alright? He is a nice man."

"No, Josh, he's dead. Now move!"

A man appeared at the doorway. Dave swiveled round and held his pistol on the man, gave one last despairing glance at Josh and ran back out. There were two more men in the courtyard. One had a carbine and the other a pistol. Dave loomed over them and pointed his own gun threateningly and the two men cowered back. From the carriage, he heard Nicholson calling out in his lisping way, "For God's sake, hurry!" It was good advice. He ran for the hack and tumbled in, and Caldwell whipped up the horses and they rattled away back towards East Las Vegas. They sped across the Gallinas Bridge and on the rise from the river to East Las Vegas Dave hauled on the reins, kicked Caldwell squarely out into the street, where he tumbled in the dust, and took the reins. He pulled up outside Houghton's Hardware Store where he grabbed several carbines and rifles and some boxes of shells and threw them in the back, ignoring the shouts of outrage of George Houghton, and he whipped the horses into a run east out of town.

Back at the jail, one man bent over Valdez but saw that there was nothing to be done. Two others were shouting and wild. One wanted to shoot the prisoner. A posse of four men was hastily assembled and they galloped out after the hack. They came close enough to exchange shots and several rounds hit the back of the wagon but they soon ran out of ammunition and Nicholson was in the back firing rapidly at them. They backed off and then walked their horses back to the jail. The hack grew smaller until it disappeared in a cloud of dust.

Later, a larger posse comitatus was dispatched and found the hack abandoned about twenty-five miles east of town. Some sheepherders there said that two men had forced them to give over two good saddle horses in exchange for the hack beasts. Dirty Dave and Slap-Jack had disappeared into the plains.

***

All this action had finally awakened Josh from his trance. As he surfaced, as it were, poor Antonio Valdez came into focus, lying on the dusty ground outside the cell. He picked up the keys from the floor of his cell and handed them to one of the jailers. "Here." The jailer took them nervously, as if still afraid of a jailbreak. But Josh sat down on the cot and put his head in his hands.

They carried Valdez into a kitchen and laid him on a table and sent for the doctor. But the jailer died shortly afterwards.

Later in the afternoon, two men came in and shackled him in leg irons. Josh shrugged but said, "That's kind of shutting the stable door after the horse has bolted, ain't it?" It was a feeble joke but it was the first time for weeks that he had spoken in any way except a monosyllabic reply.

He asked the men if Valdez had a family. He was told that he was married and had three young children. Josh shook his head. And Nicholson! What on earth was that awful man doing helping to break him out anyway? Josh had shot Nicholson during the gunfight at Close & Paterson's and later had been on the posse up in Mora that had apprehended him. Josh would have thought that Nicholson would have no interest at all in securing his release. Perhaps Dave had paid him. Nicholson would have done anything for money.

Sidney Barnes returned. He found Josh a little more responsive than the last time he had visited him, though still depressed. Of course, who wouldn't be? But Barnes had tidings which he knew would cheer the poor man. "Mr. Webb, I have some excellent news for you. Let me tell you immediately. Our appeal has been successful to the extent that the death penalty has been commuted to a sentence of life imprisonment. Sir, you are not to hang."

"I see."

"Did you not understand, sir? I said they will not hang you."

"Yes, I understood. I am not to hang."

"Well, you don't seem very pleased or relieved."

"Oh yes. Thank you."

Barnes shook his head. Was he not getting through? He had never had a prisoner react so little to such news. "Well, I have all the papers here. The jailers and city authorities have been informed. It is not yet certain where you will serve out your sentence. Normally this would not be in a county jail but in a more secure penitentiary. This could be in Fort Leavenworth in Kansas or possibly in Yuma. For the moment, however, you are to remain here."

"You mean, remain forever behind bars?"

"Why, yes, sir. That is the best we could hope for. But you will live!"

"Live."

"Life is the most precious gift of all."

"It is?"

A few days later, Josh was taken out into the *placita* in his leg irons. He was told to sit on a plain wooden chair. He sat sideways on it and stared down at the ground. They had set up a photographic apparatus in the yard and the photographer busied himself adjusting it to get the right focus and composition.

He said, "Look into the camera, please, and above all, do not move." He was not going to get his subject to look into the lens, and the resulting picture shows a sad, sideways figure, but he needn't have worried about the prisoner moving. He remained completely immobile while the photograph was taken and afterwards, and the jailers had to come and tell him to move.

Marshal John Morrison came into the courtyard while the photograph was being taken and he watched Josh shuffle off between the jailers back into his cell afterwards. He shook his head in something like pity.

Part III

Chapter Ten

Dirty Dave had done what he could. Josh had had his chance and had not taken it. Dave could not afford to try again to break Josh out. To show himself in Las Vegas now would be asking for a lynch mob. Anglo outlaws who shoot down decent Hispanic law officers are not exactly popular. It was time to move south and hook up with Billy. That would not be difficult.

Fort Sumner was in San Miguel County but about as far from the county seat as you could get. The county law officers had far too much to do with the lawlessness in Las Vegas to patrol regularly so far from their base. Fort Sumner therefore was haven for every kind of disreputable man (and woman) in the territory. There was no law there. It was why Billy Bonney had made it a kind of headquarters. Criminals abounded, driven westwards by the Texas Rangers or south from Santa Fe by the law there. Most lived by rustling cattle from the large herds on the Pecos and selling them to Mexicans or to the Indian agency on the reservation. They frequented Beaver Smith's rough saloon and that was where Dave was headed. Sooner or later Billy would appear at Beaver Smith's.

But Dave did not intend to go there with Slap-Jack Bill Nicholson. The man was a fool and an incompetent. He killed unnecessarily for the hell of it and was a liability. The murder of the jailer had been pointless and damaging. In any case, such a worthless no-good would never be accepted by Billy and his friends. Not that Nicholson even seemed to want to go to Fort Sumner. He hadn't even the intelligence to realize that he would not be able to return to Vegas. He talked about how he couldn't leave his girl. Girl, indeed. Couldn't have been much of a girl who would want him as a man. Anyway, it was time for Dave to strike out alone. The only question was when and how to dispose of his accomplice.

They rode down the Pecos valley, slowly, not tiring their horses. They camped along the way and ate what they had bought or shot. Dave wanted to be careful, for this was Chisum land and Billy was engaged in a private feud with the great cattleman. Billy said that Chisum owed him five hundred dollars for fighting on the McSween side in the county war. Chisum had been a McSween supporter, true, but had never taken an active part in the war and had been back East for most of it. He declared that he had never agreed to pay anyone to fight in that war. He said he always paid his debts but would not pay made-up ones. Billy could shoot him if he wished—he was an old man now and that wouldn't knock him out of many years—but Billy wasn't going to get a dime. Billy said he would rustle Chisum cows until he had his five hundred dollars' worth, and he proceeded to start. So Chisum range was not a good place for a friend of Billy's to be found.

The second night after leaving Las Vegas, they camped in a small clump of cottonwoods near the river, where the trees would hide their smoke. They cooked up some beans and made coffee and then lay smoking. They passed a bottle between them. Late in the evening, the second bottle was almost empty and they slumped into a deep sleep and the fire went out. It was late the next morning, probably nine or so, and the sun was full up when they were awakened by that particular noise which a Winchester repeater makes when a round is levered into the breech.

Five men stood before them, their horses tied further back. Cowboys. Chisum men.

Cowboys can be tough little fellows but they are not gunmen. Five to two was poor odds, especially when your head felt bad, but Dave had faced worse.

One of the drovers spoke. "So what you fellows doing here? Rustling Mr. Chisum's cows?"

Dave answered. "Shucks, no. We was just passing through. Don't mean to disturb no one."

The cowpokes looked at each other. The leader resumed, "Well, I reckon you are disturbing us, though. All of them pistols and carbines you got. That don't seem normal. Could be you're rustlers."

Dave got slowly to his feet. The lead cowman backed off and pulled his pistol. "Whoa! Now don't you do nothing hasty, Mister."

"I ain't about to. Look, just let us ride off, okay? I don't want to get into a situation here. Some of us might get hurt." This last he said with menace in his voice.

Nicholson, still in his blanket, looked sour. Dave had an idea that he had his pistol out under that blanket. Sure enough, in a moment Nicholson had fired and two of the cowboys fell. Dave grabbed a carbine and moved smartly behind a tree. The other three cowpokes were now blazing away and one of them caught Nicholson in the shoulder. Dave heard a loud, "Shit!" Nicholson staggered to his feet, threw down his empty pistol and rushed to his saddlebags for another. It was too late. A Winchester round caught him full in the middle of the back, piercing his heart, and he was dead before he hit the ground.

Dave hollered loud and clear. "Now hold your fire! I don't want none of this. That fellow started this, not me. Don't shoot, you hear? Let's talk this over."

"Too late for talkin,' Mister!" And the tree that sheltered Dave was riddled with shots.

Dave reckoned that he now had no choice. He checked that his Colt's .45 was fully loaded and then threw a stone away to his left. The oldest trick in the book but the nervous cowboys fell for it, firing their guns till they were empty at where they had heard the noise. Dave stepped out and shot them. One, two, three. Three shots were enough. He threw their weapons in the creek and shooed their horses away. He left them where they fell, one still groaning, and rode out. Well, one thing anyway: that settled the question of what to do with Slap-Jack Bill Nicholson.

***

Fort Sumner lies about a hundred miles or more south of Las Vegas on the crossroads where the Roswell to Vegas trail crossed the Texas Road. It had been built to control the Mescalero Apache and Navajos but closed by the Army in 1868. In 1870, the fort buildings were sold to Lucien Buonaparte Maxwell, the former owner of the largest land grant in U.S. history. Maxwell paid some $5,000 for the buildings and surrounding land and installed his whole family there. Now his son Pete ran the place. It was a bleak kind of home, even after refurbishment of the various barracks and barns to make living accommodations. To Dave, it was no better or worse than any other place really. Its most attractive feature was the complete lack of law. He tied his horse to the hitching rail and walked into Beaver Smith's stinking saloon.

***

That summer, while Josh sank deeper into depression in the jail in Las Vegas, Dave ran all over southern New Mexico with Billy and his compadres

Tom O'Folliard and Charlie Bowdre. Billy was not leader of the gang. It was not a gang like that. They just rode together.

Charlie sported a dashing imperial and liked fancy shirts and Mexican gun belts laden with bullets. His Mexican wife Manuela was full of fire and no friend of Billy's. She was sure that Billy was going to get her husband killed, and she was right in the end. Charlie had got caught up in the Lincoln County War and at Blazer's Mills it was he who fired the fatal bullet into the groin of Buckshot Roberts. After the war, he rode with the Kid out of Fort Sumner. He wanted out and if he could have gotten a pardon for the killing of Roberts would have quit the gang and, as he said, "gone straight."

Tom O'Folliard was a different type altogether. He'd come up from Texas at the age of sixteen to fight in Lincoln County and had escaped with Billy from the burning McSween house. Almost girlish, sweet-looking, he became Billy's worshiping shadow, ready to do anything for him, even hold Billy's horse all night during Billy's nocturnal adventures with the señoritas.

Occasionally others would fall in with them, like Tom Pickett, a tall, powerfully built youth who had served as a Texas Ranger and had briefly been a Las Vegas policeman like Dave, and who had had to leave in a hurry because, as the *Las Vegas Optic* said, "A job had been put up to kill him." Or Billy Wilson, known as 'the other Billy', two years younger than Bonney and stouter but no less murderous when necessary. Through the summer they rode, all of them or some of them, rustling, usually, driving the stolen beef west to White Oaks and selling them to Pat Coghlan. Or they'd steal horses. Sometimes they'd ride up to Lincoln and play cards with Sheriff George Kimball, who liked Billy and was understanding.

But that summer things changed. There was a U.S. Secret Service agent in the area, Azariah Wild, investigating counterfeit currency, and he was a determined and resolute man. Agent Wild believed that the same people were involved in the counterfeiting as in the purchase of the stolen cattle. And then Chisum got some other cattlemen together and campaigned for the election of a new Democrat county sheriff to replace the over-tolerant Kimball. This man was Patrick Floyd Garrett.

Pat Garrett had come down to New Mexico from the buffalo plains in the late 70s and was known as a very tough son of a bitch. He was in his early thirties. He wore long hair and droopy mustache. He had piercing blue eyes. Six and a half feet in his boots and hat, he was known as Juan Largo by the

Hispanic community, who liked him. He had married a Hispanic woman and when she died, he married her sister. He had worked as barman at Beaver Smith's and knew Billy well enough. He was a noted marksman.

Of course, Billy wanted Kimball to win the election but on November 2nd Pat Garrett was elected by 320 votes to 179. Although Garrett was not officially to take office till January 1st, 1881, Kimball appointed him deputy and for the rest of 1880 Pat was sheriff in all but name. Worse for Billy and the boys, he also had a commission as Deputy U.S. Marshal. This had come about by a mixture of error and guile, for two commissions were accidentally sent for John Hurley, a former soldier out of Fort Stanton deputized by Azariah Wild, and Wild simply crossed out Hurley's name on one and wrote in Pat's. So now Billy and the boys had U.S. Deputy Marshal and County Sheriff Patrick F. Garrett after them, with the full support of Governor Wallace, the Secret Service, and the stockmen's association with their unsavory hired 'detectives', most of whom were worse than any rustler. When they heard all this down in Beaver Smith's, there were those who reckoned it might be time to move on.

In the middle of November Billy and the boys stole some horses and a rifle and a saddle from Padre Polaco, a jovial Polish storekeeper up to Puerto de Luna, about forty miles along the Pecos from Fort Sumner. Billy liked Padre Polaco but liking people never stopped him stealing their property. He stole from Pete Maxwell or anyone else he could.

They rode down to the Greathouse place to sell some of the horses to Whiskey Jim, who had become a good friend of both Billy Bonney and Dirty Dave and often bought stock from them. But they were surprised by a great posse and Whiskey Jim's place was surrounded. The posse called on the gang to surrender and they, safe and warm inside and all of them except Billy drinking at the bar, laughed at that alright. The next morning there was a lot of shooting and one of the posse, a blacksmith named Carlyle, was shot and killed and the posse lost heart, cold and hungry as they were, and pulled out to come back with reinforcements. Billy and Dave and the others took advantage of that and rode away. Later the posse returned and burned Whiskey Jim's place to the ground, which he did not forgive.

***

The more Josh thought about it, and he had little else to do but think, the more he thought that he should have gone with Dave and broken out. Being stuck in one place had always upset him and prison was the worst kind of one place. As the summer passed and one day succeeded another, he became desperate to leave. The autumn days he could see though the small window were enticing, beckoning. He had come out of the depths of his depression. It had been the worst attack he had had and he still often felt morose and irritable but the worst of it was past. Now he was itchy to be gone, to roam, to have space. And he couldn't. He was confined, no longer in irons but still incarcerated, entombed.

Others were imprisoned with him: George Davis, mule stealer; John Murray, indicted on a charge of murdering a Tecolote gardener; and Jack Allen, the waiter who had shot the salesman Morehead in the St. Nicholas Hotel over the fried eggs. He found them unbearable. They worsened his confinement. He had nothing in common with them and wished them gone.

But one of them, Davis, turned out to have an invaluable talent. He could pick locks.

In the black of a cold November night, the door swung open with a slight creak and the prisoners silently stepped out. The front door of the jail was unlocked and there were no guards, or no guards awake anyway. Josh didn't like it at all. It was too easy. Was it a vigilante plot to let them out and then shoot them down? But his heart was beating too strongly and the urge for freedom was too strong to resist. Keeping to the shadows and close to the walls, they gingerly moved out. They got clean away.

As soon as the escape was discovered, early the next morning, a posse was assembled and it found the escapees camped at Chaperito on the Gallinas River, south of Las Vegas. A lot of shooting ensued but it was rather one-sided seeing as none of the fugitives had guns. Allen was killed and Murray recaptured. But one member of the posse fell from his rearing horse and Josh hit him and took his revolver and commenced firing. The place was densely wooded and Josh and George Davis were able to move gradually away, hidden by trees. In half an hour, they were clear and free. They walked east, Davis put his mule-stealing talents to good use and they headed out down the Pecos with no clear destination in mind except possibly Mexico. Josh was hungry, he had no money and only two bullets in the stolen pistol. But he was free.

***

Some time on November 12th, the two riders, who had 'traded' their two mules for three stout but serviceable horses (they had taken the horses from a field and left the mules), arrived in Anton Chico, known as 'the best town this side of Las Vegas', where Davis sold one of the horses to a Mexican farmer who didn't ask too many questions. With the money, they acquired a gunny sack of food (some tortillas and some buffalo jerky), an old six-shooter for Davis of the same caliber as Josh's pistol and rounds of ammunition for both. They had enough left for a drink or two in Manuel Sanchez's bar where they heard that the hue and cry was well and truly out for them and they best skedaddle. They rode on through the night. They had decided on Mexico, at least for a while. They would pass through Fort Sumner and Roswell and follow the Pecos right over the border.

The country between Anton Chico and Fort Sumner is high and barren and very cold on November nights. They could smell snow in the air. A cold moon lit their way but they didn't hurry. The trail was too stony and the light too weak to risk a brisk pace. Once they stopped and ate the tortillas and drank some whiskey. Then they pushed on, still with more than forty miles to go before Sumner.

The question was, should they go into the Fort? It was true that they were likely to find a haven there. They might even find Dave or Billy. Davis was all for it. He knew Beaver Smith's and some of its denizens. But Fort Sumner was after all the biggest settlement between Anton Chico and Roswell. They could find a posse there. Or they had heard that County Sheriff Garrett was on the trail hunting for Bonney: Garrett could go to Fort Sumner too. They decided it would be better to circle the place and head on down south.

In the end, they stopped, exhausted, at Dan Diedrick's ranch at Bosque Grande, about thirty or so miles north of Roswell. Davis knew Diedrick, who was a notorious dealer in stolen horseflesh. He'd buy anything on four legs, Davis said, as long as it was stolen and cheap. Bosque Grande had once been the Chisum headquarters but had since become a disreputable place rather like Beaver Smith's in Sumner, frequented by malefactors of all kinds. Josh thought it would do for them.

They were made very welcome, and for a few days Davis amused himself running with some of his friends rustling stock of various kinds. Josh stayed in the ranch and kept warm. He read a few books Diedrick had there, did some blacksmithing for him, talked to Dan Diedrick's brother Sam, who had arrived, and began to feel better. Dan and Sam were great rogues and were involved in counterfeiting, 'pushing the green' as they called it. They had some scheme to go down to Mexico with thirty thousand fake greenbacks and buy cattle there with it. They asked Josh if he wanted to go. Josh though it was not a bad idea. He was going across into Mexico anyway. There would be some safety going in a band and he would earn something. But he told the Diedricks that he wasn't going to come back driving the cattle afterwards, and they lost interest. Josh thought he would move out the next day on his own. He was grateful to Davis. The man was a very effective minor criminal in his way. He knew everyone and could manage to get out of any scrape. He was versatile and resourceful, and one of the world's survivors. If it hadn't been for him, Josh wouldn't be here. But Josh had no particular wish to stay with him. He would wait till Davis was back from his latest expedition and say his goodbyes.

***

Pat Garrett, spurred on by Governor Wallace and Azariah Wild, planned a great posse which would sweep the southern territory and net Bonney and all the cattle thieves and counterfeiters. But there were delays. Hard November snowstorms swept across the land, making it difficult to travel. And a virulent outbreak of distemper put a lot of the horses out of action. But finally, at the end of the month, Garrett and twelve men left Roswell and moved north-east up the Pecos Valley. The Bosque Grande ranch lay right in their path.

Garrett knew all about Bosque Grande and the Diedricks. He thought there was a good chance that Billy or some other rustlers might be there. Azariah Wild had told him of his suspicions that they were involved in the counterfeiting. Garrett decided that he would visit the place in force and see what he netted.

What he netted was not Billy the Kid but George Davis and J.J. Webb.

Josh had heard a lot about Pat Garrett—everyone had—but this was the first time he had seen him. The man was very tall, thirtyish, maybe two or three years younger than Josh, dark haired but already going gray at the edges, with that high forehead and hair flat to the scalp that says he'll be bald in five years. He wore a big drooping mustache and the very heavy bristle of days on the trail. His eyes reminded Josh of steel. He had an authoritative demeanor. When he spoke, everyone listened and most did his bidding. It was a mixture of his height, the badge, the experience and the reputation. He spoke articulately although like Josh he had never had a real education. There was always an almost-smile flickering about his mouth, as if he really believed that this was all a game but why not do it anyway as there was not much else to do. Garrett was the sort of man who would walk in the direction that everyone else was running from, just out of curiosity. But then he might just as easily sit down for a drink in a saloon on the way.

Josh liked him. That was odd in view of the fact that Garrett had placed him under close guard and said that he was being taken to Fort Sumner and thence back to Las Vegas to serve out the rest of his time and a bit more and he hoped Webb, who was a son of a bitch, would live long enough to make life mean life. Garrett was irritated that he had only found two escaped convicts and had missed Billy, Bowdre, O'Folliard and the others altogether. He seemed on a mission to capture them, as if it was all he wanted to do. Not a mission from God but a mission from Garrett. Josh and Davis were just small fry. Not small enough to be thrown back in the pond but still hardly worth his trouble.

So Josh finally found himself in Fort Sumner, not drinking with Dave or Billy at Beaver Smith's as he would have hoped but under guard in a room in the old barracks. Garrett, riding out to continue his search, had detached four men to watch over the two until the law in Las Vegas should come for them.

My, but it was cold in that barracks.

***

A few days later, Garrett rode back in. There had been no sign of Billy and, once he got back to Fort Sumner, no sign the Las Vegas law either. That did not surprise Garrett, who had little time for the County force in Las Vegas. Garrett said he would take Davis and Webb back to Las Vegas himself and on December 6th they left Sumner, just Josh and Davis in a wagon driven by a fellow named C.B. Hoadley and Pat and Berney Mason riding alongside. Pat spat and said he didn't need a whole goddam posse just to take two second-rate criminals to Las Vegas. That hurt Josh a bit. But they bounced slowly along the rutted road, two rather moth-eaten mules pulling the wagon and Pat looking bored, slumped on his horse.

About eight miles south of Puerto de Luna, they met thirty or so men galloping wildly towards them.

Josh heard Pat mutter, "Oh, shit."

It was a Las Vegas deputy by the name of Romero, a decent enough fellow himself but he had a band of whooping, riled-up men, several clearly drunk, some even shooting their pistols in the air, come to get back the two escapees from their jail. When they came up with the wagon, they reared their horses and shouted loud boasts. They were all decked out in bandoliers and had carbines and pistols and knives and heaven knows what else. Pat shook his head at the dismal quality of this 'posse'. Josh looked at Davis. They liked the posse even less.

The group made its way onward to Puerto de Luna, retracing its steps in the case of the posse. There they used the blacksmith's forge at Padre Polaco's and the two prisoners were placed in irons. Pat smoked and looked on distantly, you could say from a height, both metaphorically and really. Josh clanked up to him while Davis was being chained. "Mr. Garrett, listen. I'll give you everything I've got not to leave us here but to accompany us on to Las Vegas. You leave us here, they're going to lynch us, sure"

Pat looked at him as if he were something that had gotten stuck to his shoe. "How much does everything you've got amount to?"

Josh looked shamefaced. "Ten dollars."

Pat went back to his cigar. Josh turned and was about to go back to join Davis. Then Pat said, "Listen to me, you worthless no-good. I decline your paltry ten dollars. I would decline ten hundred or ten thousand. In fact, you can stick it up your ass and set fire to it. But I will accompany you to Las Vegas. I will do this because no prisoner of mine is lynched and because I consider it my duty. It has nothing to do with you and still less with your ten dollars. Get in the wagon."

Pat Garrett went further up in Josh's estimation.

They got to within a few miles of Las Vegas and the effects of the drink on the posse were obviously wearing off so they stopped in a low cantina and started to drink wine until they were sufficiently refueled and boisterous again and ready for anything, especially their triumphal entry into the town with their prisoners. Josh saw Pat quietly mount up and turn his horse. "You going?"

"I would be ashamed to enter town with this rabble. I will go in alone. They won't hurt you now. They're too keen to show you off." He rode off at a walk and none of the men saw him go.

A little while later, as he and Davis were consigned once more to the San Miguel County Jail, Josh saw Pat in the plaza, leaning against a post and smoking. Inside, Davis looked meaningfully at two new, solid-looking locks on the cell door, shiny with recent oil, and raised his eyebrows. Josh shook his head mournfully. The door clanged to behind them. Josh looked at the wall.

Chapter Eleven

Pat Garrett looked down on a small, primitive rock house. He reckoned, as he stamped the snow off his feet, that this was a terrible way to spend Christmas. At an old sheep camp called Stinking Springs with an armed band of cattlemen, freezing your balls off.

In Las Vegas, he had met up with a substantial group of armed Texans led by a 'detective' named Frank Stewart, paid for by the Cattlemen's Association and unscrupulous enough for anything. The big cattlemen were paying considerable sums to have Billy Bonney and his rustling renegades taken and put away, preferably forever. The combined forces of Garrett's posse and the cattlemen's, reinforced with a few locals made brave by whiskey, moved back down to Fort Sumner and waited for Billy to ride in.

Once the effects of the whiskey had evaporated and their courage with it, the townspeople slunk off in the night, not relishing a fight with a bevy of bandits who had become notorious, led by the most famous outlaw in America after Jesse James. Pat was glad to see them go. Trash, he said. The cattlemen were ruthless bastards but at least they wouldn't run out on you. He set a trap: he had persuaded a fellow Billy knew and trusted to take the news to Billy that Garrett had been at Fort Sumner but had grown tired of waiting and had pulled out.

It worked. At about eight in the evening on December 19th, in a dusting of light snow, Billy and the boys rode in.

O'Folliard and Pickett rode in front. They came right up to the old hospital building and O'Folliard's horse lowered its head to the trough.

"Halt!" Pat's voice thundered out. Startled, Tom O'Folliard went for the pistol in his belt. Pat fired his Winchester and O'Folliard yelped in pain. Then the rest of the men opened up and a furious fusillade crashed out in the night. Pickett also cried out, as if hit, and galloped away. The Kid, Dave Rudabaugh and the others, further back in the dark and snow, wheeled their horses about, dug in their spurs and galloped off into the night.

Tom O'Folliard's horse, unguided now, turned off its own accord and walked back to the shelter of the building, with Tom slumped in the saddle. "Don't shoot, Garrett. I'm killed." He had been shot in the chest, just below the heart. They helped him down and carried him inside and laid him down on a blanket by the fire. His voice was already weaker. "Goddam you, Garrett. I hope to meet you in hell."

"I would not talk that way, Tom. You are going to die in a few minutes."

"Go to hell, you long-legged son of a bitch." He asked for some water, drank a little, gave a groan, lay back and died.

They had one of the gang, therefore, and they may also have hit Pickett, but Rudabaugh and, above all, Bonney had escaped yet again. Stewart came up to Garrett. "Goddam it, we lost them."

"Yes, we did. But only for the moment. How would you like to be out on the prairies in this weather? We'll get them." Stewart looked at him skeptically. Did Garrett mean this or was it bravado? He didn't know Garrett or he wouldn't have wondered.

In fact, Pickett had not been hit. He had simply yelped with fright, then ridden howling out into the night spurring his horse till it fell and died on him. Dirty Dave's horse had also been hit and had fallen and Dave had ridden double behind Billy. They rode slowly in this way, Tom Pickett on foot, to the Wilcox-Brazil Ranch, where they had found shelter before.

Billy, Dave, Tom Pickett, the other Billy and Charlie Bowdre, depressed and disheartened, walked their horses up into the hills. Another vicious snowstorm swept through and they cowered and shivered in what shelter they could, not daring to light a fire.

The Texans found Dave Rudabaugh's dead horse but the snow had obliterated the trail and they went back. They buried O'Folliard and spent the evening in the warm, drinking, smoking, gambling and planning their next move.

The night had not long progressed before Garrett was kicking the men from their sleep and under the light of a freezing moon, they rode out east. The snow had stopped and Pat knew that now at last they could follow Billy's tracks. It was thus that they came up to the abandoned rock house, once the shelter of sheepmen, where Pat gazed down and could clearly hear the snores of the five outlaws.

***

Finally, after a long cold wait, the weak gray light began to spread across the landscape. A single figure, in a large-brimmed Mexican hat, emerged from the house carrying a nosebag for the horses. The whole posse took aim with their Winchesters and let rip. The figure staggered and fell back into the dwelling.

Inside, there was sudden panic. Charlie slumped to the floor and the other Billy stretched him out more comfortably. Billy Bonney looked down at Bowdre's bleeding wounds. "They have murdered you, Charlie," he said, and Dave Rudabaugh, looking grimly on, thought that was not far from the truth at that. Billy went on, "But you can get your revenge. Kill some of the sons of bitches before you die" and Billy lifted him and shoved him towards the door. Bowdre came out, staggering, but never even got to shoot. He moved slowly to where Garrett stood, murmured, "I wish…I wish…" and collapsed. Pat took the boy in his arms and watched him die.

Pat was distracted by movement below. The outlaws were pulling their horses into the house, ready to make a break. Garrett did not hesitate one moment. Taking up his Winchester again, he dropped a horse full in the doorway with one shot. He then aimed carefully at the rope tying the other two mounts and fired, cutting it, and the animals trotted off. It was an astonishing shot.

Dave looked rather admiringly at Billy as the Kid bantered to and fro with Garrett. Billy seemed in the best of spirits.

"Yo, Pat, you want to come in for a cup of coffee?"

"I'll come in alright but it won't be for coffee."

"Why Pat, now that ain't polite. Come on now. We got a nice warm fire going here. We got feather beds and champagne and some French whores too. You'd enjoy it."

"Well, come to the door and invite me in then."

"And of course you won't shoot."

"Well, I won't shoot very much."

And so on.

But they were trapped, and Dave, Tom and both Billies knew it. It was the dead horse that did for them; Garrett's damn marksmanship. And although Billy gave out the idea that he and the boys were snug in the rock house with plenty of grub and a warm fire, while Garrett's posse was freezing and hungry outside, it was in fact the reverse of the truth for Garrett was very well supplied and there was almost nothing to eat or drink in the house.

The day wore on and at about four in the afternoon the smell of roasting meat wafted from Garrett's camp down to the bandits' lair and drove them crazy with hunger. It was the last straw. A dirty white rag fluttered from a window. Dave Rudabaugh shouted that they wanted to surrender and please not to shoot. Garrett answered that they should come out with their hands up. It suddenly reminded Dave of the posse up in Mora, led by Dave Mather, when they had captured Slap-Jack Nicholson and the others. But this time he was on the other side.

Dave came out, cautiously, hands high, ready to rush back in if they commenced firing. He edged towards Garrett. "Mr. Garrett, listen. We'll come out and surrender. I know we ain't in no position to impose conditions so I won't. But I do ask a favor. It's this. You take me in, take me to Santa Fe and let me be tried there. I know full well that if I get into the jail in Las Vegas, after my pardner shot the Spanish jailer there, they'll hang me for sure and the fact that that windmill ain't there no more won't stop them one moment. Hand me in at Santa Fe."

Pat considered for a moment. Then he simply nodded. It was enough for Dave. He turned back, and after a few moments all four of them came out again, with their hands high.

As soon as he saw it, one of the cattlemen raised his Winchester and took a bead on Billy, muttering, "Son of a bitch, I'll get you."

Pat swiveled sharply, looked furiously at him, and leveled his Winchester at the man's stomach. "If you fire a shot, I will kill you." The man reluctantly lowered his gun. One look at Garrett was enough to know he meant it.

The outlaws and Charlie Bowdre's body were taken back to the Wilcox-Brazil ranch in a wagon and thence to Fort Sumner. Billy was laughing and joking all the way and Dave found his high spirits infectious. Tom and the other Billy were glum and did not join in. Tom Pickett seemed scared half to death.

Pat, his men and the captives too all drank on Christmas Eve at Beaver Smith's. The place was rowdy, it was hot and it stank. None of the inhabitants had washed in a good long while and the pot-bellied stove gave out a thumping heat. The men drank and roared at the crude timber bar and told jokes and slapped each other on the back. Pat smiled. Billy was the life and soul of the party. He gave Beaver Smith his Winchester in payment for the bill he had run up over the past months, buying other fellows drinks. "Here you are, Beaver. Don't reckon I'll be needing it. Not for a week or two anyway!"

Paulita, the beautiful daughter of Deluvina Maxwell, a servant of Pete's, came in and the men cheered and hollered. Paulita embraced Billy passionately. Dave was shackled to Billy and was obliged to almost take part. He grinned broadly. But then Manuela Bowdre entered and she was not so lovey-dovey. She railed at Pat and spat at him and screamed at him in Spanish for murdering her husband, who wanted to give himself up and go straight. She tried to beat him with a branding iron. They had to pull her off Pat. But Pat was gentle with her and gave orders for Charlie to be buried decently and said he would pay for a good suit for him to be buried in and also pay for the grave digger.

Beaver Smith had put a small pine sapling in a corner and someone got out a squeezebox and everyone sang Stille Nacht, and they made up in sentiment and earnestness for what they lacked in musical skill, and not a few tears were shed.

***

On the day after Christmas, word spread rapidly through Las Vegas that Pat Garrett was approaching with a posse and that he was bringing in Billy the Kid and three of his gang.

Pat was the hero of Las Vegas. Hardly a month before, he had brought in George Davis and J.J. Webb, and now here he was with the most famous outlaw of the whole southwest and three of his men. One of them, Tom Pickett, was a corrupt Las Vegas policeman who had run out to escape being killed. And one of them, Dave Rudabaugh, was the desperado responsible for the death of Antonio Valdez, the jailer, and he would now hang for it. The town was jubilant. People stood and gawped as the party arrived and the whole day stood in saloons and discussed nothing else.

Reporters of the *Las Vegas Optic* and rival *Las Vegas Gazette* were allowed into the jail and everyone read their accounts and discussed how easily the Kid was taking everything. He had apparently laughed and joked with the reporters and jailers.

Garrett retired to the Exchange Hotel for a bath and sleep. Henry Hoyt was there again at the bar and attended to Pat's needs, which included the sending to Garrett's room of such items as a bottle of the best whiskey the Exchange could offer, ditto a box of cigars and two rather lovely señoritas from the east end of town. Hoyt later walked across the plaza to the jail and asked to be allowed to see Billy. Said he was a friend from way back.

***

Dave had sat heavily down on the cot beside Josh. So heavily that Josh feared for its structure. "Well, Josh, remember I said to you when I visited you here that I didn't want to end up as your neighbor in the same cell?"

"I do, Dave, yes."

"Well, I shouldn't of said that, now, should I? Must of been bad luck. 'Cause here I am!"

"Yes, Dave, here you are. Here we both are."

"And between you and me, Josh, I kind of wish I was somewhere else. They don't seem to take kindly to me here. They say I shot that jailer. But I didn't, Josh."

"No, you didn't, but you know, Dave, in law you were just as guilty and they could easily hang you for it."

"Yes, I know. And what's more, they could easily also hang me unofficial, like." Dave looked gloomy. "But Pat Garrett says he's going to take me to Santa Fe to stand trial and I believe him. He's an ornery son of a bitch but he's straight as a rail on the Santa Fe."

"Good. Well, I hope you make it out okay and maybe down there they'll give you life, like me, and not let you swing. I hope so. Not that, in all honesty, I am much enjoying life imprisonment so far, Dave. I must tell you that it is not really an existence of carefree luxury and pleasure."

"Well, I believe you."

The jailer interrupted them to tell Billy that he had a visitor, and Henry Hoyt came in. Billy jumped up. "Why, Dr. Hoyt, how good to see you! Happy Christmas!"

Josh looked at Dave. "Doctor Hoyt? Henry Hoyt's no doctor. He's the barman at the Exchange."

Dave looked surprised. "He's a doctor, alright. Been practicing for years here and there on the frontier. In the Panhandle, mostly. He's a friend of Billy's."

Josh was puzzled and surprised. There was always more to Henry Hoyt than met the eye.

"Do you still have that pretty little gold watch I gave you, Billy? The one with the plaited hair watch-chain?"

"Shucks, Doc, you know that was a ladies' watch. I gave it to a certain señorita."

"You did, right, Billy. That watch was made for a beauty."

Billy was lively. "Well, well, well. And how's that racehorse I gave you, Doctor? You still got him?"

"Why no, I don't, Billy, I'm afraid. I had to give up Dandy Dick to raise money to set up a faro game. I sold him to Mr. Teats and he put him on one of his mail routes. I guess the post got through right quickly when Dandy was carrying it! But it was a fine present, Billy, and I thank you. It was mighty kind of you."

"Oh, it was nothing. You probably guessed that I didn't exactly buy that nag."

Hoyt laughed. "No, I guess not. But you gave me a proper deed and all so I guess they won't hang me for a horse thief!"

That riposte rather put a dampener on all the inhabitants of the jail as they reflected on their condition. Tom Pickett had gone as white as the wall. Hoyt looked as though he wished he hadn't said that.

When Hoyt had gone, Josh spoke to Billy. "Mr. McCarty, as I was introduced to you some time back up at Montezuma Springs, if you remember. Perhaps I should use another name now. Mr. Bonney? How do you do?"

"I remember you very well. J.J. Webb. You went off with that marshal's wife. And just call me Billy. Everyone else does."

"Why, yes, Mrs. Carson. She has since left town and no one seems to know where she is. You know, her husband was murdered in Close & Paterson's saloon."

"Yes, Dave has filled me in on all your excitements here in Las Vegas. Seems to have been a lively place! And I hear they gave you life."

"Yes."

"Well, Mr. Webb, Josh, I can tell you one thing. They want to hang me for sure. But whether I am in the condemned cell waiting for the rope or serving life in some pen, I shall escape. They won't keep me in. No sir."

"Well, I wish you luck. I can tell you, however, that it won't be easy getting out of here. George here and I did it thanks to George's lock-picking skills but see, they changed the old iron key for this masterpiece of the modern locksmith's art and George says it can't be done."

"Oh, here, the next jail, wherever it may be. It can be done. It can be done alright." And he smiled broadly and sat down on his bed.

They talked for most of the night. Billy, Tom and the other Billy got to know all about Las Vegas and the story of Hoodoo and the robberies and all, and Josh and George Davis learned the story of Billy's dealings with the Governor and Pat Garrett and life in Roswell and Fort Sumner. Dave, of course, was the link between the two and enjoyed the conversation greatly, often embellishing and correcting. Dave told Josh how Billy and Jesse and he, along with Mysterious Dave and Doc Holliday, had held up the train to Raton, and how Jesse said he was Billy the Kid and Billy had to be Jesse James.

They discussed Josh's shooting of Kelliher and what part Hoodoo had had in his downfall. And they speculated on where Hoodoo and Dutchy were now and whether Mrs. Carson was with them. They all vowed friendship to each other and swore to help each other out of any fix should it be in their power. But they all knew that such selflessness was not likely to be called upon. Only Billy was constantly cheerful and seemed utterly confident that all would go well and no one would hang. The others buoyed themselves with this optimism and clung to it, rather as a drowning man clings to a stick.

***

In the afternoon of the 27th, Pat came back to the jail and with his Winchester signaled the jailers to open the cell door. The two Billies and Dave were taken out, shackled together.

Dirty Dave shook Josh's hand and said, "Goodbye, Josh." The Kid waved cheerfully and smiled and Billy Wilson turned his back and waited. The prisoners were put into a wagon, around which a hostile crowd was already beginning to mill. They weren't after the Billies. In fact, the Kid was rather a hero. But they didn't want Dave Rudabaugh to escape their clutches. They

179

wanted him to hang in Las Vegas for the murder of Valdez, not in Santa Fe for some cattle rustling down south.

The wagon rolled down to the Gallinas Bridge, with Pat and a few men on horseback beside. They reached the railroad station and had to wait for the westbound train, which was late. By the time the train pulled in, an angry crowd had rallied, loudly demanding that Rudabaugh be left behind. They surged onto the tracks and covered the engineer with rifles. The train was delayed forty-five minutes and there seemed to be a stand-off. Billy was enjoying it and, making a gun of his hand, pointed it at the men and hollered, "Bang! Bang!"

But Dave didn't look happy at all. He put a hand on Garrett's arm. "Mr. Garrett, now you promised up there at the sheep house. You said you would hand me in to the authorities in Santa Fe."

Pat looked him with disgust. "Don't you dare to remind me what I promised, you dirty son of a bitch. I know damn well what I promised. Now keep your filthy mouth shut."

One of the crowd suddenly felt brave, stepped forward, cocked his pistol and shouted for Garrett to give Dave over.

Pat said, "I've had enough of this" and went to the door of the car. There he stood with his Winchester seated on his hip and said very clearly, though without shouting, "Now, the first man who comes near I will shoot in the gut. Furthermore, I will release the prisoners and arm them. Now, who is first?" And he slowly bought the Winchester to bear on the man who had spoken.

There was a moment of hesitation, then their spirit broke and they started to disperse, grumbling.

Pat turned back into the car. "That's what you get with mobs," he said. "Even though they outnumber you a hundred to one, no one wants to be the first to get shot in the stomach." And he threw the Winchester up onto the baggage rack and sat down, stretching his long legs across into the next seat. The train moved slowly out. Pat looked sour. Billy Bonney leaned out and shouted to the retreating crowd, "Happy Christmas, boys!"

***

Josh languished in jail in Las Vegas. The deep depression did not attack him again but he nevertheless was desperate to be free. Being cooped up was terrible to him. He would almost rather hang. The winter months passed. Spring came slowly but made Josh's restlessness worse. He had no visitors. Other prisoners came and went. The one he knew best was Davis but they were cut from different cloth, somehow, and were only polite, not close. Then one day he too was gone, taken down to Santa Fe.

On March 3rd, 1881, the previous day's copy of the *Las Vegas Gazette* came into his hands. It carried a story taken from the Santa Fe *New Mexican*. The article told how Dave had been sentenced to death by Chief Justice L. Bradford Prince who had ordered that he be brought back to Las Vegas to hang for the murder of Antonio Lino Valdez. He and Billy and the others had been surprised an inch away from a jailbreak in Santa Fe. They had been tunneling their way out. Their bed ticking was discovered to be full of stones and dirt, and a deep hole was uncovered. As a result, they had been shackled heavily and more closely guarded.

Josh muttered to himself, "Nice try, Billy. But you see, it ain't quite as easy as you made out."

In April, Dave Rudabaugh was brought back and incarcerated with Josh. Dave's execution had been set for May 20th. They made a glum couple. Dave told Josh that Billy the Kid had been taken down to Lincoln for trial and would likely hang. They were confined in the middle cell with some other prisoners, fellows they hardly knew, one held for the murder of a store clerk and the others for robbery.

Dave's lawyer won a stay of execution while an appeal was being prepared and the spring turned to summer. They didn't get regular access to newspapers but picked up bits of news from prisoners who came and went and the odd conversation overheard. Most of it was local gossip and accounts of what had happened last night in the town, shootings and brawls and such.

But one day in July they did get access to an out-of-date newspaper and knew that all the talk they had been hearing was true. Billy the Kid, unarmed, had been shot dead in Fort Sumner by Pat Garrett on July 14th.

Josh looked at Dave. "Read this about Billy."

"Read what about Billy?"

"It's true. He was shot and killed by Pat Garrett on the 14th."

"Billy is really dead?"

"Yes. We knew he had escaped from the Lincoln Court House and killed Olinger and Bell. But it says here Pat caught up with him at Fort Sumner and shot him dead when he was unarmed. I am surprised. I did not think that was Pat's way."

Dave was ashen faced. The shock had washed all the color out of him. "It's his way, alright. I saw him shoot Charlie Bowdre down without a warning, without a word. He just fired that Winchester of his till it was hot and Charlie was full of holes. He's one ruthless son of a bitch."

***

Autumn came. In October, the whole country was talking about a gunfight down in Tombstone between the Earps and the Clanton clan. Two McLaury boys and Billy Clanton had been killed by three Earps and Doc Holliday. Virgil and Morgan Earp had been hit but not mortally. Doc and Wyatt had been untouched. Ike Clanton had run away. It seemed there had been a real feud which had flared out. Josh reckoned that was Wyatt's way. He'll take a lot but provoke him too far and he'll fight, and fight hard.

Dirty Dave thought there was something fishy about the whole affair. He said that if Holliday was involved you could be sure it was not on the up and up. Josh thought he might have had a point. But then Dave had never been an admirer or friend of the Earps and least of all of Doc Holliday.

In November, news came that Dave's appeal had been turned down and the death sentence was confirmed. He was to hang after Christmas.

Dave said quietly to Josh, "Well, friend, however we do it, we have to get out of here. And soon. It's that or hang for me and that or rot for you."

Josh looked him in the eye, reflected for a moment and then simply nodded.

***

When the jailers came to bring breakfast to the prisoners on the morning of December 3rd, they discovered the central cell empty. There was a hole in the adobe wall, only seven by nineteen inches. How a man as big as Dave had gotten through was a mystery. The jailers didn't know it but in fact the escapees had almost had to leave Dave there, stuck in the hole and red-faced and panting. In the end, he had only got through by taking off all his clothes and being hauled through, painfully, by the others, scraping his skin.

The *Las Vegas Optic* identified the escaped prisoners as David Rudabaugh, J.J. Webb, T. Quilian, who had been arrested by Pat Garrett on a charge of killing a deputy sheriff in Texas, and four men identified only as Shroeder, Kelly, Goodman and Kearney. The jailers had found stones and earth in the mattresses.

A knife and a pick were discovered, discarded, near the cell. It was not known who had given the prisoners these tools or how they had been smuggled in.

Early in the morning, a man who lived near the railroad tracks reported having seen two men, one big and tall, the other stocky and strongly built, walking along together, and chains dangling from the legs of both. How they had broken them was not known, nor how they had left town. But the clear suspicion was that Josh Webb and Dave Rudabaugh had left Las Vegas, New Mexico Territory the same way they had come in about two years before, using the railway.

Chapter Twelve

Two men on foot, one stocky, the other big, walked into Bernalillo, a small but prosperous burg on the Rio Grande a short distance above Albuquerque, in the early hours of a cold December morning, and headed for a two-room adobe building on the main street in the center of town. They knocked at the door and a tousled fair-haired boy of about sixteen opened it.

The spotty youth said his name was Jack McCutchlin and he minded the office when the Doctor was out. Dr. Hoyt was presently away treating Don José Antonio's pneumonia. The lad didn't know when he would be back.

Josh said, "We'll wait" and he and Dave entered and sat on a small wooden bench. Jack looked uncertain but, in the end, just got on with his work.

Why Hoyt had smuggled those tools into the Las Vegas jail and later broken their chains, Josh and Dave did not really know. Nor did they know why the doctor had told them where he would be and offered them a safe house. You never understood much with Henry Hoyt. There was always something behind. Something deeper.

They were woken from their sleep on the floor by the sound of the door opening and the booted step of the doctor, who had somehow now sprouted eyeglasses. "Hello, boys. Good to see you again."

Josh and Dave shuffled to their feet and wiped the sleep out of their eyes. They shook hands with Hoyt. The boy had gone and Hoyt himself prepared something to eat. He put a bottle of whiskey on the table but did not drink any himself.

When they had eaten and Dave and Josh had lit the cigars which Hoyt offered them (though he did not smoke himself), Josh asked the doc why he had helped them in Las Vegas. Hoyt looked doubtful, as if he genuinely didn't know why, but he said, "I heard about Billy and it was my way of getting back at them. I do not approve of Patrick Garrett and I hold New Mexican law officers very low in my esteem."

Josh looked at Hoyt. "Doctor Hoyt, whenever I think I know who you are, you surprise me."

"Oh well, I may be young but I've knocked about this country for a fair time now, you know, and have my ideas. There are people I like and people I don't."

"But doctors don't usually, well, run faro games and break people out of jail."

"I suppose it is true that I am not the usual kind of doctor. I'm quite a good one, though, and cured a lot of people of the smallpox in Texas. In fact, I haven't finished my medical studies and am saving to go to New York to enroll in a college. I was in Deadwood in '77. I've punched cattle and done this and that to get some money together." (Josh thought that 'this and that' did not half cover it.) "They've just made me postmaster here. But the money always seems to disappear somehow. I think there must be a hole in my pockets." He smiled and poured Josh and Dave more drinks. "Anyway, I'm glad I could have been of help to you boys and I hope you make it out of this Territory. Good luck to you. I have horses and pistol belts and grub for you. Don't tell me where you're going."

"Doc, we don't know how to repay you."

"You don't have to. Only, if you ever run into Patrick F.J. Garrett, and you have a loaded pistol on you..."

Dave piped up. "We sure don't aim to run into that son of a bitch again. Not if we can help it."

***

They traveled west through the bleak, empty lands between the Navajos to the north and Apaches to the south and crossed into Arizona Territory. There was some small comfort about being out of the jurisdiction of such city and county authorities as might be searching for them, though they knew they were not out of the reach of the U.S. Marshals. They turned south.

Josh enjoyed these weeks. It was freezing cold at night but brightly sunny by day. The Apaches were quiet, his horse sound, even lively. Dave was comfortable enough company even if he was no sparkling conversationalist. Above all, Josh felt, he was free. Free to roam and follow his horse's head. Free to wonder what he might find in Arizona or Mexico or go where he wanted, and free to dream a little. Free just to breathe the fresh air. It was a good feeling. Oh, he probably didn't deserve it. He knew he was no saint, and

185

people who go around shooting other people in saloons probably ought to end their days in a miserable cell in Las Vegas or on some chain gang, but that didn't stop him luxuriating in his freedom. As they crested a rise and the evening sun added even more pinkness to the rosy Arizona landscape, he looked over at Dave and for the first time in he couldn't remember how long, smiled.

Dave caught the mood and before long they were trotting and joking and passing a bottle between them.

In Tucson, they felt bold enough to check into a hotel as Mr. Howard and Mr. McCarty, cattle buyers. They had money they had won in a poker game in the silver-town of Globe and from having sold two mules they had found in a field. It was curious weather for the season, quite hot and humid, and in the evening a dramatic thunderstorm burst out. The street suddenly became a river and as they wanted to cross to enter a saloon, they took their boots and socks off and walked across carrying them. The water was warm and pleasant between the toes and Josh was suddenly reminded of wading in the shallows with Masie one Kansas evening.

From there, they struck out towards Contention. They thought about taking the Butterfield stage but decided to stick to their horses and take rarely-used trails. They ran across a grizzled old Mexican constable named Bob Valdez who indicated the way for them. Josh remarked how the wily old man had silently sized them up then decided to leave them be. He had obviously been an Indian scout. He had that look about him and that quiet, calm perspicacity and courage.

They arrived in Tombstone, A.T. on December 15th.

***

There was a strong movement against the Earps. There had been a mighty turnout for the funeral of the McLaury boys and Billy Clanton after the October gunfight and many townsfolk feared retaliation. Josh found the town edgy, jumpy. It was nothing like Las Vegas. Here, the whole town seemed involved and backing one faction or the other. The idea was spreading that the gunfight had deterred Eastern investors. Virgil had been suspended as town marshal. The *Nugget* kept up its virulent attacks on the Earps.

Josh met Wyatt and Morgan and they seemed pleased to see him. They said he was welcome and they could do with another gun. Whereas in the old days, in Caldwell or Dodge, that would have appealed to Josh, now somehow it didn't. He was polite, he wished them well, but he had other plans. It had come to him quite suddenly. He would go to St. Louis.

Dave didn't understand at all. "St. Louis? But whatever for? I thought we was going to Mexico together."

"We shall go to Mexico, Dave, if you want. But not quite yet. I must do this. I won't be long. I'll get the stage to Contention and take the train to Tucson then north. I'll be back in a couple of months. I reckon you have enough to occupy you here for that time, if I'm any judge."

"Well, alright. I'll wait. In fact, I might ride with the Clantons."

"The Clantons? Dave, whatever do you mean?"

"The Clantons are my kind of folk. They are rustlers first and foremost. That's what I do. I learned them skills long ago and I also learned a lot riding with Billy. What's more, I don't like the Earps. They're too big for their boots. They act like they own this town. And as for Holliday…"

"I thought you liked Holliday. They say he taught you to play cards and you taught him to shoot in return."

"Well, whoever told you that yarn is a fool. I never liked Holliday and still don't. He's a back shooter and he's, er, what's the word?"

"I don't know. What do you mean?"

"When someone says clever and nasty things about you and laughs at you."

"Do you mean sarcastic?"

"Yeah. Sarcastic."

"Well, yes, I guess he can be sarcastic."

"Okay, you go off. But Josh, I'll be waiting for you. We're pards now, right? You wouldn't run out on me like Mysterious did?"

"I'll be back, Dave, and if for some reason I don't return, I'll write you. I promise."

***

Josh had forgotten what a big city was like. He had been in the West so long that he had grown used to scruffy towns, low adobe or wooden buildings and dirt streets. In St. Louis, he found the address of Mr. and Mrs. Samuel King in a directory and rode a streetcar between banks and mansion houses, watching elegant ladies and bowler-hatted gentlemen thronging the sidewalks. Even in his best suit, he felt poorly dressed.

He was admitted by a rather haughty servant and told, rather than asked, to wait. Sam King was not as Josh had expected. He had always imagined him to be a solid, even middle-aged banker. In reality, he was a young man with glossy back hair, a shine in his eyes and a fresh, open face. He extended his hand in a warm, friendly gesture. "Mr. Webb, how good of you to call. Of course Masie used to talk about you and I almost feel that I know you. Do sit down."

Josh said, "Thank you." Then a sudden chill passed over Josh's heart. "Used to?"

King looked startled and then understood. "I see. You didn't know. Well, I regret being the one to tell you, Mr. Webb, that Masie passed away last March. You knew of course that she had been ill for some time. Well-known doctors attended her and she had the best attention and care but nothing could be done. I am sorry." Josh must have looked blank and uncomprehending for King said, "Mr. Webb?" Then he rose and brought Josh a glass of water.

Josh rose. "Thank you. I must be going."

"Please, Mr. Webb, do stay a little. You don't look well. Allow me to tell you more."

"No, I don't want to hear more."

"Well, I could show you the grave. Perhaps you'd like-"

"Why go to the grave? She ain't there."

In five minutes, Josh was back in the street. He thought he might have appeared churlish to Samuel King. He hadn't meant to be. The man must have suffered just as much.

Josh stared around the broad avenue and stood motionless in the bustling crowd. He suddenly wondered where he was and why. What was he doing here? Why had he come? If Masie had been alive, what would he have said or done? Now that she was gone, he felt directionless, like a ship with a broken rudder.

He walked mechanically back to the small hotel he had chosen, just for somewhere to go. When he arrived, he entered his room and sat on a chair staring at the bare wall.

When he looked up, it was dark. The windows were black.

He went back to Tombstone only because Dave expected it, and for somewhere to go. Before he got back, Josh read that Virgil Earp had been maimed by a shotgun blast and pistol shots three nights after Christmas, stepping out of the Oriental Saloon. Three men had immediately run out of a derelict building down an alley and into the night. The marks of nineteen shots had been found in the awning posts and walls of the Oriental afterwards and it was a miracle Virgil had not been killed instantly. The paper said he was like to die from his wounds. He had staggered back into the saloon to find Wyatt, and doctors had been called. Josh guessed that Ike Clanton had been the prime mover and wondered uncomfortably about Dave.

Josh arrived back in town on March 18th, a Saturday. He found the Earps all holed up for safety in the Cosmopolitan Hotel, right across from their rivals' haunt, the Grand. Wyatt was grim faced and told him that Ike's hat, with his name in it, had been found in the derelict building. Ike had a wonderful talent for messing everything up. He mixed incompetence and cowardice in unique proportions. Wyatt also said that because of the shooting he had been appointed Deputy U.S. Marshal and had the authority to select his own deputies. He wondered if Josh would be interested. But Josh did not want his name mentioned anywhere just now, at any price, and declined.

It got him to thinking and he wrote to Jim Scott, a friend in Arkansas, who duly sent a letter to the *Dodge City Times*. The letter read:

Sir, John Joshua Webb is dead. He died on 12th inst. of smallpox in Winslow, Arkansas. He had the best attention and care but there came a sudden change in the weather and I suppose he caught cold for he died very suddenly. You can tell his friends of his death. Signed, J.A. Scott.

It did not seem to Josh a very convincing letter but it worked. The story was picked up by the *Las Vegas Optic* and no one hunted any more for J.J. Webb.

In a small town in southern Colorado, the local town marshal put down his copy of the *Dodge City Times* sadly. Will Hardcastle had been very fond of Josh Webb. Too many people died from smallpox. Will was not an old man, only in his thirties, yet it seemed that everyone he knew or liked or loved had gone.

Further north, in Cheyenne, Wyoming, a widow with gray hair drawn back tightly in a bun also read the letter in the paper. It was in her mind to rejoice that the man who had killed her husband was dead. But she could not. Kitty Kelliher was even faintly sorry for the man.

In the Tennessee city of Nashville, Hoodoo Brown threw the paper down at the letters page before his companion. "Well, he's gone. I would have preferred that he be hanged but at least he's dead."

Mrs. Carson read the letter from James Scott and recalled Josh Webb in her bed. She remembered him as an attractive man but a sad one. One who had lost something—or someone—and had never gotten over it. She was sorry he was gone and regretted also that he had been taken by an unpleasant disease. She had always assumed that he would die bravely in some gunfight, defending a friend perhaps. A truly beautiful sixteen-year-old girl sitting beside them glanced at the letter and looked curiously at her mother, wondering who this man Webb was. But then there was so much of her mother's past that she did not know about. Sometimes she wasn't sure that she wanted to.

***

Meanwhile, law and order had not improved in Cochise County, Arizona. Faro games raged all through the night in Tombstone and Charleston, drink flowed, shots were fired. There were two stage robberies on the road to Bisbee, and Wells, Fargo threatened to remove the routes. The Mexican army had built posts on the border which greatly reduced the profitable smuggling and cross-border rustling that had been a staple of the criminal community, and the 'Cowboys', as they were called, needed new targets. They flocked into Tombstone and crime became rampant. The most dangerous elements were John Ringo and Curly Bill Brocius.

John Ringo had been a leading light in the Mason County War in Texas where with his friend, the ex-Texas Ranger Scott Cooley, he had killed the local deputy sheriff. Cooley had then scalped him and thrown the body down a well. Ringo had killed other men too, including Charley Bader, mistaking him for his brother Pete. For that, Ringo was locked up and found himself the cellmate of the notorious John Wesley Hardin. Come into Arizona where there was less law to hinder him, Ringo had shot a fellow named Hancock in a saloon for preferring beer to whiskey. He was dangerous, unstable and manic. He and Doc Holliday loathed each other. They were maybe too similar.

As for Curly Bill, he was an altogether different character, flamboyant, dashing, and prone to bouts of almost hysterical hilarity. He dressed in flaming red shirts and broad-brimmed Stetsons and he carried two guns in a specially designed belt and holster arrangement. He loved twirling his silver pistols and firing them in the air, though it was said he was the worst pistol shot in the southwest. He was known for having held a church service hostage, making the preacher dance and demanding the hymns he liked, conducting the choir with his pistols. He evidently liked dancing for he had also made all the occupants of a Mexican saloon strip naked and dance while he whooped and drank and fired his guns into the ceiling. He had ridden with the odious Jesse Evans in the Lincoln County War, alongside Billy the Kid for a time, and he had robbed a stage in El Paso and had his right ear shot through there by Texas Ranger Thomas Mode. There was nothing moderate or restrained about Curly Bill. In October of the previous year, Curly had shot and killed Marshal Fred White and Wyatt had arrested him and taken him to Tucson to avoid a lynching. There he got off, and in fact Marshal White had said, almost as his dying words, that the pistol had discharged by accident.

Wyatt suspected both Ringo and Brocius of involvement in the shooting of Virgil. Doc Holliday had a face-off with John Ringo, the Cowboys' leading gunfighter. It was said that Ringo had eyes for Holliday's companion Big-Nose Kate. In any case, the men had been restrained at the last minute and gunplay avoided. But the town had never been edgier.

In March, the Lingard Theater Company brought to Tombstone their production of 'Stolen Kisses'. Many of the town's residents and all its sporting community had no intention of missing that performance. Morgan Earp was eager and was tired of being cooped up in the Cosmopolitan. His was not a character that bore inactivity easily and certainly not glumness, and boy, was he ready to have fun.

On a fresh March night, Morgan sponged himself in water laced with eau de Cologne, oiled his hair, put on a clean shirt, dandied himself up with a frock coat and a hat of which he was particularly fond, and set out with a spring in his step. Thirty years old, handsome, with sparkling eyes and a drooping mustache copied from his idolized brother's, full of spirit, Morgan was the liveliest of the clan. He was particularly close to Wyatt because when elder brothers Newton, James and Virgil had gone off to the war, he and Wyatt had had to remain and they shared therefore a love of adventure and a hatred of farming.

As a police officer, Morgan had killed a man in Butte, Montana and with Wyatt he had been a shotgun messenger for Wells, Fargo. He had been wounded at the October gunfight on Fremont Street by a bullet across the shoulder and back but had not stopped firing and afterwards had recovered well. There was no weakness about Morgan. When Virgil was maimed, Morgan had sensed danger and sent his young wife Louisa back to the Earp parents in California and safety. Now, it was not that he felt himself a bachelor again and free to dally but still, he was a young man in his prime and he was not averse to handsome ladies, nor were they to him. And a show of the kind promised by the title 'Stolen Kisses' was certainly not to be missed.

And indeed, 'Stolen Kisses' had lived up to its promise. It was racy, musical and hugely enjoyable. In fact, Morgan had purchased a ticket for the following night's performance.

It was a blowy night and rain and wind did damage to Morgan's coiffure and dampened his coat, to his annoyance.

"Morgan, good, I've found you. Come on, let's get back to the Cosmopolitan."

"Why, Wyatt, you come searching for your little brother 'cause you don't think he can look after himself on a stormy night?"

Wyatt took his brother by the arm. "Listen, Morgan, I've heard things. Goodrich tells me there's something brewing against us. I think we ought to get back."

"No, Wyatt, out of the question. I have my mind set on a game of pool. Bob Hatch tells me he has fifty dollars says he can beat me. Now that's fifty bucks in the bank, Wyatt, in the bank!"

Morgan would have his way and Wyatt accompanied him to the poolroom in Campbell & Hatch's Saloon. Bob Hatch planked a fifty-dollar gold piece on the edge of the pool table. Wyatt sat indulgently at the side and began to smoke. Bob and Morgan began to play.

At about eleven in the evening, as Morgan was sizing up a shot, a rifle bullet smashed through the glass-paned door and shattered his spine. Another shot crashed out, aimed at Wyatt, but he had instinctively ducked at the first noise and the slug slammed into the wooden wall just where he had been sitting. The door gave onto a narrow, dark alley and although footsteps running away were heard, by the time Wyatt had wrenched open the door, the alley was empty.

He rushed back to his brother and he and Bob Hatch carried Morgan to a lounge next door in the card room, upon which he lay in agony, bleeding. A doctor arrived, then another, but there was nothing to be done. Morgan was clearly in great pain and clearly dying.

In the hour that followed, various people came in, or tried to. Wyatt ordered that no one be admitted without his express permission. Josh Webb was one of those allowed in and offered his hand to Wyatt and asked what he could do.

"Nothing, Josh, nothing. He's dying and that's all. But if you want to help, just watch our backs, and keep your gun handy."

"I'll certainly do that."

Josh saw Wyatt bend low over his brother again and again and it was clear that a whispered conversation was being held but it was too soft to be heard and in any case, Josh did not want to listen. It was not proper. Only one remark he heard, which was when Morgan faintly said, "This is the last game of pool I'll ever play."

Josh went out into the alley and looked carefully around. Although it was dark, he could see the imprints of footsteps of perhaps three men. There were two spent Winchester shells in the dirt. And a kerchief.

When Josh went back in, Morgan had died.

***

They laid Morgan out in one of Doc Holliday's blue suits and prepared his body to be shipped back to Colton, California, where it could be buried in the family plot. James Earp would go with him. Virgil, too, had decided to return with his wife Allie.

Wyatt either accepted this or even had ordered it, almost as if he wished to clear away any further risk to his family so that he could concentrate on the job he had to do. Only Warren was to remain, as a useful gun.

Wyatt and Doc Holliday escorted Virgil and Allie, with the casket of Morgan, up to the railhead at Benson. In Tucson, at the railroad station, Frank

Stilwell and Ike Clanton tried to murder Virgil but Wyatt shot Stilwell down with his ten-gauge as he was pleading for his life and Ike, as usual, ran away.

Wyatt was a changed man. He would never before have cut down a man begging for his life, face to face with a shotgun blast to the body. Josh had never seen him like this, in Dodge or Las Vegas or anywhere. All circumspection and thoughtfulness were gone, swept away in the tornado of his grief and anger. It was now the time for action, and only action. And Josh had never seen such single-mindedness. It was a thirst for revenge and a determination to bring to justice those responsible that drove him, and Wyatt did nothing else nor thought of anything else until it should be accomplished.

When Josh spoke to him, he seemed distant. When Josh offered to ride with him, for he had liked Morgan very much, Wyatt said yes, okay, if you like, but he was far away. As if it didn't matter how many guns he had with him, or even any; he would do it alone or accompanied, it was indifferent to him. This applied even to his friend Doc Holliday.

The next three weeks were a wild time. A crew of some of the hardest men Josh had ever seen gathered round Wyatt and they rode out all over the Territory. With Wyatt and Warren, there was Doc Holliday, Josh, Turkey-Creek Jack Johnson and Texas Jack Vermilion. Others, such as Wells, Fargo agent Fred Dodge, Charlie Smith or Johnny Green, joined in the posse from time to time.

Turkey-Creek was a tough nut who had fled Webb City, Missouri after a vicious and lethal street gun battle with miners. He had been a marshal up in Nebraska and later had killed two men with two shots at thirty yards in Deadwood in '76, where he had met Wyatt. Stocky and powerfully built, he kept his hair cropped short to his head and sported a long handlebar mustache. He wore range clothes always and looked like a cowboy. He toted a heavy .44 and was an expert rifle shot. He was known for his temper and for his partiality to the bottle. He was not a man to cross.

Texas Jack Vermilion, tall and thin, was a Confederate veteran who had fought with J.E.B. Stuart. He had a photograph of himself as a young man, posed with sword in one hand and pistol in the other, which he was proud to show to anyone he met. After the war, he had been a lawman in Missouri but his wife and two young children had all died of diphtheria while had had been absent and it had almost deranged him. He had gotten to know the Earps and

Holliday in Dodge. Holliday liked him because they were both Methodists and Doc, whose own father had been a Confederate veteran, admired Texas Jack.

They had other things in common: Texas Jack Vermilion was also wanted for shooting someone dead in a card game. No one knew why he was called Texas Jack and when asked he said it was because he was from Virginia. His hair was long, flowing down from under a huge-brimmed sombrero, and he wore a fancy Spanish gun belt tricked out in silver.

It was also strange because Wyatt's posse, under the warrant of his U.S. Deputy Marshal's badge, was harried by the County Sheriff Johnny Behan's posse, with a Tucson warrant for Wyatt's arrest for the killing of Frank Stilwell, and this band contained many of the Cowboy clan and known rustlers including Phineas Clanton and John Ringo. Not that the two posses ever met. Josh thought it would have been interesting if they had.

On March 22nd, Wyatt, Doc, Warren, Josh, Turkey-Creek and Texas Jack came to a wood camp at South Pass in the Dragoon Mountains. There they found Florentino 'Indian Charlie' Cruz. Cruz was well-known as one of the Cowboys and rode with the Clantons. Wyatt sat his horse carefully and looked down at Indian Charlie.

"I'm looking for the men who killed my brother Morgan the day before yesterday."

Indian Charlie looked rattled. He had a right to be. Alone, facing a posse of expert and ruthless gunmen led by the implacable Earp, there was good reason to be afraid. "I don't know nothing about that."

"I think you do." Wyatt just waited.

"Listen, Mr. Earp, I didn't shoot nobody. You got to believe me. I didn't kill your brother."

"But you were there."

"No, I wasn't there. I swear."

"Be careful what you swear, Charlie, because in a very short time you may have to answer for it."

"Well, I was there, in town, but I didn't—"

"What did you do? Act as look-out? Hold the horses? Spy out the alley? That would be in your line." Indian Charlie was silent. Josh saw that he was sweating. Wyatt suddenly barked, "Well? Which was it?"

"I was look-out, Mr. Earp, but they made me do it, I didn't want to, and I took no part in the shooting."

Wyatt continued quietly, "Well, Charlie, you better go for that gun. We ain't got all day. We got other trash to run down."

"I don't want no gun shooting!"

Wyatt turned to the others. "Boys, I would be grateful if you would leave this one to me." Indian Charlie looked panicky. Wyatt said, "Come on, Charlie. Let's get to shooting."

At that point, Cruz's nerve broke and he made a rush for a nearby wagon, jerking the pistol from his belt. Wyatt drew and shot him through the thigh and he fell. Then he shot him again, causing a wound to the pelvis and groin, a wound like that which Morgan had received, and then he dismounted, walked over to the groaning Charlie, and coldly shot him through the side of the head. It was, to all effects, an execution.

Texas Jack looked at Turkey-Creek and raised his eyebrows. Turkey-Creek shrugged and wheeled his horse round. Wyatt remounted and rode out without a word and the others followed. Josh took a last look at the mortal remains of Florentino Cruz, known as Indian Charlie, and went after them.

***

Iron Springs was a waterhole in the Whetstone Mountains. It was a pretty place. A stream ran into a small lagoon there and it was surrounded by cottonwoods that whispered in the breeze. As the Earp party, minus Warren, who had been left behind to await a messenger, drew near it on the Friday, looking forward to watering their horses, Josh noticed Wyatt look uneasy and unlimber his shotgun. Something was not right. They were plumb out in the open and the thicket of trees round the waterhole made too good cover. Suddenly, Cowboys leaped up from the bank and began firing. Straight away, Texas Jack's horse went down and pinned him to the ground by the leg. Curly Bill stood out from the other Cowboys in his bright red shirt, firing his pistols till they were empty and then snatching up a rifle. Wyatt saw him, leaped down and tried to hold his horse but the animal was rearing and bucking in the gunfire. A shot ripped through the tails of Wyatt's coat and another struck his boot heel.

While the others were wheeling their horses and trying to get out of the hail of lead, Earp didn't hesitate even for a moment. He walked slowly and deliberately towards Curly Bill, ignoring all the gunshots, until he was near enough for a shotgun to kill, then fired both barrels into Curly's chest. The red shirt was shredded and soaked with another red as Curly was thrown violently onto his back, making a great splash in the spring.

Wyatt threw the empty shotgun down and walked back to his horse to snatch his rifle from the scabbard but the animal turned and twisted and he could not get the gun. So he drew his pistol and fired methodically into the thicket where the Cowboys were hidden and heard a yell as one of them was hit.

Holliday was shouting at him to get down, to find some cover, but Wyatt seemed uninterested. Doc had dismounted and came back to rescue his friend Texas Jack, tugging him out from under his horse.

As he dragged him away, Texas Jack kept shouting, "Wait, I want my rifle!"

Doc replied testily, "Fuck your rifle. Let's get out of range first!"

Wyatt, Doc and Texas Jack now scurried for some cover.

Behind some rocks, Doc took Wyatt's arm and said solicitously, "You must be shot to pieces."

Wyatt looked at him and said simply, "No." He showed his broken heel and his bullet-holed hat and held out his coat which had a great tear in it. But not a single bullet had touched him. He had not even a graze. It was extraordinary.

All this while, Josh had waited back with Turkey-Creek Johnson, flat to the ground and covering the others with his rifle, doing his best to drive the Cowboys back into the trees. While reloading his Winchester, he looked up and there, among the cottonwoods, between two other cowboys, Josh caught a sudden glimpse of Dirty Dave Rudabaugh.

***

"Wyatt, can I speak to you a moment?"

"Sure."

"Well, I think I'd like to leave now. We have done the work, the main work and well…"

Wyatt looked at him surprised. "Of course, Josh, whatever you want. There is still work to be done, though. There's Ike Clanton, for one, and I particularly want Ringo. But I thank you for coming this far. I guess it was a bit hot back there."

Josh looked at him sharply. "I hope you don't think it was because of that shooting. I have other reasons for wanting to go."

Wyatt realized he had offended Josh. "Of course, of course, think nothing of it. But we're heading out for Hooker's Ranch, get a bit of rest, feed the horses and all, so why don't you come that far, then you can ride out wherever you're headed."

"Well, the thing is, I kind of need to leave right now."

Wyatt looked at him strangely. "Well, whatever you want, Josh. Listen, I can pay you for the posse work you done. Warren's coming up with a thousand dollars."

"I don't want any money. I wouldn't take any, leaving halfway through like this."

"I thought you said the work was nigh on done!" Wyatt smiled, trying to make a joke of it. It was the first smile Josh had seen on Wyatt's face since Morgan had been killed. They shook hands, rather stiffly, and Josh rode over to bid farewell to Doc and Turkey-Creek and Texas Jack. He said to Doc, "Say goodbye to Warren for me."

Doc simply said, "God speed." Texas Jack slapped him on the back.

Josh sat his horse and watched the band as it grew smaller and more distant until all that could be made out was dust, and then he turned his horse and rode back to the spring.

He didn't really expect to find any of the Cowboys still there but in fact Dave and three others were loading Curly Bill's body onto his horse and tying it down. Josh dismounted and yelled, "Hello in the camp!" There was immediately much movement in the bushes and cocking of firearms. Josh continued, "I am alone and have come to speak with you. You won't shoot now, will you?"

Dave had recognized his voice and he called out, "Come on in, Josh. But just to be sure, you better hoist them arms aloft."

The reunion was friendly on Dave's side but cool on the part of the other three. Dave introduced them. They were Pony Deal and the two Hicks brothers, Bill and Milt. These men were clearly unsure. They probably knew that Josh had been riding with the Earps. Dave sent Pony and the Hicks boys ahead to the Patterson ranch near the Babocomari River, where they would find a welcome and could bury Curly. Then he and Josh sat down beside the spring and made some coffee.

Talking about what had befallen each of them since they had last met before Christmas the previous year, Josh felt that they were both skirting the real facts. They alluded, indirectly, to the attack on Virgil Earp and the killing of Morgan but Josh did not ask right out if Dave had been involved and Dave did not volunteer information. The closest they came to it was when Josh said, "I see you lost your favorite kerchief."

***

In early April, they heard that Jesse James had been shot dead in St. Joseph by Robert and Charley Ford. Of course the whole country was talking about it and every newspaper was full of the story. Josh felt that with the end of Billy and now Jesse, law and regulation were coming to the West and men like him and Dave would be increasingly leftovers from the past.

It was the 1880s, after all. Things advanced. Railroads and telephones arrived. Towns got streetcars and temperance committees and churches and no-gun ordinances. Dave didn't see it like that. He just thought it was bad luck, was all, and both Billy and Jesse had been shot by cowards while not in a position to defend themselves. Other fellows would take their place. And even if it got too civilized in the States, there was always Mexico. For now, anyway, Mexico was safer. Josh reckoned that he didn't know about the Fords but one word which could never justly be applied to Patrick F. Garrett was coward.

They rode over Mule Pass down to Bisbee. A traveling tinker warned them of the dangers of the route. Between the depredations of the famous outlaw gang of Ben Wade, renegade Apaches and Mexican rustlers it was not the most law-abiding of countries. But they pushed on without incident and eventually crossed the border into Old Mexico at Naco.

Chapter Thirteen

Mexico was not just another country. It was another world. Josh had not seen such misery or such a dull look in the eyes of country people. Diaz may have brought stability but only at the price of repression and grinding poverty. There had been plenty of poor farmers in New Mexico and Arizona, especially Hispanic ones, but this was something different. And in the north of Mexico there were wandering bandits organized into gangs preying on the villages and towns. One was particularly feared, a chief named Calvera. Josh thought it sounded ominously like *calavera*, the Spanish for skull.

Josh and Dave worked as hired guns to protect a village but the farmers had so little money to pay them or even food to give them that they moved on. They worked on a ranch as cowpunchers and before long Dave was rustling cattle again, indiscriminately from the ranch owner who paid him or from others. When it became too hot for them, they headed south through Chihuahua and arrived in the town of Parral.

Parral was quite impressive. It was a silver-mining town and silver had put up several imposing buildings and laid out a park with palm trees. Many of the people looked prosperous. There were cantinas and hotels. They ate well there, burritos, grilled meats and beef tacos, food that neither Josh nor Dave was used to but both came to like. There was also a cooked milk confection called *dulce de leche* which Dave took a liking to. Parral was at least a town, not an impoverished village, and they decided to make it their home for a while. They needed to make some money and wanted to stop traveling for a time. The weather was very fine. Dave had his eye on a pretty Indian girl, whom he referred to as his own little *dulce de leche*.

1882 became 1883. They picked up better Spanish and made some money, gambling and riding shotgun on silver shipments, and they started up a small freighting business.

***

Dirty Dave liked to drink. He had always liked to drink. And he liked to gamble too. In most people, the two don't really mix and Dave was no exception. Drink made Dave play badly, recklessly. And it made him say things that would better have been left unsaid.

Some of the Mexicans came to dislike him. He was too free with the unpleasant word 'greaser', which he used thoughtlessly and casually, without meaning to give offense but nevertheless giving it. And they knew he was dallying with a young Mexican girl who was only sixteen and they did not like it.

Still, for the moment they tolerated him. There was not much else they could do. The gringo carried a gun and seemed the type of man who knew how to use it. He was big and strong and had once laid a Mexican man out cold with one blow of his fist. And he gave them work in his freighting business and sometimes bought them drinks. They won money from him when he was playing badly. So they bided their time.

Josh could sense the animosity but was unable to explain it to Dave beyond suggesting that he do not use the pejorative term so freely. Dave answered that he wouldn't call the greasers greasers anymore, but of course he did.

In a stifling evening of the summer of 83, Josh and Dave were playing cards in their favored cantina and drinking wine. Dave had drunk a great deal of wine, a very great deal of wine. He was loud and aggressive and unhappy that he was losing. He made a grab at the waist of the passing saloon owner's wife; said she should sit on his knee and bring him luck. He didn't really mean much by it but he never had the sense to see how he gave offense.

A tall Mexican came in and stood at the bar, looking idly at the game. Suddenly his brow darkened and he put down his drink and walked over to his friend Gonzalez, playing with Dave and Josh. He addressed Gonzalez quietly in Spanish. Josh had enough of the language by now to follow. "Hey, Jesus. Why are you playing with this American? Don't you know that he's the one who killed the jailer up in Las Vegas?"

The three Mexicans at the card table looked sharply at the man, then at Dave. Gonzalez threw down his hand. "Is that true, Señor? Were you the man who killed Deputy Antonio Valdez in New Mexico?"

Dave's manner changed. He became steely and wary. "No, I didn't kill that jailer. I was there, but I didn't shoot him. And I'll fight any man says I did."

There was a moment of silence.

Gonzalez rose from the table. His companions followed suit. Dave looked angrily at them. "You saying you don't believe me?"

"We are not saying anything, Señor. We are just leaving."

"Look, you goddam greasers, I did not kill your greaser jailer and I want to win back the money I have just lost. So sit back down right now and play."

"I am sorry. We have business to attend to."

Then it all happened incredibly quickly. Dave drew his handgun, Josh put a restraining hand on his arm, a man threw over the table, the gun went off, then went off again, there was screaming and breaking glass and blood seeping into the floorboards from a man on his back.

Dave was backing towards the door and Josh had his pistol out and was with him. Josh saw the tall man who had been at the bar reaching under it, presumably for a shotgun. Josh shot over the man's head into the glass shelving behind the bar where the bottles were kept, and the man and the barman ducked down fast. A Mexican rushed towards Josh and Dave with a knife and Dave shot him in the head.

Then they were out in the street.

Two horses tied at the rail were frightened and rearing, trying to free themselves. Dust was raised. Josh and Dave looked at each other and understood. They took the horses, quieted them, and rode off fast down the street as two men came out of the saloon and leveled pistols at them. But they were too far away by then and were safe.

Out of the plaza, they reined in. Josh looked at Dave. "Dave, I think this town just got too hot for us."

Dave looked hard and grim. "I left money on that table and my hat on the chair."

"Well, we're not going back to get killed for a hat."

"You do what you want. I'm going back."

"Dave, that ain't smart."

Dave glared at him. "You always thought I was dumb, didn't you? You never said it, but I knew you always thought it."

"Dave, I don't think you are dumb. Not as a rule. But going back now for a hat, that would be dumb. Come on, let's go."

"I done told you. You go where you want." And he wheeled his horse about and trotted off back down the street.

Josh sighed and put his horse into a walk to follow him. As he rode, he replaced the spent cartridge in his forty-five. He didn't see Dave doing that. Dave reached the cantina again and dismounted. He didn't bother to tie the horse but walked right in. Josh drew up, dismounted, and tied his horse. In the time this took, there were more shots inside.

He ran in and saw Dave on the floor, lying prone and gasping for air. He looked to have been shot through a lung. The tall man was there with a shotgun in his hand and there were three or four others with machetes. They looked at Josh. The man with the shotgun covered Josh and the others turned back to Dave. With a cry, they suddenly fell on him with their machetes. Josh thought of drawing his pistol but at that range the shotgun would finish him.

He called out, "Hold! Stop that!" but it was too late. The hacking and chopping continued, then one of the men rose with Dave's severed head in his hands.

Josh backed out and walked carefully down the street, pistol out, covering himself from all attack. No one harmed him. It was not him they hated.

Later in the night there was a procession. A boy beat a drum and women held torches and sang. One of the machete men held aloft a long pike with Dave's head affixed to it. They had put his hat back on his head. In the plaza, the parade halted and a Mexican policeman in a helmet was photographed holding Dave's head in his hands. The head was almost too big to hold. The eyes were closed but in every other way Dave's expression seemed normal. The large mustache flowed. The young policeman's face showed pride and satisfaction.

Josh watched from the shadows then went up to the stable where his horse was kept, mounted and rode out of town northwards. He thought he would go back to the States.

Epilogue

"Ah, my good friend, how nice to see you again. Pray do join us. Allow me to introduce you."

Josh leaned over the table and stretched out his hand. "Hello, Dutchy. How are you?"

Dutchy looked up and gave a half-smile. Then he shook hands and nodded. Josh sat down.

"So you know each other then?"

"Oh yes, we know each other. We worked together for a time."

"Really? Well, it's a happy reunion then!"

"Yes, it is. So Dutchy, any news of our mutual friend?"

Dutchy shook his head. Then he said, "I heard they was in Tennessee."

"They?"

"Yes, they."

"I see."

Dutchy nodded again.

Josh took the drink he was offered and raised the glass to Dutchy. "Well, here's to the future."

Dutchy inevitably nodded.

Their companion resumed his part in the conversation. "So, do you like El Paso, Mr. King? Or I hope I may call you Samuel?"

Josh looked at Dutchy who did not even blink at the use of the name.

"Oh yes, Mr. Armstrong, George, I like it well enough. It will do for the moment anyhow."

"Oh, but I assure you, Samuel, that El Paso is set to become a great city, one of the greatest of Texas, nay, of the whole United States. You should stay, sir, and I feel confident that you will make yourself prosperous and successful."

"Well, maybe I'll do that."

Printed in the USA
CPSIA information can be obtained
at www.ICGtesting.com
LVHW012143141023
761050LV00008B/169